100

Perseverance

Perseverance

The First Black Millionaire

Carolyn Holm Bakken

Dedication

For my husband Paul, who listens and encourages, and to my mother, Violet Syverson Holm, who instilled in me the love of reading and writing

Acknowledgments

I THANK MY critique group, who read the manuscript and gave helpful insight. Thank you to my husband Paul, who listened and encouraged, and to Gary Palgon, who researched and made available so much information.

C H A P T E R   1

1828

ON THE SIXTH day at sea, the wind and rain picked up, pelting the ship. The schooner tossed about like a leaf in a rushing river, and each wave sent a torrent of water onto the deck. The crew scrambled about securing the sails, but the assaulting rain continued flooding the bottom deck.

"All hands!" the captain shouted above the howling winds. "You too, Vill! You can help bail vater out below. Ve'll use the pump, but ve need all de able bodies."

William stumbled behind the captain, the fierce wind bulleting and stinging him with shards of rain. Blinded, he clung to the ropes as he edged to the ladder that took him below to the bilge pump. He fought to maintain an upright position as he staggered down the stairs.

"In a storm, de deck can't drain fast enough, so vater ends up in the bottom of de ship. It's foul smelling and fills up fast. Gotta station sailors to keep an eye on it," the captain hollered.

Will inhaled the smell of briny seawater. It smelled like rotten eggs, and he choked. Covering his nose with his free hand, he used the other to steady himself as he slogged through the muck at his feet.

One of the sailors threw Will a bucket and yelled, "Bail. Get busy! We don't want to go down!"

Two Weeks Earlier

William shoved the desk chair back and strode to the window. The crisp blue of the Caribbean Sea held no appeal today. Despairing, he returned to the desk, picked up the pen, dipped it in the ink, and began again on the incessant numbers. "Numbers, numbers, numbers. All I see are numbers. There is no end to adding and subtracting and straight orderly columns," he mumbled. He raked his fingers through his soft black curls and searched his brain for possibilities but found none. He was trapped in the four walls of the office with its two mahogany desks, two matching leather chairs, two neat stacks of paper, and two matching silver candlesticks on each of the two desks.

Feeling a gust of air, William looked up to see his foster father enter the office. Albert Forest held a letter in his hand. "Good morning, William. I just received this from my brother in New Orleans. I think you will be excited about its content." He waved the crisp white paper before him. "He would like you to come to his cotton plantation to help him manage it." His words were clipped, precise, just like him; he was a well-built man, neat in appearance and brusque in manner. "He has some health issues, and since we have no heir but you, he needs your help. You have learned the sugar business; I can't imagine the cotton business in America is much different."

Suddenly, William's world changed. "You mean go to America? Leave my friends, my mother, you, the only home I have known, and become a complete stranger in a new land?" From his desk, he could see a schooner anchored at the pier, waiting for the sugar to be loaded.

His father stood tall and erect, waiting, his shoulders squared, his brown hair cut close to his head. No emotion flitted across his disciplined face, but William knew the tenderness that lay beneath the polished exterior.

"I have read my uncle's letters about Louisiana and its wild ways: the Negroes, the Indians, the French, and the Creoles that live along the Mississippi River. He called it a land of opportunity." His brow furrowed, and a shadow trailed across his face. "What about my mother? I am all she has. Who will take care of her?"

"Your mother has served us well, and my wife will never let her go. She is like one of our family and will always have a place here. You think about it, talk to her, and we will discuss it more tomorrow." He gave Will a reassuring pat on the back before he sat down and began rifling through the organized papers on his own desk.

Returning to the task before him, Will plodded away at the numbers, while his thoughts darted elsewhere. By early afternoon, he had accomplished nothing other than dropping a large black ink blot in the ledger, smudging the numbers.

Interrupting his father, he asked, "I'd like to do some research on New Orleans and look through the atlas you gave me. Do you mind if I leave the office for the rest of the day?"

"I knew it would be difficult to keep your mind on the figures after I gave you the news. I don't want any more mistakes, so, yes, you may go." Will sensed his lingering gaze on him as he left the room.

Sprinting the short distance to his home, Will approached the Danish Colonial house in which he had been raised. It stood big and grand, clothed in yellow brick, the Danish uniform. Green wooden shutters framed the large white windows of the two floors. A wide, sprawling staircase announced the imposing entrance.

He entered the foyer. Smelling the scent of baking bread, he knew his mother was busy in the kitchen. Instead of greeting her, he climbed the stairs two at a time to his room where his shelves, made of island hardwood, were stacked with his favorite books and the playbills he had collected while a student in England. A shell of a large island turtle rested next to seashells he had gathered as a young boy.

Kneeling by his bed, he pulled out a wooden box from under it and removed an atlas, a gift from his father. He opened it to the map of America and traced the path from Saint Croix to the Gulf of Mexico and along the eastern coastline of America until he found New Orleans. He would have to sail by ship, crossing part of the Atlantic and the Gulf of Mexico.

Putting the atlas aside, he took out the letters from his uncle. He scoured the pages looking for any information on New Orleans, the people, the weather, the lifestyle, and the slaves that worked the plantations. He was the son of a slave, although his Danish birth father had given him a lighter skin tone than most of the other islanders..

He waited anxiously for his mother to finish her work in the kitchen so they could talk. As Will paced the length of his room, pleasure and excitement argued with concern and uncertainty. Finally, from his window, he saw her leave the kitchen below, her shoulders stooped, her steps slow and measured as she made her way down the graveled path to the cottage in which he had been born. His heart warmed as he watched her snatch the red bandanna from her dark hair. The ebony kinks sprang free, uncontrollable. He slipped the atlas under his arm and raced down the steps to catch up with her.

She was at the door when he reached her. He saw the pride in her eyes when she smiled at him. He always saw it. Together they entered the small worn cottage. The faded, yellowed paint peeled from the corners of the single room. One window, opened to the sea, allowed a sliver of light. A single bed stood against the wall next to a washstand, and a faded threadbare quilt was pulled over the mattress stuffed with moss. The wicker rocker creaked when she sank into it. Kicking off her tattered brown shoes, she wiggled her toes. Will pulled out the chair by the table and spread his long limbs into the center of the room.

"I have news, Mama. News I must talk to you about," he said impatiently.

"Lemme rest my feet a bit, and we'll talk. Massa Forest, he did tell me somethin' about New Orleans and his brotha there. He run a cotton plantation?" She raised her eyes to her son.

"Yes. He wrote to ask if I could come to New Orleans to help him manage his cotton plantation. I'd have to cross the ocean by schooner. It will be a long trip, at least two weeks."

He opened the atlas and laid it on the small table. "Let me show you where America is. Come and see." When she stood, he pointed out the route. He watched her trace the course with her finger.

She didn't say a word until she returned to her rocker and whimpered, "I donna wan' you go. You be my only son." She reached for his hand. "Please donna go. Please. Please." Tears trickled down her cheeks. She brushed at them with the back of her hand and then rocked heatedly, gripping the arms of the rocker.

Will knelt at her feet. Soon the rocking slowed and then stopped. He grasped her small brown hands and peered into the face he loved so much, the face of the one who cared for him when his birth father abandoned them both. "Maybe this is an opportunity I should take just like you did when you gave Mr. Forest permission to raise me as his son." He paused, waiting for her to say something.

She squeezed his hands and brushed away the last of the tears. "Yessah, Son, I not sorry I did tha'. You got educated in Englan' at the fines' school. You smart." That proud smile flitted across her pretty dark-skinned face once again as she patted his hand with her calloused one. "I still ge' to see you mos' ev'ry day. But if you go to 'merica, I migh' never see you agin." She lowered her eyes and reached for the rag stuffed in her sleeve.

The little cabin was hot and stuffy. The one window did not allow the breeze to circulate. William felt enclosed, suffocated. "Let's sit outside, Mama." He pulled her up with both hands and led her to a wooden bench on the side of the cabin where they could see the stars and hear the surf pound the shore. He sat beside her and cupped her hand in his. "I will miss you, but Mr. Forest assured me he would always provide for you. I will not be gone forever." He sat quietly. The moon slipped behind a cloud, creating dark dancing shadows in the palm trees. Mama said nothing.

Finally Mama said, "I s'pose you shoul' go. It be good for you. I see you agin soon…"

Will kicked the gravel under his feet; the pebbles skipped and fell back into place. "Thank you for understanding, Mama. Just today I was dreaming of adventure and travel. I am eighteen and a man, and I'd like to go to America to help my uncle and learn about the cotton industry...but I will miss you." He turned so she could not see the tears welling up in his eyes, threatening to spill onto his white shirt, belying his independence and budding manhood. "I will tell him first thing in the morning." He bent and hugged his mother before he planted a kiss on her forehead. In the darkness of the night, he returned to his own room.

CHAPTER 2

WILLIAM AWAKENED EARLY. He nestled into the softness of his bed and pulled the blanket up to his chin clinging to just a few more minutes of sleep. Then he remembered. He kicked off the covers and jumped up—there was no time to waste. He pulled on his cream linen pants, tied the drawstring, and buttoned up the white cotton shirt. After slipping on his sandals, he took the stairs two at a time to reach the kitchen. His mother was there, fixing eggs, ham, and biscuits, which he ate in haste, having no time for formal dining this morning. He kissed her on the cheek and grabbed a cup of coffee. "I'm going to the office to finish the accounting," he explained as the door banged behind him.

The ledger remained open on his desk, exactly where he left it. He cringed at the black blot that marred his perfect page of numbers. Drawing a single line through the disfigured item, he entered it again on the next line. Satisfied, he continued working with the sums, subtracting the expenses and recording the profits from sales to the sugar-refining plants. Today, the figures skipped before his eyes and then fell into the lines appropriated for them. The plantation was doing well.

The door opened, and his father entered with the morning sun. "You are up early and working already. That must mean you have made a decision." He stopped in front of Will's desk, waiting, his face void of expression.

Will returned the gaze thinking how hard it would be to leave him since he had shown such kindness. He pushed back his chair and stood, grinning. "Yes, I have decided. I want to go." He walked to the window, taking in the green of the island and the blue of the sea he loved. "I talked with my mother last night, and she agrees it would be good for me, although I know she is sad and will miss me." He turned and faced his father. "You will take care of her?" he questioned again.

"Of course we will. I give you my word."

Assured, Will asked the next questions: "When do I leave, and what do I need to prepare?"

"I will arrange passage this afternoon. Get your clothes packed and the things you want to take—your books, I imagine. The schooner is scheduled to sail at the end of the week, after it's loaded with the sugar. That will give you time to say farewell to your friends." He put his hands on Will's shoulders. "I will miss you, William; you are a good son and a good worker, but you must remember the one thing you promised." Silence hung heavy as he captured Will's gaze. "You are never, under any circumstances, to reveal the truth of your birth and that I am not your father.

Never allow anyone to guess that you are a Negro and not my natural-born son." He paused, his brow furrowed. "I must caution you. My brother tells me there are Creoles and free Negroes in New Orleans. Your skin color is that of a white man, but your features are those of a Negro."

He pulled an official-looking envelope out of his pocket. "I had my lawyer draw up papers for you stating that you are a free man. Carry those with you at all times. My brother says even free men of color may be sold as slaves." He handed Will the envelope and continued speaking as he swept his hand across the room. "Someday all of this will be yours, if you keep that confidential."

Will took the letter warily. He was very aware of the arrangement Mr. Forest had made with his mother when he was just five years old. He remembered the day his life changed forever, but hearing that his freedom might be in danger was startling new information.

Will stood in the center of his large bedroom satiated with so many memories. His bed was piled with trousers, shirts, and the three overcoats he took from his wardrobe. What should he take, and what should he leave behind? Would he need a jacket in New Orleans? Would he need formal clothing for dining?

His steamer trunk stood empty at the foot of his bed. Needing to start somewhere, he threw in his warm wool stockings and undergarments. Next, he added one of the thicker overcoats and then began layering his trousers and shirts. He decided to take his black formal dinner suit. He folded it carefully and added the red cravat. That left room at the top for his beloved books. Which ones should he take?

He sat on his bed and leafed through some of the collection he loved so much. Finally, he settled on Sir Walter Scott's *The Talisman* and a new publication, *The Last Moments of Napoleon*. He picked up the atlas that lay open on his bed, and his eyes wandered once again to the Gulf Coast, the Mississippi River, and the town of New Orleans. He lay the book aside. He would pack it in his valise to keep with him so he could follow his journey on the map.

The packing done, he slipped on his swimsuit and headed to the beach where his friends were waiting. He ran past the old plaster houses with their once brightly colored paint that was now faded to soft pastels. He brushed aside the bougainvillea that threatened to conceal the path in a blaze of pink, purple, and orange and pushed out onto the beach. He stopped and gazed in wonder. It was the most beautiful spot in the world. Two giant mahogany trees stretched to the edge of the crystal-blue water.

Agwe and Umar, boyhood friends, were already swimming, diving, and frolicking in the clear water. He watched for a moment, drinking in the beauty before he kicked off his sandals and raced head-on to dive into the warm water. He came up seconds later, gasping for air, and then dove again, deeper this time. Vivid purple, red, and magenta coral colored the ocean's floor. Yellow fish bathed in the beauty, swimming leisurely. A large leatherback turtle glided beneath him before he surfaced again to fill his lungs with air.

"Let's swim to Buck Island," he shouted to his friends, and a race ensued. Will, an avid swimmer, reached the sandy shores first, where he fell breathless. Agwe arrived second and then Umar, who joined them under the sandbox tree, so named because nobody (including the monkeys) attempted to climb it. Its yellow-gray bark was covered with short, squat fleshly spines. The fruit was green and not ready to break open, not yet at its poisonous stage. It was safe.

Once he caught his breath,, Agwe suggested, "Let's explore the elkhorn coral reef. Maybe we'll see a spotted eagle ray or some fire coral."

Late in the afternoon, after swimming back to Saint Croix, they sat under the shade of a palm tree, the gentle trade winds fanning the branches overhead. "I'm leaving the island. I'm going to my Uncle's plantation in New Orleans. I'll be leaving tomorrow on the ship sitting at the pier." Will waited to see his friends' reaction and then added, "I'm going to help him with his cotton plantation."

"Wow Will! What an adventure, I'd like the opportunity to go to America. You are lucky," Agwe said. He plucked a ripe pineapple and sliced it open with his pocket knife. "We will miss you," he said, handing Will a piece. "Do you think New Orleans grows pineapple?" He wiped away the juices dripping down his chin.

"I don't know. It will all be new for me." Will grew quiet. "I am going to miss you and all this." A huge wave of sadness enveloped him. "I don't know much about America except people of color need to carry their freedom papers with them at all times." He looked into the dark faces of his childhood friends and saw his own freedom slipping.

Will jumped to his feet. "Come on," he said. "Let's go down to the pier and see the schooner that will be my passageway to adventure. I watched it sail into port yesterday and looked it up in the sailing book my father gave me." They jogged the short distance to the pier and sat down on the knoll.

"See, it has three masts." He pointed. "The first mast is both fore rigged and aft rigged. All the other masts are aft rigged. All those ropes hold the sails together. This boat has a smaller crew than the bigger ships, so the crew has to work harder."

Umar and Agwe listened as Will continued, "My father told me about the *Star of Hope* schooner sailing from North Carolina to England carrying a cargo of cotton that was caught in a strong gale in the Mersy approaches in Liverpool and went down. I pray that doesn't happen to me." Once again, silence masked his fears.

CHAPTER 3

ON THE MORNING of departure, Will's father agreed he could walk with his mother to the pier. Anxious, he arrived early at her cabin. She was just putting away the biscuits and honey, remains from her breakfast.

"Come on, Mama, we need to hurry. I don't want to miss the schooner," he urged.

She tied a blue bandanna around her dark hair and patted it down, tucking in all the loose tendrils. She did not speak but picked up a handwoven basket and closed the door behind her, not looking at Will, although he could see the sadness written on her face.

"What's in the basket, Mama?" he asked as he lifted a corner of the red cloth and peeked in. "Mangos, baked yams, fried plantains, cassava, and beans. My favorites." He dug deeper and spied corn bread, too. "I will miss the callaloo soup you make just for me," he said. Still she said nothing.

They walked on silently, she clinging to the basket, her last gift to her son, and Will gripping a small valise that held his personal belongings he would need on the ship, a warm wool blanket for the cool evenings, his freedom papers, and his books. His steamer had been delivered to the docks and loaded earlier. Only the crunch of the graveled pebbles beneath their feet broke the silence as neither mother nor son wanted to say the words that hurt most.

When they reached the knoll that overlooked the intense blue of the Caribbean, his mother stopped and laid her hand on his arm. She reached inside the pocket of her gaily colored skirt and brought out an envelope. Knowing his mother did not read or write, Will asked, "What is this?"

"I axed the pastor at the church to wri' this for me. It is fo' you to read on the ship, not befo'e." She pulled away as Will reached for it. "Not yet, not till you on the boat." She tucked it under the red cloth of the basket and said simply, "Later."

Thick brown ropes anchored the vessel to the wooden pier. The sailors were busy loading barrels onto the ship. Native women in bright-colored dresses and ragged crewmen bargained loudly over coconuts, bananas, pineapples, and strings of rainbow-colored fish. Other passengers stood watching and saying tearful good-byes to loved ones. He turned to his mother and put his hands on her shoulders. "I will miss you, Mama, but I hope to come back and see you soon." He clutched her to him and held tight. "I love you, Mama."

"I love you too, my son. I pray for yo' saf'ty. May God keep you." She clung to him before reluctantly stepping back so Mr. Forest could say his good-bye.

William shook his father's hand and said, "I will miss you, too, Father, but I am grateful for this opportunity. I hope to make you proud."

Mr. Forest returned the handshake but then, in a moment of sentiment, grabbed Will and gripped him in a firm hug. "You always make me proud, William. You will get along well with my brother; I have written him much about you. Give him my greetings; he is expecting you." He turned away so Will could not see the emotions he was trying so hard to mask.

Will joined the other passengers ascending the gangplank. When he found a spot on the deck near the railing, he turned to wave for the last time as the ship disembarked and moved slowly out to sea. There they stood: a tall, wealthy plantation owner and an attractive black woman, side by side, the people he loved most in the world. He glanced at the strangers surrounding him. He knew no one. His eyes clung to the two shapes as they faded into the distance. Soon they were only a speck on the horizon along with his beloved island. He stood there for quite some time, watching the emptiness, his hair disheveled by the wind and dampened by the saltwater.

Finding a quiet place on the deck and away from the busyness of the crew, his hands trembled as he pulled out the letter his mama had given him. The envelope was yellow and ragged as though it had been opened many times or carried in the pocket of his mama's skirt for some time.

Dear William,

Your mama asked me to write for her. I tell you her story.

I first met your daddy when I was just a girl of sixteen. I sold cakes, apples, figs, and pineapples down on the wharf, and when the ships and sailors arrived, I be there. Your daddy thought I was beautiful and he tell me he buy only from me. Each time his ship come in, he see only me. He be so tall handsome, and fair. He have blond hair because he be Danish, and I fall in love with him. He tell me I be the only woman for him. Soon he has to sail away on his ship again. I am pregnant with you.

Your gramma work on the plantations, and I live with her in the cabin. I work in the fields alongside her until I just too big, and I go to the cabin to wait for you to be born. Soon you come burstin' into this world. You still burstin' You just like yo daddy, which is why I give you his name, William Alexander Leidesdorff Jr.

Everybody tell me what a handsome boy you be, big brown eyes, big dark curls, and your skin the color of caramel. You not black like me. No wonder you catch Massa Forest's eye. One day you come runnin' home and a man on a big black horse follow you. You tell me he wanna talk to me. I stand there and not look at him, but I knowed who he was. He from the big house. He walk over to my cabin and touch the paint peelin' off the walls and see the sagging roof that leaks when it rains, and he only shake his head.

I just stand there not lookin' at him but waitin' Finally he talk.

He say, "I Mr. Forest I live in the big house on the plantation. I been watching your son play with his friends. He is a very good-looking boy."

William flipped to the next page and kept reading. It was hard for him to hold back the tears as the memories flooded his mind. The daylight was beginning to fade, and the sea breeze chilled him. He dug his wool blanket out of his valise and wrapped it tightly around him, cocooning himself in its warmth.

I know who he be, but I just kep my head down. Then he say, "I would like the boy to come and live at my house like my son since I have no children of my own. I will educate him and take care of all his needs."

I gasp. I canna hep myself. He wanna take my son, my only son. How I tell him no? 'Mos' massas just take the chillum. They don't ask.

He talk more. "You can continue living here but come and work in the kitchen in the big house. That way you will see him every day, but you are never to tell that he is not my natural-born son."

I think, girls in the big house get better clothes and plenty of food. I still see you every day, and you get a better life. I nod my head.

He say, "You can start tomorrow, and bring the boy when you come. What's his name?"

I say, "William Alexander Leidesdorff Jr. I name him after his daddy."

The next day I bring you, and we go to the big house. Mr. Forest there waitin' for you. He take your hand and show you your big room with your own bed and your very own books. I see the smile on your face.

The hardest part was when he send you away to England to get learnin' You gone for a long time, and I get so lonesome, but you smart. When you come home, you speak three languages. You look so growed up and handsome, and I be so proud. But you still call me mama.

Don't ever forget that I your mama and I love you.
Anna Marie Sparks

Recorded in this letter by Pastor Jacobs, May 14, 1828.

Brushing away the tears that gathered in the corner of his eyes, Will was aware he might never see his mama again. Looking around cautiously, he folded the letter and hid it inside the zippered pocket of his valise along with his freedom letter, both for his eyes only.

He found a spot on deck to string his hammock. Opening the basket of food, he ate some of the baked yams and one of the juicy mangos until his stomach was satisfied.

As the sun disappeared below the gray horizon, the cooling westerlies began blowing across the bow. He buried himself deeper in the warmth of his wool blanket. The moon came out and lighted a silvery path in the now-black waters. The stars shone like diamonds in the sky, and William was able to pick out the Big Dipper and follow its handle to the Little Dipper. It was almost 1,800 miles, as the crow flies, to his destination—a long journey. Tomorrow, he would track their course in his atlas. Falling asleep to the lull of the ship's movement, he dreamed of sailing his own schooner.

The next morning, the sun and the noise of the crew awakened him. Sailors were busy covering the backstays with mats so the yards would not harm the rigging. Two deckhands swabbed the deck. Another climbed to the crow's nest so he could anchor the shrouds of the topmast.

Will lay watching and listening to the constant patter of busy feet. He tried to sit up, but his stomach lurched, and his head pounded. He lay down again but groaned, rolled over, and spewed his last meal on the deck.

A sailor, dressed in worn, ragged trousers with a calico bandanna tied over his matted hair, threw a bucket of water on the vomit. "It'll pass in 'bout three days. Most new passengers get seasick the first couple a days." He left with the bucket and then returned with a tin cup and handed it to Will. "Some water to rinse the ugly taste from your mouth."

For the next two days, Will contorted over the starboard railing of the ship, thrusting dry heaves. On the fourth day, he awakened and lay quietly in his hammock. He waited: no headache, no lurching stomach pains. After gingerly eating some of the cassava and baked yams and drinking a cup of tea sweetened with molasses, he felt stronger.

Strolling around the deck, he watched the sailors tie off the rigging, tend the sails, and trim them with each gust of wind. He learned how to read the direction of the wind by watching a flag tied to the top of the mast and how to adjust the sails to catch the most wind as they flew across the waves gaining speed.

The captain, Pete Peterson, was a Dane just like Will's birth father and a seasoned captain, although he was only thirty-eight years old. Strong as an ox, he was six feet four inches tall and did not carry a surplus pound of flesh on his body. He knew how to take accurate observations of the heavenly planets and had a reputation of handling a ship in all kinds of weather. Will imagined he was much like his birth father and soon made his acquaintance as he hovered about asking questions. "I hear the sailors say *belay*; what does that mean?" Before the captain could answer, he asked another: "What is a block?"

Wiping the sea spray from his eyes, the captain patiently answered, "Ven a sailor fastens a line around a cleat or belaying pin, it's called *belay*. A block is a set of pulleys used to raise de sails."

For the rest of the trip, the captain allowed Will to shadow him as he tolerantly answered his inquiries. "I'm fascinated by ships and sailing. I want to learn as much as I can because I am going to have my own schooner someday."

Will was not prepared for the horrendous storm that occurred on the sixth day. Hurricanes occasionally created chaos on his island and the other islands and he knew crossing the ocean could be dangerous, he just didn't know how dangerous..

After heaving water out of the bilge, the next morning Will felt muscles he didn't know existed. He rolled out of his hammock and fell to the deck when he tried to stand, his legs quivering. He watched the sailors scampering about tending to the sails and admired their tenacity. Amazingly, the sea was calm—no wind, such a difference from the blustering winds and pelting rain the day before. The ocean was smooth as glass. That meant no wind and no sailing, the doldrums. He finished the last of the yams, had some salted beef, and munched on some hard bread. He wiped his mouth and thought, *I may never again taste my mama's callaloo soup, but at least I am alive after the storm.*

He found the captain at the helm and asked, "How many more days until we reach New Orleans?"

"Did de storm scare you? It's part of life at sea, ya know." He pointed to a far-distant spot of land. "Von't be long now. See dat? Dat's Cuba. We'll sail by dat, Central America, and then into de Gulf of Mexico." He wiped his nose with the back of his hand and then stepped back. "Here, you take de helm for a vhile." Will gripped the wheel with both hands, his knuckles white.

New Orleans

THE SAILORS BEGAN dropping the sails and binding them up with ropes. Stationed near the captain, Will sensed the rising excitement of the crew as they neared New Orleans. Once finished with the sails, the men carried out wooden buckets of water and scrubbed the weeks of grime from their weathered bodies, shaved scruffy beards, cut the tangles from their hair, and donned new flannel shirts, duck trousers, stockings, and shoes. The captain handed each of the sailors two silver dollars.

On the approaching pier, Will could see the men in business suits, merchants and sailors who lined the wharf. Negroes and Indians peddled their wares while roustabouts or dockhands basked in the sunshine waiting for the boats to moor. The levee was lined with tiers of arks, keelboats, flatboats, steamboats, and barges.

"De Mississippi River is a major vaterway dat flows right into de Gulf of Mexico in New Orleans. About a tousand sailing ships and hundreds of steamships have entered de port dis year alone, I'm told," the captain explained.

"One, two, three, four..." Will counted thirteen big steamboats. "Why so many?" he asked.

"De're de main mode of transportation on de river." He pointed to one ornate boat trimmed with wood. Will was close enough to see the stairs, the velvet plush chairs, and the gilt edging. "Not all are dat nice," the captain added. "It depends on de owner's taste and pocketbook." He patted his own pockets with his weathered hands. "De're usually made of wood but only need about two feet of water to navigate."

"I see the passengers on the upper deck. What's below?" Will asked.

"De main deck holds de boiler. All cargo is carried below de main deck. She is propelled by a horizontally mounted engine dat turns a single stern paddle wheel," he said, pointing to the big wheel.

Two burly men, using large oars to propel a boat from the rooftop, maneuvered right next to them. "That looks like a floating house. It must be carrying at least two hundred barrels of cargo. It's stacked all the way to the second deck. I'm surprised it doesn't sink," Will said.

"Dat's a flatboat and comes from Kentucky. De're called arks because animals are carried on dem, too. Like Noah in de Bible," he laughed. "Cattle are on de first floor and people on de top floor. See de livestock on dat one?" Two brown horses and three black-and-white cows poked their heads over the edge of the floating box. A dog ran wildly on the deck, barking, and chickens cackled in wire cages.

"Dey can't go back upstream, so de're torn apart and used for building houses and streets."

"Even London didn't look like this," Will said in amazement. The skyline was peppered with towering masts. Black clouds billowed from the tall chimneys of the steamships, making the air hazy and dense with smoke. Diminutive rowboats bobbed from ropes that anchored them to the wooden pier. Stretches of canvas, looking like sails on a ship, covered barrels waiting to be loaded onto the departing ships.

The captain continued to explain, "Dese are international docks in New Orleans, and products are shipped from America overseas, especially cotton and sugar."

Will could hear the many languages and dialects being spoken, including French and Spanish.

"Products come from overseas to be shipped inland as vell, and it all happens at dis port." The captain motioned to a riverboat loaded with bales of cotton stacked high enough to block the windows of the staterooms and the grand salon.

Moving to the railing, Will dug his hands into his pockets and began pacing up and down. The wooden pier stretched for miles. How would he find his uncle in this crowd? His anxiety increased as he continued scanning the people waiting at the ship's pier.

A fine-looking gentleman stood aloof from the crowd. He was dressed in a long brown overcoat and striped trousers and wore a fashionable top hat. When William spotted him, he raised his hand pensively. Was he the uncle? The man touched his hand to his hat. "That must be my father's brother. He looks just like him," he said, pointing him out to the captain. "He is tall and thin just like my father."

He shook hands with the captain and thanked him for the journey and the answers to all the questions about sailing. Saddened to say good-bye to the crew and the captain but excited to meet his uncle, Will descended the gangplank and approached the man on the pier, who stepped forward to meet him. "You must be William," he said. He sported a fine black mustache that stood out because of the paleness of his face. Will remembered his father said he had health issues.

"I am, sir, and you must be Mr. Forest. You look very much like my father. How do you do, sir?" Will extended his hand, and the gentleman gripped it firmly.

His uncle smiled, his features softening. "You may call me Leif or Uncle." He turned and began walking briskly toward the horse and buggies that lined the wharf. "Gather your belongings, and let's find my driver so we can get to my house in the French Quarter before it gets dark."

Will collected his trunk and motioned to the driver to load it on the buggy. He grasped his valise containing his freedom papers close to his side and stepped into the carriage.

CHAPTER 5

THE CARRIAGE JOLTED, and Will bumped into Mr. Forest. He grasped the side of the carriage, his face flushed. His valise tumbled into the mud. "Stop. Please stop. I must get my valise." He scrambled out and retrieved his splattered satchel. Hugging it close, he climbed aboard and brushed at the grime.

"There are many potholes in the streets because of the rain, and New Orleans is below sea level, so it floods often. Be prepared for a rough ride," his uncle said. "My brother tells me you are good with numbers and with the workers. You are quite a young man to have that much responsibility."

"My father trained me well and taught me much about the running of a plantation. He also told me you raised cotton. I am looking forward to learning about the cotton industry, too," Will replied politely. He studied his uncle discreetly and thought, *I think I am going to like him.* Continuing his perusal, he noticed Leif was tall, lean, and dressed impeccably. His brown leather shoes were highly polished, and he spoke and carried himself with confidence.

"It is a day's journey to my plantation farther along the Mississippi River. I keep a house in New Orleans, too, so we will spend the night there and leave early in the morning." Reaching forward, Mr. Forest tapped his slave driver with his cane and said, "We will be staying in my house on Bourbon Street tonight." Then he continued, "Sugar does very well in this area, as you will see when we travel to the plantation. We will go by many fields."

Bumping over the rough streets, they arrived on Bourbon Street. "What is that horrible smell?" Will asked, wrinkling his nose.

"The slaughterhouse is just over that levee." His uncle pointed to a mound of dirt. "All the slaughtering is done there. You should smell it in the rains. Ugh."

Only one cart and horse could traverse the very narrow lane called Bourbon Street. The road was muddy and dirty and the buildings dingy. Peddlers were stationed in their shaded stalls selling food, furs, clothes, cloth, and tools. Rough-looking sailors, dressed in ragged clothes, their hats pulled down jauntily, lounged in the open doors, making crude comments while the sound of mournful piano music filled the street.

Will slid low in the seat and pulled his hat over his forehead.

Seeing his uneasiness, Mr. Forest explained, "Bourbon Street is the heartbeat of New Orleans. It becomes very loud and raucous, but don't worry. We are safe." He laughed lightly. "We are protected by a cavalry of police called the Orleans Gendarmes. Each of them is armed with a broadsword and a pair of pistols, and they patrol the city until dawn on their horses."

"That is good," Will responded, somewhat relieved, and he sat taller. He watched the Negro ladies selling their wares, the round trays on their heads piled high with pineapples, oranges, sweetmeats, and bananas. *Just like my island and my mother when she met my father,* he thought. They too wore brightly colored clothing and swayed their hips as they hawked their goods down the narrow street.

"There are many free men and women of color in New Orleans, too, but they must carry their papers with them at all times and cannot be on the streets after nine," Mr. Forest continued. "The city fathers argued whether they should shoot a cannon or ring a bell at curfew time, but they agreed on a bell, a much more agreeable sound. Cannon shots have a tendency to frighten people."

Will clutched his valise close to his chest, knowing his papers were safely hidden in the zippered pocket but worrying anyway: *Will I be safe here? Will I lose my freedom?*

His uncle tapped the driver's shoulder once more with his cane. "Take us by the Cabildo on Jackson Square. I want to show William where the Louisiana Purchase was signed." The Negro driver nodded and did not turn around or say a word but just clicked his tongue to the horse and turned off Bourbon Street onto Saint Peter Street.

Mr. Forest leaned back against the seat, breathed a tired sigh, and continued, "New Orleans was named after the royal ruling family of France at the time it was founded as a French colonial outpost. This was all French territory at one time." He waved his outstretched hand, encompassing the area. "In 1803, the United States purchased the territory called Louisiana from France. The transfer ceremony took place right here at Jackson Square in that building called the Cabildo." He pointed to a large white three-story building with Spanish arches and a French mansard roof. "That is the Saint Louis Cathedral right next to it. Catholicism was strong during the French reign, and all slaves had to be baptized Catholic. It states that in the Code Noir." [1]

His interest piqued, Will asked, "What is the Code Noir? I know *noir* means *black* in French."

"It was a code promulgated by Louis XIV of France and the Catholic Church, and it regulated slave behavior in French overseas colonies. Sundays and holidays were strictly observed. The slaves could not work on those days. They also had to be baptized Catholic and were granted certain rights. I have a copy you can read if you wish."

"I would like to see it," Will responded. They settled into silence until Will commented, "I see wicker chairs and wooden rocking chairs on the porches, and most of

---

[1] "Code Noir." Dictionary of American History. 2003. Encyclopedia.com. (March 11, 2015). http://www.encyclopedia.com/doc/1G2-3401800891. html

the houses have covered verandas. The people must like to sit outside, just like in Saint Croix."

"The weather is very warm and humid in the summer so they enjoy living outdoors under those roofs. They decorate the houses with cornices, wainscoting, and chair rails." He pointed to a gas lantern hanging by the front door of the house they passed where an elderly lady rocked leisurely in the early evening. "Most houses have gas lighting too."

They turned back onto Bourbon Street. The humidity and heat caused Will to perspire profusely. He wiped the sweat from his forehead and commented, "It seems the shops are on the first floor, so the owners must live above the shops."

"Yes. You will see the shop doors open right onto the street. It makes good business sense." He turned in the carriage to adjust his legs and continued, "My home, however, does not have a shop on the first floor." They stopped in front of a house with two dormers on the roof containing leaded-glass windows. Four double french doors opened to the street level, and ornate gingerbread adorned the home tucked closely between the neighboring houses.

"We have arrived. My housekeeper will have refreshments for us. I can imagine you are hungry." Mr. Forest motioned for Will to enter the house with him.

Although the home's exterior was not pretentious, Will was surprised to see the opulent interior. A large crystal chandelier hung in the center of the foyer from an intricately carved medallion. Gold brocade curtains covered the two windows of the salon beneath elegant cornices. The reflection of the gas lamps danced on the gleaming marble floor. In the left corner, he saw a gilt Venetian figure draped modestly at the waist. A mahogany side table was set with cheese, fruit, and crusty bread.

Neither man spoke as they enjoyed the grapes and pineapple slices. *They must have pineapple,* Will thought, thinking about Agwe's question.

After finishing his bread and cheese, Mr. Forest covered a yawn with his hand and said, "Your room is ready for you. You must be tired. I know I am." He swallowed the last bite and rose from the chair slowly, painstakingly, and said, "Come, I'll show you." He led Will up the stairs. "We'll leave first thing in the morning. I am eager to get back to the plantation." He turned to go into his room and then stopped. "I'm glad you made it safely. I'll send a message tomorrow to my brother telling him you arrived."

"Thank you. He will want to know. Good night," Will said and opened the door to his room. A wrought-iron bed stood against the mint-green wall flanked by two mahogany nightstands. A comfortable Queen Anne leather chair made its home in one corner of the room, and an oak chest stood at the end of the bed. He dropped his valise on the trunk and quickly changed into his nightshirt before nestling into the softness of the mattress filled with spanish moss. He fell into a troubled sleep thinking about all the new things he had encountered: new land, new uncle who is not in the best health, new acquaintances, new home, so many new things.

CHAPTER 6

HE TOSSED AND turned, trapping himself in the sheets. His papers were missing when he opened his valise. Frantic, he searched all through his grip and his trunk, but he was not able to find them. He heaved a sigh of relief when he awakened and realized it was a dream, a nightmare. Just to make sure, he jumped out of bed and opened his valise. His papers were just where he left them.

Hurriedly dressing in his black trousers and gray top-coat, he brushed his unruly curls. His black leather shoes were shined and ready for him outside his bedroom door, the mud and grime from the streets of New Orleans removed. He grinned in satisfaction as he slipped them on. Feeling and looking like a gentleman, he carried his luggage down the stairs and sat down to a breakfast of eggs, biscuits, bacon, and fruit, so much better than the ship's fare.

Stepping outside, he found the weather was already warm and humid. Will dug his handkerchief out of his pocket and mopped his forehead, surprised that the heat and humidity didn't seem to bother his uncle. Unaware of Will's discomfort or choosing to ignore it, his uncle began pointing out the unique architectural features of the houses as they made the long journey to the plantation.

"Louisiana is a mix of many nationalities, and each brought its own influence to our city. Look, there is a Creole house." He pointed to a big white house with a pitched gable roof and a long covered veranda and then continued his description. "Creoles are Louisianans of mixed French, African, Spanish, and Indian heritage and are the first born in a new country."

Mr. Forest has no idea that my birth father is Danish and my mother African and Caribbean. I could be considered a Creole although I wasn't born here. These could be my people, he thought. But he listened closely and learned as his host spoke.

"They build houses using a Norman truss-roof system and heavy braced timber frames. They fill the space between the timbers with bricks or bousillage, a mixture of spanish moss and mud." He stopped speaking and gazed at the houses as they rode silently. "You will see the trees draped with spanish moss, and the people make good use of it. You slept on a mattress filled with it last night." He pointed to a house on the left. "Their houses are built with multiple french doors and large galleries beneath spreading rooflines, just like that one."

Continuing, Mr. Forest explained, "The Creole people added much to the Louisiana culture. Originally, the Spanish word *criollo* meant 'children born in the Caribbean,' but it has come to mean 'homegrown.' More generally, it means native-born Louisianans who descended from continental European stock." He looked at Will, who was listening intently. "Enough about architecture. Tell me about your education and my brother. I would like to know how he is faring."

"He is doing well, and so is his sugar plantation." Will shifted in the buggy so he could see his uncle. "Where shall I start? When I was twelve, my father sent me to Eton in England, where I studied. I learned to speak French, Spanish, Danish, and a couple other languages. I also attended plays and did a great amount of reading. I am most interested in astronomy, science, and sailing." Will wiped away the ever-present perspiration from his forehead. "When I was sixteen, I returned to Saint Croix to help my father with the sugar plantation. We also spent many evenings in our library reading, as he is an avid reader like me. He likes to order the latest books, and we read them together." He hesitated and then continued, "I am very interested in the sea now that I have spent some time sailing. I hope to have my own ship someday."

"Well, I must say, you seem to be everything my brother told me. You speak perfect English, and you seem ambitious. You do have much to learn about life in New Orleans, especially if you are going to help manage my thousand-acre plantation and the slaves needed to run it," he told the handsome lad sitting next to him. "I have a slave who oversees most of the field hands. His name is Silas. His wife works in the house and manages the house slaves. I don't know what I would do without them."

Mr. Forest changed the subject. "I have met many Creoles during my stay in America. Family is important to them. They have good manners, entertain lavishly, and love music and dancing. The Queys are Creoles and friends of mine. They have a daughter named Lynne about your age. Maybe someday you will be invited to their home." Mr. Forest seemed to tire as he sat silent for some time, leaning back on the seat and closing his eyes.

As they left the town of New Orleans and continued their drive, Will noticed the huge sugarcane fields where rows of stalks stood in perfect attendance. As they traveled farther north, cotton fields dominated the landscape. Will noted the slaves working in the fields and knew that both cotton and sugar could not be harvested without the manpower of the slaves.

When Mr. Forest opened his eyes, Will asked, "How many slaves do you own?" He was thinking of his own heritage, his grandmother and mother.

"I have about a thousand acres of land all in cotton, and to work that land I need many slaves. Without them, I could not harvest the plants. Part of your job will be to manage them, although like I mentioned, I do have a good slave overseer named Silas. You will meet him tomorrow." He closed his eyes again and leaned his head back against the carriage.

Troubled, Will's thoughts traveled back to Saint Croix and his slave roots, his grandmother, his mother, the hard life. He would manage his own people, but he could not tell them. As he rode along, he developed a plan. *I will be kind and maybe someday help them gain their freedom,* he thought. *My father told me they earned money and could buy their freedom. I will pay them as well as my uncle allows. I would like to educate them, too.*

Disturbed, he watched the ever-flowing Mississippi River going he knew not where. He listened to the continuous *clip-clop* of the horses' hooves on the hardened dirt road.

Chilled now, he pulled the lapels of his jacket close around him. The sun was beginning to set, painting the sky a pink and red hue, and the evening air cooled. The driver turned into a well-traveled lane lined with beautiful canopied oak trees.

Sensing they were close, Mr. Forest opened his eyes. "Because it gets so hot in the summer, we planted trees to channel the breezes from the Mississippi River to our front door. We open wide those doors and invite the gentle wind in to cool the house." A majestic white house stood at the end of the path. "That is my home," Mr. Forest said proudly. "Eight pillars in the front in Greek Revival style. Like the Creole style of home, mine, too, has a covered veranda and a second-floor balcony that spans the entire front of the house. Your room is up there." He pointed to the top floor where white french doors opened to the veranda.

"It is a beautiful home," Will said. He wondered why Mr. Forest did not have a wife and family when he had such a large house.

"Come on. I'll show you around, and you can meet the housekeeper, Bella. She is Silas's wife. Although slaves cannot legally marry, they jumped over the broom and live together as husband and wife. They have five children. She will help you get settled, and I can imagine you are hungry. I know I am ready for a good meal."

He entered the foyer. Will stood in stunned silence. The floor was covered in white marble, and two grand staircases with banisters of black scroll ironwork on either side led to the second floor where a chandelier hung, its crystals dancing in the gentle breeze that whispered through the open french doors of the grand home.

Mr. Forest cleared his throat. "This is Bella." She stood demurely, her head lowered. She wore a blue and white cotton printed dress and, like his mother, a bandanna around her head. Her flour-sack apron covered her ample front and was smudged with flour. She reminded him of his grandmother, although she was younger. She adjusted the blue bandanna atop her black curly hair. Will trailed her to his room, vaguely smelling vanilla, while the driver followed with his trunk.

A mahogany four-poster bed stood against one wall. Two Queen Anne chairs were positioned comfortably in front of the brick fireplace. A small desk occupied one corner of the room. "This is perfect," Will said, dropping his valise onto the desk.

"Supper be ready when you come down," Bella said as she closed the door. "You tell me if you need somethin'."

After providing a satisfying supper of fried chicken, rice gumbo, and biscuits, Bella poured warm water into a tub in the hall bath, and Will basked in its comfort before retiring to his room. The bed stuffed with spanish moss felt like resting on a soft cloud after the arduous trip. He immediately fell asleep and dreamed of running along the sandy beaches of his island, free.

Sunlight flooding his room awakened him the next morning. He quickly washed the sleep from his eyes in the basin of water in his room, pulled on his trousers and cotton shirt, and headed down the stairs to the dining room. It was a large well-lit room with tall windows flanking the white wainscoting and white mantled fireplace. Scrambled eggs, bacon, and warm biscuits with honey awaited him on the sideboard. Mr. Forest was dressed and already at the table. Will noticed his coloring was much better.

"Good morning. I hope you had a good night's rest," he said. "Help yourself to the food and sit down." He gestured to a chair. "There is much I want to tell you about life on this cotton plantation before we go out. I want to teach you about the cotton gin. It revolutionized life on the cotton plantation."

Will helped himself to breakfast, filling his plate with pancakes and bacon, mounding them with butter and burying them in syrup. After filling his cup with hot black coffee, he sat down.

His uncle leaned back in his chair and began, "Eli Whitney invented the cotton gin about thirty years ago—1792 exactly. Prior to the gin, as it is called, short for *engine*, it was difficult for the slaves to separate the cotton plant from its seed. It took a slave an average of ten hours to produce about one pound of clean cotton. With Whitney's invention, a slave can produce up to a thousand pounds of cotton per day. Quite an improvement, don't you think?" He looked at Will, waiting for a response.

Will nodded. "Yes, and it means you do not have to have as many slaves."

"I do have far fewer slaves than when I originally came to America," he replied, adding cream to his coffee. "After we finish our coffee, I will show you a gin. It uses wire teeth hammered into a rotating wooden cylinder to snare the cotton fibers and pull them through a grate. It really is quite amazing and an ingenious invention."

Sipping another drink of coffee, he stretched his legs under the table and continued. "There is one problem though that hasn't been resolved." He frowned, running his fingers through his hair. "The fiber quality isn't as good as it is with the hand-separated cotton, so our English buyers are not as ready to purchase the cotton, and the price has dropped some. The southern states export over one million tons of cotton annually to the textile mills in England and up north. That is why all those ships are in the port of New Orleans. It is a huge industry." He stood, pushed his chair in, and stated, "It's time I show you the place. Do you ride?"

Will swallowed the rest of his pancakes. "Yes, I learned on the island. We had much land to cover." Gulping the last bit of coffee, he followed Mr. Forest out to the stable where a sorrel pony was saddled and waiting for him. As they rode by the fields, Will watched the plows at work, both with single and double mule teams that were held by sturdy women.

"Why women on the plows?" Will asked.

"Women are cheaper to buy and have babies to raise as slaves. They often do the work of men." Twenty of them were plowing together, with double teams and heavy plows. They twitched their plows around, jerked their reins, and yelled to their mules, all with apparent ease. Everything seemed to run smoothly. He noticed a large muscled Negro man standing to the side of the field observing. *That must be Silas,* he thought.

As they approached, Mr. Forest dismounted and stopped in front of the burly man. "Silas, this is my nephew, William. He has just arrived from Saint Croix." Silas grunted but did not look up.

"I look forward to working with you, Silas," Will said. Silas shuffled his feet in the dirt and muttered, his eyes downcast.

Not seeming to notice the lack of respect, Mr. Forest turned to Will and said, "Come. I want to show you the buildings so you know your way around."

Silas looked up to watch them ride off, Will dipped his head to the man who had just ignored him.

The outbuildings on the plantation were many. "There is a separate kitchen so that when it gets hot the ovens won't heat the house. The food is prepared in the out kitchen and carried into the dining room in the big house," Mr. Forest explained. "There are privies, barns, quarter houses, and buildings to maintain the equipment. The slaves live in those quarter houses." He pointed to humble buildings that were situated with geometric precision, showing the status of his plantation and the slaves.

The cabins appeared in good order. Will recalled the cabins in Saint Croix had chimneys that were prone to catch fire, roofs that leaked, dirt floors and walls with gaping holes. He remembered his grandmother telling him, "In my day, we din' have no floors in them cabins, but we kep' those dirt floors swept clean wit' our sage brooms. The beds in them cabins was made of rough poles fitted into holes bored in the walls and planks laid across them. We had tickin' mattresses filled with corn shucks."

His uncle was speaking, and Will turned his attention to him. "Napoleon actually claimed the Louisiana Territory for France, which is why there are so many French-speaking people in New Orleans and the French Quarter. They have a strong presence in politics, too." His uncle turned to look at him. "You remember the building we drove by where the papers were signed? Louisiana is named after King Louis XIV of France and became a state in 1812, the eighteenth state of the Union." He turned back to his horse and spurred him into a full gallop.

"I just finished reading a book about Napoleon, *The Last Moments of Napoleon*. Maybe you read it?" Will said into the wind, his uncle already far ahead. He nudged his sorrel to keep up with the black stallion Mr. Forest was riding. *My uncle is an educated man and knowledgeable,* he thought. *My father told me he was in politics, so he must be a very important man, and certainly a wealthy one judging by the size of the plantation.* Refusing to feel intimidated, he sat up straighter in the saddle, held his head high, and pushed his horse into a full gallop until he caught up to his uncle.

CHAPTER 7

AT SUPPER ONE evening, after Will had been on the plantation for about a month, Mr. Forest turned and said, "I want to discuss the politics of Louisiana with you. The constitution of 1812 set the ground rules for voters and state officers. To be a governor, one has to own at least five thousand dollars in property. I own that much land, so I meet the qualifications to serve in the legislature."

Conversation stopped for Bella to pour coffee, the chicory brew that Will liked, and then Mr. Forest continued, "The voters do not directly select officers; rather the legislators choose the governor from the top two recipients of the popular vote, and the governor then selects most of the other governing officers, including the attorney general, state treasurer, and state judges. The vote was close, but I was selected and appointed to the legislature."

Will could see he was quite pleased with his position and popularity, and he nodded his head in approval.

"The governor is a personal friend of mine, and I hold him in high esteem. He frequently dines with me."

"That is quite an honor. Will I have opportunity to meet him?" Will asked, trying to hide his awe.

"As a matter of fact, he will be coming to supper on Saturday evening. I have invited some of the other plantation owners as well. It will be a formal event. Did you bring attire appropriate for the evening?" he questioned Will.

"Yes, I did. I made sure I packed my formal evening wear, which will be quite proper. I even have a red cravat to wear," he said.

"Good. I want to introduce you to my friends. There is an unstated dress code among my friends, and I want you to make a good impression." He smiled at Will and then continued elaborating on the growing conflict between the Creoles and the Anglos regarding sugar and cotton cultivation, an issue that was close to his heart.

After supper was completed, Mr. Forest beckoned Will to follow him into the library, where leather-bound books lined the shelves and a blazing fire warmed the evening chill. Two tall candles in silver candlesticks burned brightly on the mahogany desk. Mr. Forrest opened a drawer and pulled out a leather-bound ledger, which Will recognized immediately. He had spent hours writing in his father's account book. "I want you to understand the banking of Louisiana."

He trusts me! he thought. *He wants me to be involved in the finances of the plantation.* A sense of elation filled Will, and he leaned over the ledger eager to learn.

"Two financial institutions have been created under Governor Johnson. One is the Louisiana State Bank, and the other is the Consolidated Association of Planters of Louisiana. The latter is where I do my banking." He took out a large checkbook and pointed to the name of the bank. "My brother tells me you kept his financial records. I would like you to do the same for me. I have notified the bank of my approval."

Standing straight, Will looked directly in his uncle's eyes and said, "I am honored that you trust me enough to give me this opportunity. I will do my best."

"I know you will. I see your integrity. I will help you until you learn, but there is something else. Let's sit down." He put the checkbook and ledger back in the drawer and motioned to a couple of burgundy leather armchairs in front of the fireplace. "Governor Johnson has also created the Internal Improvement Board to maintain and improve our roads and canals. It is a board on which I serve, and I would like you to attend with me."

Will did not respond immediately. When he could speak, he said, "I am honored once again to be thought worthy of attending with you." His thoughts swirled. *If only I could tell you my story. I am the illegitimate son of a slave woman, not yet twenty years of age, and carry in my valise the papers of freedom, and I am to meet the governor of Louisiana, attend a board meeting, and dine at a formal supper with the elite of New Orleans.*

CHAPTER 8

THE DAYS PASSED quickly as Will adjusted to his role as plantation manager. His father had given him plenty of opportunity to learn the day-to-day management of a huge estate. When he was around Silas and the rest of the slaves, he felt a kinship with them, although his Danish blood concealed any distinct physical likeness to the Negro population. His bond with his uncle was growing deeper every day, and Will sensed his growing dependence on him as Mr. Forest spent more time in his office than riding his beloved black stallion. It seemed to take him forever to walk the distance to the barns after breakfast in the morning.

Friday evening after the meal, Mr. Forest said, "Come into the library. We can have our coffee in there. I want to tell you about the people who will be attending tomorrow's supper."

The fire again warmed the room; flames danced off the deep mahogany wood and flitted over the leather-bound books that stood straight as soldiers on the shelves. The Queen Anne chairs were pulled close to the cordial fire. Will settled into the depths of the overstuffed chair and sipped his steaming coffee with just a bit of chicory.

Mr. Forest began, "I've told you we have a very strong French influence in New Orleans. After the sale of Louisiana to the United States, there was an influx of Anglos, and the two groups do not always agree. Both are trying to assert their power. Right now, there is a battle as to where the capital should be located. The Anglos want it out of New Orleans, and the Creoles want to keep it in the French area of the city."

He rubbed his legs and continued talking. "Some of my guests will be French. One of those men is Pierre Mercier. His family is from southwest France. Like many of the French families, they send their children back to France to be educated, and because of that, they speak excellent French and maintain the French traditions. By the way, do you speak the language?" He paused and looked at Will.

"*Oui, Monsieur, je parle français très bien puisque j'ai passé quelque temps à Paris alors que j'ai été éduqué en Europe,*" he said fluently.

"Good. In some homes, only French is spoken. It is used in the cotton industry too. It will be of great benefit to you to speak the language." He lifted a beignet pastry from the dessert plate Bella set on the side table beside the coffee, and a cloud of powdered sugar descended on his chest. He brushed at it impatiently. "Monsieur Mercier has been educated in Paris and is a lover of literature."

"I have read the French novelist and playwright, Balzac. I studied the author when I was abroad. I'll look forward to a lively discussion with Monsieur Mercier," Will said as he reached for a second beignet.

Mr. Forest also reached for another beignet, more carefully this time, knocking the surplus powdered sugar back onto the plate. After the white cloud settled, he went on, "Mr. Louis Canonge will also be attending. His father is a distinguished lawyer in New Orleans. You may have heard of him as he originally lived in Saint-Domingue before his family came to Louisiana. Louis received his education in Paris as well, and he, too, is a lover of literature and the arts. He is considered by the people of New Orleans to be the prototypical Frenchman. He is said to have fought many duels defending his honor and that of his friends. Be careful that you don't offend him." Mr. Forest chuckled. "Being of English origin, I do not understand the fiery French temperament and quickness to challenge one to a duel when offended. It's foolishness, but nevertheless it happens." He reached for his coffee, his hand shook slightly, spilling its hot contents on his shirt. He dabbed at it with his handkerchief, murmuring under his breath.

"As for the young ladies, Hortense Marginy and Lynne Quey will also be our guests. I spoke earlier of Lynne, a belle Creole—a beautiful young lady. Her parents are very wealthy. She has many suitors already although she is just seventeen."

The thought of meeting young people his age was enticing. Will's uncle seemed to be well connected in social circles, which made Will wonder why his uncle had not married, but did not feel it his place to ask. There were no pictures of family in the sitting room or parlor. He assumed he had no family other than his brother in Saint Croix. He never spoke of anyone else. Did his health deter him?

His uncle was speaking again. "Another guest will be John Grimes, a Virginian who is a strong advocate of Louisiana. He is an excellent lawyer and was only twenty-five when he was appointed district attorney to the United States." He reached for a copy of the newspaper, the *Courier*. "I want you to read this article about him. I think you will find it amusing."

It is said that Mr. Grimes never wears the same suit for more than two consecutive days and that he changes his colors often and as rapidly as a chameleon. Today, he is in full black, apparently in mourning. Tomorrow, he will surprise the public with a green cockney coat with fox-head buttons, buff pants, white hat, and red neckerchief. The next day, he will appear in spotless white.

After Will read the article, he handed the newspaper back to his uncle, chuckling. "I can't wait to see what he will wear to your dinner!"

Mr. Forest covered a yawn with his hand. He leaned forward in the chair and rose with difficulty. "I am tired. It is time for me to retire. Good night, Will."

When the evening of the supper arrived, William dressed with great care for his introduction to New Orleans society. After a refreshing bath, he stepped into the corset, or girdle, and shoved and pulled it up to his waist, cinching it in the fashion of the day. *Not very comfortable, but the military is wearing them, so I guess I can suffer through one evening,* he mused. His hand shook as he buttoned his white linen shirt with the tall standing collar and puffs at the sleeve head. He tied the wide red cravat in a bow at his neck. Peering at himself in the looking glass, he pulled at the black velvet coat with the high shawl-like collar that framed his face. He turned to see his black formal trousers that were cut full through the hip and thighs, tapering to his ankles. He adjusted the straps that fastened under his square-toed black shoes to hold his trousers smoothly in place. *This will have to do. I hope it meets with my uncle's approval.*

Trying to conceal his nervousness, Will descended the staircase slowly. His oiled, unruly hair lay sleek against his well-shaped head. He noticed every man in the room had sideburns just like his. After scanning the room, he saw the gentlemen were dressed very much like him. *I can do this,* he said to himself, *it only takes perseverance.*

He stopped suddenly. His eyes were irresistibly drawn to the most beautiful girl he had ever seen. Candlelight bounced off the red highlights of her chestnut hair, the curls framing her peach-colored cheeks. Simple pearls adorned her ears and neck. When her cerulean eyes caught his and held them, he was captivated. He could not move. He was aware that staring was rude, but he was mesmerized.

She turned to her companions, a girl with very dark hair and deep-brown eyes and a young man who seemed smitten by the dark-haired beauty, as he did not let her out of his vision. She spoke to them, and they turned to look at Will. She slipped him one more glance with just the slightest flirtatious smile before turning again to her friends.

He knew he must meet her before the night was over. Searching the room, he saw Mr. Forest talking to an important looking gentleman. As he neared the men, he heard the man speaking of President Jackson and Lafayette. "Yes, when General Lafayette came to the United States this year, I was selected to give the welcoming speech in French," the man said and turned to Will when he approached them.

"Ah, William, let me introduce Mr. Marginy, he is the mayor of New Orleans and a strong supporter of our President Jackson.. You have heard me speak of him," said his uncle.

Will extended his hand and gripped the hand of Mr. Marginy. "How do you do, sir? I have heard much about you. I too am a strong supporter of President Jackson. It is good to have a president from our part of the country who understands us and the importance of our cotton plantations to the development of the South."

"Well spoken, young man. From what Forest tells me, it sounds like you are doing a fine job of managing the plantation. That is good, as it frees him to spend more time in politics and in helping us run the fine city of New Orleans and our state as well." He turned as his wife, coming alongside him, tucked her arm in his.

"Don't be selfish with this young man. You must introduce us." She smiled a winsome smile, including both Mr. Forest and Will in her gaze. He looked into the same deep-blue eyes as those of the young woman who attracted his attention earlier.

"Of course, dear. This is the young man of whom we spoke. He is Mr. Forest's right-hand man and nephew. His name is William. William, this is my wife, Mrs. Marginy." He smiled, laying his hand over the small one resting on his arm.

"How do you do? Oh, I have heard of you." She graciously offered him the fingertips of her gloved hand. "How are you enjoying your time in Louisiana? Do you find it much different from your island, or are all plantations the same?" Not giving him time to answer, she continued, "You must come to supper some evening with Mr. Forest. I am sure you can manage that?" she questioned.

Carolyn Holm Bakken

Will turned to his uncle. "I am certain we can accept your invitation, can we not?" Mr. Forest nodded in assent.

"Good. How about next Saturday evening?"

Mr. Forest responded, "Thank you. We would enjoy that." With that, he excused himself and spoke to Will, "I want you to meet some more of my acquaintances. If you are to get involved in our city and our state, you need to be familiar with the people."

Following his uncle across the ballroom floor, perfectly waxed and buffed for the night's event, Will felt his heart pound as they approached the governor, Mr. Henry Johnson. He was dressed much like Will. He combed his thinning brown hair off his high forehead in gentle waves. His eyes were dark and astute and his speech loud and commanding. The group of men who surrounded him were talking politics. "Yes, it was certainly to my advantage to have the marquis de Lafayette visit me in New Orleans," he bellowed." The division among the Creoles helped me with my election, and having him as my guest aided in getting the votes. Of course, changing the capital from New Orleans to Donaldsville helped, too, as it was a compromise between the Anglos and the Creoles. I didn't want the riot we had in 1824." He turned as Will and Mr. Forest approached him. "Well, here is our host. Nice party, Forest, and who is this young man?" he asked, nodding toward Will.

"This is my nephew and new manager, William. My brother sent him from his sugar plantation on Saint

Croix. He is a great help to me as he is a quick learner and very efficient. I shall be bringing him with me to the Internal Improvement Board meetings. You don't mind, do you?" he questioned.

"I am glad to meet you, William, and by all means, do join us at the board meetings. We need young minds and new ideas if we are to improve our state." He smiled and continued, "Do you have an interest in politics?"

Will responded humbly, "I do not feel knowledgeable enough to answer that question. I do know I am eager to learn and will enjoy seeing how the board meetings are conducted."

Governor Johnson nodded his approval and turned his attention back to the circle of men surrounding him. Will, forgotten for the moment and still dwelling on Mrs. Marginy's invitation to dinner, asked Mr. Forest, "I have heard you talk about the Marginys' suppers at Lake Pontchartrain. Do you think we will be entertained at Fontainebleau, his home right on the lake? I have heard that he is somewhat of a hero."

"Let's walk out of earshot, and I will tell you more." He led William to the potted ferns in the corner of the large room, where he could view his guests and explain. "He spent two years in France as a guest of Lafayette, so it was understandable why Lafayette would stay with him in his home. As I mentioned earlier, he also speaks excellent French. He does love a fine table and good conversation with his friends." He stopped and swallowed, Will assumed from his mouth watering as he described the delicacies. "I have heard say that the turkeys are fattened on pecans. He serves softshell crabs from the beach and oysters from his own reef and green trout and perch from the bayous. He has it all right there, and his staff knows how to fix it. To dine at his home is a treat indeed."

He scanned the room, observing the clusters of people as they visited. "Come now, we mustn't be rude to our guests; let's return to them. We will talk more tomorrow, and I will answer your questions." He left Will and circulated among the guests.

Will stayed in his secluded spot for minutes longer; long enough to hear the servants whispering about one of the guests. "Miss Quey be so be'utiful but she cause way too many duels. Now it be massah Cononge who wants her hand."

Will left the seclusion and the gossiping servants and wandered among he guests.

Just then he heard Mrs. Marginy call his name. "William, come here. I want you to meet my daughter." She led him to the group of women he had just been observing. The girl with the deep-blue eyes turned to face him. She was wearing a dress of the softest cream with a pink rose tucked in her bodice. Her puffed sleeves slipped just off her perfectly formed shoulders. Her chestnut hair was parted in the middle, curled on both sides, and swept up in the back with more curls cascading to her shoulders. "This is my daughter, Hortense Marginy. Hortense, I would like you to meet William. He is Mr. Forest's nephew and plantation manager and has come from the island of Saint Croix."

Hortense gracefully curtsied. "I am so pleased to make your acquaintance," she murmured in a low voice and smiled, lowering her long eyelashes. "Have you had the opportunity to meet any of the young people in New Orleans?" she asked politely.

Will swallowed, wanting to make a good impression, but when he spoke, his voice cracked. He cleared his throat. "Unfortunately, I have been very busy learning this cotton plantation and its workings. This is my first opportunity to meet people my age. I have been in New Orleans on occasion for business, but I am looking forward to attending the Théâtre d'Orléans I have heard so much about. I understand many people go on Sunday nights to see the plays."

"Oh, yes, and the grand opera on Tuesdays and the comic opera on Thursdays. I will be attending on Tuesday night, and if you come, please do call at my booth now that we have been introduced. It is on the second tier, and you will see me if you bring your opera glasses." She added demurely, "Of course, we will be chaperoned."

"I would like that very much," Will responded, his heart racing at the thought of getting to know this beautiful woman more intimately. At that moment, Mr. Forest announced it was time to go in for supper. Will offered Hortense his arm and asked, "May I escort you?"

Hortense looked to her mother for permission, and when she nodded, she took his arm, and together they entered the dining room. The table was set with fine white linen, and brilliant crystal candelabras sparkled, reflecting off the fine white china and silver flatware at each table setting. He pulled out the chair for Hortense, making sure her full dress was tucked in before he helped her slide the chair under the table. Sitting next to her, he realized Mr. Forest had arranged the seating with Bella prior to the supper. He glanced at his host, who was watching his reaction to the arrangement. Will felt the warmth of his blush and hoped it didn't show too much.

As they were served sumptuous pheasant, roast pork, assorted vegetables, and sweet potatoes, a staple of the South, Hortense asked, "Do you enjoy reading, William?" She used the linen napkin to daintily wipe the corner of her mouth before placing it back in her lap. "I have read *Le Père Goriot*; have you?" Nodding his assent, she went on, "I have been there, as I studied in Paris. My parents sent me there for finishing school. It was there that I gained an interest in literature and reading. My tutors required me to read many of the classics. My dream is to write someday like Honoré de Balzac." She blushed a very lovely peach and lowered her eyes. "Have I spoken too forthrightly for our first meeting?" she asked.

Will responded, "Not at all. I prefer a woman who has ideas, and, yes, I have read the book and also the play he wrote, *La Comédie Humaine.*" He took a bite of one of Bella's biscuits he loved, savored it, and then continued, "My schooling required me to read many of the classics also. I acquired a love of literature, although I have no desire to write."

He grew quiet, thinking, *I am just like Rastignac in* La Comédie Humaine. *He pursued his ambitions by being introduced to Parisian high society. Here I am, the grandson of a slave, sitting at a table with the governor and leaders of New Orleans and the state of Louisiana. Unlike Rastignac, I will not break my promise and tell Hortense that my grandmother was a slave. He glanced across the table where Mr. and Mrs. Marginy were seated, talking and listening with perfect decorum. They would not take kindly to their daughter being attended by a slave descendant. But here I am, and I feel like standing and shouting, like Rastignac at the end of the novel, "Beware, New Orleans, here I come."*

Realizing he had been lost in his thoughts too long and not wanting to be rude to the beautiful young lady by his side, he said, "Tell me more about you. What do you like to do besides read? I have heard that one must just write every day. Do you schedule a time to write?"

"Oh, no," Hortense replied, "I am not that disciplined…Someday I want to write. I do write in my journal most days, and tonight I shall pen my thoughts of this lovely party and of meeting you." She adjusted the napkin in her lap, her eyes downcast. "I also like to go to the opera and the theater as I mentioned earlier. I do hope to see you on Tuesday evening," she said decorously. "One of my favorite things to do is ride in the mornings. My horse's name is Duke, and he is a beautiful gelding." She turned to him, asking, "Do you ride, William?"

"My uncle and I ride most days. He has a black stallion, and I have a sorrel. We have acres to cover, and I do enjoy riding. But what I really hope to do is own a ship and sail, maybe to New York or Hawaii. I think it would be great to go west too, to see the Pacific Ocean." His eyes were shining. He spoke more animatedly as he continued, and soon Hortense was laughing at him.

"I see you have an adventurous spirit. I admire that. I think it would be exciting to travel, too. I enjoyed my time abroad, and I would like to go back to England and France again someday. I liked my time on the sea as well, except when it got too rough." She made a disparaging face that Will found charming.

Just then Mr. Forest stood to his feet and tapped his goblet with his fork. "It is time for some dancing. Please escort your lady into the ballroom where the orchestra is waiting." He smiled directly at Will and moved to the lady on his right, offered his arm, and led the way into the ballroom.

Standing, Will pulled out Hortense's chair and offered her his arm. She graciously accepted, and they followed Mr. Forest and his guest. The orchestra was playing a waltz, and the chandeliers lighting the ballroom sparkled off the pale-yellow walls. The night was magical and Hortense enchanting. He guided her out onto the highly polished floor, grateful for his dance lessons and the practice he so detested. He floated across the floor, the soft touch of Hortense's hand on his shoulder sending thrilling shudders down his spine. She fit perfectly in his arms.

The evening flew by, and soon the guests were retrieving their coats and wraps and leaving. "I hope to see you at the theater on Tuesday evening," Will whispered to Hortense, holding her wrap for her.

"Don't forget to bring your opera glasses so you know which booth is mine. I will be watching for you. Please do come and see me." She smiled and swept out the door with her parents, her full skirt whispering behind her.

Will waited for the last of the guests to leave before he and Mr. Forest went into the study to have a glass of wine. Mr. Forest looked ashen and tired. "Well, I noticed you and Hortense seemed to be enjoying each other tonight. Will you be seeing her again?"

"I hope to go to the opera on Tuesday night. She will be there, and she has asked me to come to her booth. Do you think I will be able to go?"

"I don't see any reason why you can't attend. Hortense is one of the most desirable young ladies in the community. She is not only beautiful but interesting as well. Did you find her so?"

"Yes, she loves to read, and she wants to be a writer. She also likes to ride horses, and she has a good sense of humor. I look forward to getting to know her better. I shared my love of the sea with her, and she too likes to travel and have adventure. Like me, she studied in France and England, so she has already been abroad."

Looking at the clock on the mantel, Mr. Forest stifled a yawn and stood. "It's late and time for me to go to bed. I get tired so easily. I will see you in the morning for church."

His uncle attended the Methodist church regularly, as did most people in New Orleans. Will's birth father made sure he was baptized a Lutheran, but Will had been attending church with Mr. Forest since his arrival. "I want to ride to the south-section field first thing Monday morning. We may have some blight in the cotton, and I want to get a closer look at it to see if we need to do something about it. Good night, Will." He handed him a flyer. "Read this so you know what I am talking about."

> Bacterial blight is a disease that requires an initial source of inoculum for infection to occur. Unless a field has been in cotton production for a number of years and the disease has previously been identified, the organism doesn't have a point source for subsequent infection. In those situations where cotton has either never been planted in a particular field or the field has been out of cotton production for a number of years then the initial source of the bacterium is believed to have been from infested seed.

Will hurriedly read the information. He was not quite ready to leave his delightful evening for a lesson in bacterial blight. He was aware of the danger to the cotton crop, and he knew it could ruin a man.

CHAPTER 9

HIS UNCLE KNOCKED on his bedroom door as the sun rose Monday morning. "Come on, Will. Let's get going before the heat of the day makes it unbearable. I had Bella pack us some biscuits with ham. We can eat them on the way. I'll meet you downstairs."

Will rubbed his eyes and stumbled out of bed, threw on his clothes, splashed some water on his face, and ran down the steps. Mr. Forest was out front with Silas, who was holding both horses. Silas acknowledged Will with a nod of his head. Their working relationship had improved once Silas saw that Will was a capable manager. As the sun rose over the horizon, Will felt he had never seen anything more beautiful. The cotton fields looked as though they had been covered with a soft white blanket that stretched for miles. Mr. Forest explained, "If there is a blight and we catch it soon enough, we can stop it from ruining the whole cotton crop. If just a few of the plants have been invaded, we will uproot and destroy them." He pulled his hat down over his eyes to shield them from the rising sun. "I rotate the crops to support the land, so I have rich soil. It helps prevent diseases."

When they arrived at the field, some of the slaves were already there. Mr. Forest directed, "Move down the rows looking for anything irregular on the plants."

The first plant Will looked at had no trace of blight. As he walked down the rows, gingerly exploring each plant, he found nothing unusual. The plants looked healthy. They mounted the horses and road farther into the field, stopping occasionally to examine the plants, but no sight of the blight appeared.

Breathing a sigh of relief, Mr. Forest turned to Will. "It looks like we are fine, but I do want us to keep a close eye as neighbors have sighted some irregularities. We'll check some of the other fields tomorrow."

The ride back to the house was much more relaxed, and Will's thoughts wandered to Hortense. "Do you have any opera glasses?" he asked. "I need some for tomorrow night so I can locate Hortense. By the way, you are welcome to go with me to the opera. Would you like to go?"

"No, no, I have seen my share of operas, and I have a meeting tomorrow night with some of the other plantation owners. I want to stay on top of this blight, and I need to see if any of the other planters have found traces in our community. You go and enjoy yourself."

On Tuesday morning, Mr. Forest did not come down to breakfast, which was very unusual. Normally he was there before Will each morning. "Where is my uncle, Bella? It isn't like him to miss breakfast."

"Oh, he has a touch of the cholera agin. He had a bad attack when he was younger, and e'ry once in a whil' it come back to bite him. You prob'ly noticed he skinny. He jus' don' seem to gain weight no matta how much I try to fatten 'im up. He spend the next few days in bed and then be up agin. He beats it ev'ry time."

This was news to Will, and it saddened him to think that Mr. Forest was not doing well. It did explain his thinness and his desire for Will to learn everything. "Is there anything I can do for him?" he asked.

"He did ask fo' you to come up and see him. He wants you to check on the east section today."

Will climbed the stairs and knocked gently on the door.

"Come in," Mr. Forest whispered.

He opened the door and was shocked to see how pale his uncle was, his face the same color as the white sheets. Perspiration beads glistened on his forehead. When cholera reared its ugly head, it brought with it diarrhea and vomiting, which led to dehydration if the patient could not keep fluids down. A half-filled glass of water stood on his nightstand and a bucket at the side of the bed.

"I was exposed to cholera when I first came to New Orleans, and if I am not careful to get adequate rest, it flares up. I have to rest and drink lots of fluids. I should be up in a couple of days." He paused, leaned over the pail, wretched, and lay back down exhausted.

Will waited while he caught his breath. He reached for the glass to offer his uncle a drink, but Mr. Forest waved it away.

"I want you to ride out to the east section today with Silas and some of the slaves and check the plants. We have to be cautious with this blight." He closed his eyes as if the effort of talking were just too exhausting.

Will quietly left the room. Outside the door, he leaned against the wall in disbelief. The management of the plantation would be solely on his young shoulders if anything happened to his uncle, and the weight seemed too much for him to bear. His thoughts had been only on attending the opera so he could see Hortense, but with this new situation, he thought it would be better if he stayed home. Stuffing the disappointment into the back of his mind, he ran down the stairs.

Other than the heaviness of Mr. Forest's illness, nothing could take away the beauty of the early August morning in New Orleans. Later, the heat and humidity of the day would make being outside unbearable. Will reveled in the feel of his horse beneath him and the view of the cotton fields stretching for miles. Harvesting would start in September. He turned to Silas, who rode comfortably and silently beside him. Silas had been with Mr. Forest ever since he came to New Orleans. Bella and the two youngest children were often in the house. By this time, the three older ones were already working on the plantation. They reminded Will of his time in the big house in Saint Croix.

"I see your children in the house with Bella." Knowing that normally slaves were not allowed to be educated, he asked, "Have your children learned to read?"

"No, sir, there be no un to teach 'em. I never learned to read either. I sure would like 'em to get some learnin'."

Knowing the importance of education and the opportunity it had provided him, he decided, with his uncle's approval, to provide a tutor for Silas's children. "I will see what I can do about that once Mr. Forest is feeling better." Changing the subject, he asked, "How is it that you and Bella have stayed together on the plantation all this time?"

"Massa Fo'est—he be real good to me and my fam'ly. He see the impo'tance of families staying together. He be a real good manager. He don' whup the slaves like som do."

Will had noticed that, and it made him think even more highly of his uncle. Once again he thanked the Lord for his good fortune. To come to New Orleans with a good plantation owner and one who treated his slaves well made it so much easier for him. His foster father in Saint Croix had been like that, too, giving Will his opportunity in life.

They rode on silently, both lost in their thoughts, until they reached the east section. They dismounted and walked the rows, searching for anything unusual in the plants. They found nothing. Mounting again, they slowly walked their horses down multiple rows, but they found no blight or irregularity. "Looks good to me. I think we can safely let Mr. Forest know there's nothing here. Let's go home."

When entering the house, Will noticed a somberness that seemed to fall over the house slaves. Seeing Bella descending the stairs from Mr. Forest's room, he asked, "How is he? Is he getting any better?"

Bella's face told it all. With downcast eyes, she mumbled, "He not be gettin' any better—in fac', he seem worse. I ain't ne'r seem him this lowly befo'. I just prayin' to the good Lord that he come outta it."

"Can I go up and see him?" questioned Will.

"He won' talk much, but I thin' he will see yo'."

Will slowly mounted the stairs. In his years of living, he had not come in contact with a seriously ill person or with death, and he did not know how to respond. It frightened him. He rapped quietly on the door, but not hearing any answer, he opened the door cautiously and peered into the room. His uncle was just as he had seen him earlier, but his eyes were closed, and he did not open them even though Will coughed softly. He heard the rasp of his breathing as Mr. Forest struggled with each breath. He stood quietly for a few minutes, waiting. When there was no response, he left the room to find Bella, who was in the kitchen preparing chicken soup.

"Did you call the doctor?" he asked.

"Yes, suh, he been out to see him this mornin', but he say they be nothin' we kin do but let him sweat it out and keep pourin' in the fluids. The thing is, he don' want to drink anythin' 'cause he just loses it agin. It's mighty hard on 'im." A muffled sob escaped even though Will could tell she was trying hard to keep her composure. "I ain't never seen 'im this bad."

Heavyhearted, Will left the house and went to the office. With Mr. Forest that sick, he would have to assume the management of the plantation. Fortunately, his uncle was a man of detail, and his books reflected that. Will took the log off the shelf and looked up the previous year. Flipping through the log, he noted that harvesting started September 28. That was less than two weeks away. Closing the book, he went to look for Silas, who was in the machine shop.

"Mr. Forest is not doing well, and looking through his records, I see that harvesting starts in two weeks. Is the machinery ready, and are the slaves prepared for the picking? Do we have enough bodies to get the picking done?"

Silas stopped and, seeing the concern on Will's face, responded, "We been doin' this for a lotta years, and yes, suh, we prepared. Ev'rybody come out and work, includin' the women and chillun. I blow the cow horn, callin' all the people to get out in the field. At the end of the day, we carry it all into the buildin' where the women and chillun sep'rate the white cotton from the yellow cotton, and we put it thru the gin and then the cotton press. It gets pressed into bales, which we sell. We put in long hours, and it gets hot, but we all pull together to help Mr. Forest 'cause he been good to us. He pay us if we get it done right fast." He stopped to wipe his brow with a rag he carried in his pocket. Then his face broke out in a grin. "After that, we have big feast celebratin' the harvest. We all love that. We gonna do it agin this year?" he asked.

"If I have anything to say about it, we will. We need to celebrate when everyone works hard, and there's nothing like some good southern cooking to make everybody happy," Will responded.

Somewhat relieved but still filled with anxiety, Will returned to the house. He remembered what it was like to harvest the sugarcane and how much work it took for everyone. He had never been in complete charge of harvesting before in his life, and the prospect frightened him.

CHAPTER 10

SEVERAL HOURS LATER, Will stopped at his uncle's room and put his ear against the door. He heard the murmur of Bella's voice and knocked softly.

"Who is it?" Bella asked.

"It's me, Will; can I come in?"

"Shor', come on in. Mr. Forest be awake."

Gently opening the door, Will pulled a chair up to the side of the bed where his uncle was sitting against pillows stacked behind him. "How are you feeling? Do you feel any better yet?" Will asked.

"No, I can't say that I do," and with that he began coughing, his body contorting with the effort. He fell weakly back against the pillows, and in between coughs, he choked out, "The doctor says I have to stay in bed for at least a few days, and then I can start getting up for small amounts of time if I am feeling better." He turned and looked at Bella. "Bella has been insisting that I keep enough fluids in me. I am very weak, and it is really hard to keep anything down. I think I should rest now." He closed his eyes, and Will got up, ready to leave, when his uncle whispered, "It's you this year, Will, with the harvesting." With that, he slipped back down under the covers, and Will heard his rasping breath.

Will went on to his own room as the sun was setting and evening descending like a dark blanket on the face of the plantation. He stood at his window and watched the shadowed oak trees swaying in the wind. It reminded him of the breezes on Saint Croix, and suddenly he was very homesick. He missed his mother. He checked the time on the clock on the desk and saw that it was almost time for the opera to begin, and he would not be there. He wondered if Hortense would miss him and if she would think he had forgotten. He didn't know how to let her know that Mr. Forest was very sick and he felt it was his responsibility to stay with him. Maybe he could send one of the slaves with a message to her that Mr. Forest was sick and he wouldn't be able to attend. He went to find Bella, who was in the kitchen, peeling potatoes for the evening meal. "Is there someone I can send to the opera with a message?" he asked.

"Sho', I tell Billy to take it. He ride real fast, and he'll get there befo' it start. You give it to me, and I'll take care of it."

Will returned to his room and took some of the stationery out of his desk. He sharpened the quill, dipped the pen in the ink, and wrote,

Dear Miss Marginy,

I regret to tell you that I will not be able to attend the opera tonight as Mr. Forest is very ill. I feel I must stay

*here with him. I do hope he will be well enough to attend
the supper your father has invited us to at your home
on Saturday.*

*With sincere regrets,
William*

He folded the note, slipped it into an envelope, and wrote
Miss Hortense Marginy on the outside. He uttered a sigh of
relief. Hortense was the first young person he had met,
and he found her very attractive. He desired to know her
better, to spend more time with her. He concealed his
disappointment by collecting all his thoughts and tucking them away to savor later. He had Saturday evening to
look forward to with anticipation.

True to her word, Bella had Billy waiting at the bottom of the steps, so when Will came down, he handed
him the note, and Billy galloped off to the opera house.

Will asked to have supper in his room, rather than eat
alone in the dining room. He was reading *The Adventures
of Ulysses* by Charles Lamb, and he was eager to have
some time to himself before he went to bed. He wanted
to continue to learn more about sailing. Ulysses was a
daring man of the sea and appealed to Will. He was also
trying to refresh his French since he knew the language
was spoken in cotton trading.

Through Wednesday and Thursday, Mr. Forest
remained pretty much the same, although, over time, it was
easier for him to keep down the chicken broth that Bella

made for him. He seemed to be sleeping better through the night, without so much interruption and coughing. On Friday morning, when Will entered the room, Mr. Forest was actually sitting in a chair near his bed. "Good morning. It is so good to see you out of bed. I was really worried about you," Will stated. "How are you feeling today?"

"So much better, and it feels so good to be out of bed. I hope to get dressed and come downstairs for breakfast this morning. I really don't like to be in bed when harvesting is so close. Are we ready, Will? Are the machines in order?"

Will assured him, "Yes, Silas and I have made sure all is in working order and the slaves are ready to start. Silas asked about the celebration at the end of harvest. He wanted to make sure it was still going to happen."

Mr. Forest nodded. "They love that time of celebration, and they deserve it, working as hard as they do. They are up before dawn and in bed after the sun sets. Yes, they certainly deserve a celebration. Will you speak with Bella about that? She's the one who organizes all the food."

Will didn't know how to bring it up, but he was so eager to see Hortense again and wanted to know if Mr. Forest would be able to go to the supper tomorrow evening at the Marginys'. He stood at the door, hesitating.

Seeing his reluctance at leaving the room, Mr. Forest asked, "Is there something else, Will? You seem apprehensive this morning."

"I know you have been feeling ill, and, well, I was just wondering, do you think you will be able to go to the Marginys' supper tomorrow night?"

Chuckling, Mr. Forest said, "If I am able to walk, we will be there. I know how much this means to you. I was in love at your age, too, and I wanted to spend as much time as I could with a certain young lady. I will not tell you more—so don't ask—but, yes, I will try to make it. We will not cancel yet. Leave the room now so I can get dressed, and I will meet you at the breakfast table."

Will ran down the stairs, his feet barely touching the floor. He would see Hortense tomorrow night, only thirty-six hours away. He planned to wear the suit he had worn on the night of Mr. Forest's party. He couldn't wait to see her again.

Saturday was a busy day since Mr. Forest still wanted to check the cotton fields. He sent Will and Silas out on horseback with orders to report back to him. Next week, harvest was starting, and he wanted to make sure everything was in order. He sat in his office. Will was his legs as he was still too weak to ride. It also gave him opportunity to lie down on the office chaise if he got too exhausted.

Will was impatient all day, although he tried very hard to hide it. He pictured Hortense in his mind a thousand times throughout the day, and each time she became more desirable. When evening arrived, he was ready. They had received a formal invitation to dine at Fontainebleau. Will had been practicing his French, so if Mr. Marginy did choose to speak to him in French, he hoped to respond correctly.

CHAPTER 11

WILL ADJUSTED HIS cravat. He smoothed his well-oiled dark hair into place once again. The evening was warm, making him perspire as he tried to focus on the fields they were passing. He flicked a feather that had landed on his trousers through the carriage's open window.

"Are you nervous, Will?" his uncle asked.

"I want to make a good impression on Hortense and her family. I like her very much."

"I'll help you out by telling you a little about Fontainebleau." He turned so he could face Will and spoke loudly over the crunching wheels of the carriage as it jostled over the country dirt road. "Mr. Marginy has a very large sugar plantation, not cotton. He founded his site on Lake Pontchartrain across from New Orleans. He named it after a beautiful forest near Paris, France, which is a favorite recreation area of the French kings. It is so peaceful separated from the business of the port and activity of New Orleans. He entertains lavishly in the style of a monarch."

More questions crowded Will's mind, but as Mr. Forest leaned his head against the black leather headrest of the carriage, he sensed he wanted to rest before they arrived. Soon his mouth dropped open, and a gentle snore rippled his mustache.

Horses and carriages lined the drive when they arrived. The butler, wearing a dark suit, white shirt, and white gloves, greeted them at the door and ushered them into an impressive salon where drinks were served. Blue velvet curtains hung at the leaded-glass windows. Persian rugs in deep orange and blue covered the finely polished wooden floor. "Where is Hortense? I don't see her. I think the girl with the dark hair is Lynne Quey, but I did not meet her the other night," he said, pointing her out to Mr. Forest discreetly.

"She is Lynne Quey, the belle Creole I told you about. She is a good friend of Hortense, and her family often dines with the Marginys. I will introduce you; follow me."

As they approached, Will noticed her tumbling dark curls were tied up in a scarlet ribbon that matched her red dress. Her skin was olive, and she had a very tiny waist, which he knew would fit in the span of his hands. He could hear her bubbling laughter, and it piqued his interest.

"Miss Quey, I would like to introduce you to my nephew William."

"*Comment allez-vous? Je suis ravie de vous rencontrer.*" She lowered her head in graceful acknowledgment, her curls falling over her dancing dark-brown eyes. "*J'espère que vous appréciez votre temps à la Nouvelle Orléans. C'est une belle ville.* You do speak French, don't you? If not, please tell me, and I will speak only in English."

He smiled. "Yes, I do speak French, but I am out of practice. If you speak slowly, I will be able to follow your conversation. I am refreshing myself in the language as Mr. Forest tells me that many of the merchants who buy and sell cotton speak French." He took a breath. *"Je suis fine et un débutant au français.* How was that?" He waited for her approval, which she gave willingly.

"I will tutor you." She grinned impishly. "Hortense has already told me much about you. She is looking forward to tonight and seeing you again." She slipped her arm in his and said, "I think supper is served. Let's go in and see where we are seated."

Shocked by her forwardness, Will followed her into the lavish dining room. The walls were decorated with deep-burgundy brocade, and a crystal chandelier sparkled. The table was set with crystal goblets, fine silver, and bone-china plates. Candles glowed in silver candlesticks in the center of the table. Will had never seen such extravagance. Everything Mr. Forest told him about the Marginys' home was true.

After he seated Lynne, he noticed the place cards and that he was seated right between Lynne and Hortense. He wondered who planned that. He found Lynne very attractive and vivacious, yet he thought Hortense beautiful, too.

Hortense arrived minutes later, and Will stood to pull out her chair. "Good evening, William," she greeted him with a warm smile. "I am so glad you could come tonight. Mr. Forest must be feeling better; I saw him earlier." He pushed her chair in and sat down himself. "I am so sorry you missed the opera on Tuesday. It was quite entertaining." She smelled like violets when she leaned over him to peer at Lynne. "I assume you have met my best friend, Lynne. We have been friends since childhood." She greeted Lynne, and they settled into polite conversation.

At one point, Will slid his chair back so the ladies could converse more easily, giving him a chance to observe both of them. They could not have been more different. Hortense was fair, charming, beautiful, well-read, and educated. She was very intelligent and kind. Lynne, on the other hand, was dark, precocious, outspoken, adventurous, and she laughed easily. Mr. Forest had told him she had many suitors and men had fought duels over her. Will found both women interesting and attractive.

Louis Canonge, seated across the broad span of the table, kept his eye on Lynne most of the evening. It was not convenient for Louis to speak to Lynne, but Will sensed his interest and caught the dark looks each time he spoke to her. She seemed to be avoiding him and never once looked his way. He did not want to be called out in a duel for sure.

Will was glad when supper was served and he could focus on the meal rather than worry about his attentions to Lynne. Just as anticipated, turkey fattened on pecans from the grounds, softshell crabs from the beach, oysters from Mr. Marginy's own reef, and green trout and perch from the bayous were generously served.

After the meal, he excused himself and joined the rest of the men in the smoking room. Dark paneled walls held family portraits of generations gone by. The oil lanterns burned brightly, casting a soft glow on the paneled walls. The conversation turned to cotton and sugar harvesting. Will decided that much of the harvesting of both was similar. He liked to listen to the men talk, especially his uncle, who was very knowledgeable about the subject. The pleasant smell of tobacco filled the room, and smoke filtered the light of the candles. He found himself quite content until he heard Mr. Marginy say, "We must whip the slaves when they show any disrespect, or we'll have an insurrection on our hands. They must know their station in life. We don't want an uprising."

Will watched Mr. Forest, who did not comment but averted his head, a flash of annoyance wrinkling his brow.

Standing, Mr. Marginy announced, "Well, gentlemen, I think it is time we joined the ladies, or my wife will be in here to remind me." The others followed as he opened the double doors that led to the grand ballroom.

William stood for a moment at the door. The view was breathtaking. The wooden floors were polished until they gleamed like mirrors in the reflecting light of the five chandeliers that hung from the ceiling. The walls were a pale yellow, which warmed the room with a golden hue. Like flowers on a spring morning, the ladies in their ballroom gowns created a garden of intense colors. Will listened to the strains of a waltz being played by the five-piece string orchestra. He sighted Hortense and went to sign his name to her dance card before it was filled. Lynne met him crossing the floor and handed her card to him.

"I know you want at least one waltz with me. It is almost full, but I have saved the first dance for you."

Although taken aback again by her forwardness, Will did sign her card before finding Hortense. Hortense had the last dance open, and Will had to hide his disappointment, knowing it would still be long before he held her in his arms. The orchestra struck the notes of the first song, and he went to find Lynne. She greeted him with open arms, and soon they were moving in step with the rest of the couples. She danced lightly on her feet, conversing with him the entire time. She seemed to have no end of things to talk about.

"Do you know duels have been fought over me? Did you see that man across the table from us as we dined? He asked for my hand in marriage from my father. I do not like him or want to marry him, but he never seems to give up. I will not have him!" She stamped her foot and set her chin firmly before she began talking of someone else.

Will found her exciting but very self-occupied. Not once did she ask about him or his interests. He felt relieved when the song was over and he found a more docile partner. He was very aware of Hortense, who glided effortlessly with each of her partners. Occasionally, he caught her watching him, and when he did, he smiled. She returned the smile.

Hortense was waiting for him by the beverages, and when he approached, she stepped eagerly into his arms. "Have you enjoyed the evening?" she asked.

"Yes, very much so, but I have to confess I have been waiting for this moment the entire time."

She blushed and lowered her eyes. "I have been waiting for this dance, too. Sometimes I get exhausted being the gracious host to the men my father invites to our home. I think he is ready to see me married and settled. He seems to think I will be a spinster if I am not married before I turn twenty."

Will took her in his arms, where she fit so perfectly. The scent of violets titillated his senses. He wanted to hold her close, to breathe in her fragrance. Instead he said, "I know you like to write and enjoy riding. What are some of your other interests?"

"I have not told many people my dream because I think they would tell me it is not right. I watch the little slave children work so hard in the fields, and I would like to teach them to read and write. Think how their worlds would change if they could read! I love to read; it takes me to a different place, somewhere pleasant when life isn't so pleasing."

"I think that is an admirable idea. Have you told your father you would like to teach the plantation children?" Will asked.

"Oh, no! He would never approve." She drew back in alarm. "He thinks they need to accept their station in life. He thinks they are not smart enough to learn. I disagree and would like the opportunity to show him."

Thinking of his previous conversation with Silas about teaching his children to read gave him an idea. "I haven't discussed this with Mr. Forest yet, but our slave Silas has five children, and two of them are young and in the house with their mother. I was thinking just the other day that I would like them to learn to read. I need to get my uncle's permission first. Let me talk to him, and maybe you could start with them."

The last dance ended far too quickly. Before leaving, Will asked, "Can I see you again? Are you attending the opera this week? Mr. Forest is feeling better, and he may not mind if I go. I will not be able to go during harvest as we will be too busy, but that doesn't start for two weeks."

"I would like to see you again, and, yes, I do plan to be at the opera. If you come, remember your opera glasses," she said as she held her hand to him. He bowed over it, touching it to his lips.

Humming the strains of the last waltz on the way home, his uncle asked, "Did you have a good time this evening? I noticed you had the last dance with Hortense. She is quite an enchanting young lady—and intelligent, too."

"Very," he agreed. "By the way, I would like to discuss something with you that has been on my mind. How would you feel about Silas's younger children learning to read? I know the older ones are already in the field, but I would really like to give them the opportunity to learn. Hortense told me tonight that she would like to teach children, and this would give both of them that chance. What do you think?" He waited as Mr. Forest's forehead wrinkled in thought. He could tell it was a new idea and not one that had occurred to him. Only the *clip-clop* of the horses' hooves could be heard as they struck the hard gravel on the well-traveled path.

"I am going to have to give that more thought. It could change their station in life so they become unhappy working in the fields. You are aware of the political conflict over slavery. As new states are added to our growing Union, there is a strong consensus that states allowing slavery should not be admitted. We could not plant and harvest cotton without our slaves." He paused, giving himself time to ruminate over the idea. "I am not sure it is a good idea. The Missouri Compromise has helped some with the issue. Northern states are not allowing slavery, so if our slaves run away to the North, we could face trouble. Let me ponder it some more."

They continued the ride in silence, both men lost in contemplation.

CHAPTER 12

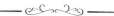

THE WEEK PASSED quickly as preparation for harvest continued. The fall mornings were crisp and cool. Thursday night arrived, and it appeared as though all was in order. "How are you feeling, Uncle?" asked Will. "If you are well, I would really like to attend the opera, *Ivanhoe*. Both Hortense and I have read the novel by Walter Scott.."

"Of course you must go. I am feeling fine, and you need a night out with your friends," his uncle responded, giving Will a pat on the back.

The Theatre d'Orleans stood grand and imposing between Royal and Bourbon Streets. Seven arches spanned the lower level with ornate columns dividing the arches. Will climbed the steps and entered the grand hall. Removing his binoculars from his pocket, he scanned the second row for Hortense's booth. He could not find her. Stepping back, he looked again and saw her. She was wearing a yellow dress, and when she saw him, she stood and waved a white handkerchief. Will quickly climbed the red carpeted stairs and arrived at her booth breathlessly. Her mother and Lynne were also in the box with her. He was surprised as he did not expect to see Lynne.

"Hello, William, I am so glad you came. We saved room for you. Here, come and sit by me," Lynne invited. She patted the chair next to her.

Hortense nudged Lynne before she added, "No, William, you are my guest, and I want you to sit by me." She moved closer to Lynne so there was only room beside her.

Feeling awkward, Will smiled at Lynne before sitting beside Hortense, who said, "I can't wait to see the opera. I know you have read the book." He nodded, and she continued, "The tension between the Saxons and the Normans reminds me of the tension between the South and the North because of the slavery issue."

Knowing that Ivanhoe concealed his true identity by returning to England as a religious pilgrim and then as a disinherited knight made him nervous because he was hiding his true identity from Hortense. How would she respond if she knew he had Negro blood? He knew she was sympathetic to the slaves so maybe his bloodline would not bother her. But then, he had made the promise to his foster father that he would never reveal his true identity.

The opera was delightful and did not disappoint Will. As they were saying good-bye, Will asked, "May I call on you next Saturday evening?"

Hortense looked at her mother, who nodded her assent. "I will look forward to it," she replied, offering her hand again. He held it lingeringly, so small and helpless.

When Will arrived back at the plantation, he went into the library and lit the candles. Scanning the titles on the shelves, he discovered a book on courtship; most of the books were about planting, harvesting, government, and politics. Why one on courtship? He pulled out the book written by George Routledge called *Courtship and Marriage*. With no woman in the house to instruct him, he was not sure about the rules of the game. He read:

> The gentleman must be a person of good breeding and right feeling, he will need no caution from us to remember that, when he is admitted into the heart of a family as the suitor of a daughter, he is receiving one of the greatest possible favors that can be conferred on him, whatever may be his own superiority of social rank or worldly circumstances; and that, therefore, his conduct should be marked by a delicate respect towards the parents of his lady-love. By this means he will propitiate them in his favor, and induce them to regard him as worthy of the trust they have placed in him.

Marking the page with his finger, he paced the length of the room. Hortense's father would never see his ranking

as superior. Anxiety simmered inside him as he read farther into the book:

The Proposal.

When about to take this step, the suitor's first
difficulty is how to get a favorable opportunity;
and next, having got the chance, how to screw his
courage up to give utterance to the "declaration."
We have heard of a young lover who carried on a
courtship for four months ere he could obtain a
private interview with his lady-love. In the house,
as might be expected, they were never left alone;
and in a walk a third party always accompanied
them. In such a dilemma, ought he to have unbur-
dened his heart of its secret through the medium
of a letter? We say not. A declaration in writing
should certainly be avoided where the lover can
by any possibility get at the lady's ear. But there
are cases where this is so difficult that an impatient lover cannot be restrained from adopting
the agency of a *billet-doux* in declaring his passion.

Dropping his head in despair, he thought, *I certainly am
not ready to propose to Hortense, but I like her very much. She
and her family have no idea of my true heritage. Would they
even consider me a suitor of good breeding? I think not, especially after hearing her father the other night. He would never*

give his consent to teach the slave children to read, much less to marry his daughter.

He looked up as Mr. Forest entered the library dressed in a burgundy velvet smoking jacket. "What are you reading?" he asked.

Will closed the small book sheepishly and tucked it behind his back but not soon enough.

His uncle walked over and held out his hand, and Will handed it to him reluctantly.

"Courting, huh? It's too bad we don't have a woman in the house who could answer those burning questions. Maybe I can help you, although it has been a few years."

Will walked to the fireplace and turned his back to his uncle. "Did your brother tell you about my birth? According to the rules of courtship, I must be of good breeding. I am not sure the Marginy family would find that so."

"One of the things I really appreciate about you is your honesty and integrity. My brother did not tell me, but I do know it took some time for you to come along. You stand in line to inherit from us as we have no heirs other than you. Don't do anything to jeopardize your heritage." He rested his hand on Will's shoulder, hoping to give him some comfort. "Hortense seems to be a girl with a good head on her shoulders, although she is an independent woman."

CHAPTER 13

Cotton Harvesting

SILAS BLEW THE long cow horn, calling the slaves to harvesting before the sun spread its blazing glory Monday morning. Every slave, including men, women, and children who were big enough to walk, picked and carried cotton, dotting the white puffed fields. Some carried big woven baskets, while others carried sacks made of heavy cotton ducking. Bella and the other women sewed them in various sizes, some three to four feet and others twelve to fifteen feet in length with diameters of sixteen to eighteen inches. The children filled the smaller sacks and the men and women the larger sacks. A strong strap, sewed to the opening, went over the neck and rested on the shoulder. The long sacks were heavy to drag when they became full, but the smaller ones had to be carried to the wagon to be dumped much more often. Both were tiring.

Silas explained to Will, "There be two ways to pick cotton: pickin' the cotton out of the bolls and pullin' the boll and all. This year is a good crop, so the loose and fluffy cotton is easy to get out." He waved to one of his sons, who was busy filling his bag. "It take about eight hundred to fifteen hundred pounds to gin a five-hundred-pound bale for de market. We use the seed left from the gin for next year's crops."

Each slave brought his or her own lunch to the picking, and when noontime arrived, Silas sat down next to the men and other slaves on the soft but crude cotton-filled bags and pulled out dried beef, snap beans, and purple hull peas. After that came greens, fresh vine-ripened tomatoes, and new boiled potatoes. Bella set out large jars of ice tea and buckets of water.

As the day wore on, the temperatures climbed to the nineties, with the humidity much higher. Thirsty pickers took breaks at the water bucket, which hung in the shade of the wagon. Everyone drank from the same dipper, and when the bucket was dry, a child was sent to fetch another bucket. Some spilled water on their heads and let it run in rivulets down the front of their clothing, momentarily cooling them.

Will watched as one of the young girls dropped her basket and fell to the ground from heatstroke or dehydration. Will ran quickly to her, gathered her in his arms, and carried her to the shade of the wagon. "Go get a dipper full of water," he shouted to a young boy, who scampered off. Gently, he held her head up so she could swallow the liquid. "You must drink lots of water, or you will become dehydrated. Rest here in the shade awhile." He set her against a tree. She smiled shyly at him. Will noticed her some time later picking in the field again. He walked over to Silas and said, "Keep an eye on her; she fainted earlier. Pull her off if she looks like she cannot do it."

The intensity of the harvest continued, as it took quite some time to pick a thousand acres of cotton. Each day, Will was out in the fields, checking the progress. Riding his horse next to Silas, he commented, "We're getting close to the end of harvest and the time for the big celebration. Is Bella prepared?"

"Yes, suh, she got all the kitchen crew workin' their tails off. The pies be baked, and the corn bread be done. All she need now is to make sure the greens be cooked and the meat done. Wait until you see the singin' and dancin'. It's a sight to behold." He chuckled. "Young and old, we love the harvest celebration, and Mr. Forest be real good to let us do it."

In the library, the embers flickered in the fireplace, taking the chill off the fall evening. Outside, the leaves burned a golden bronze and blazing orange, as the sun went to bed earlier each day. His uncle, who seemed to be very tired as of late, rested in his leather wingback chair, an open book lying on his lap. Will relaxed on the leather tufted couch, his legs stretched out in front of him.

"You did a fine job managing the harvesting, Will," his uncle said. "Everything seemed to go smoothly. I think it is time I tell you of another business I own. My brother may have mentioned it to you—a shipping business."

Will sat up abruptly and shook his head, his eyes widened in interest. "No, he never said anything about it. How many ships do you own? I'd really like to learn to sail." His broad smile revealed his excitement.

Mr. Forest watched, a pleased look on his face, "When I realized cotton and sugar are shipped all over the world from our port in New Orleans, I decided to invest in the shipping business. I did not mention it before as I wanted to see how you handled things. I can see you are very capable. You may have your opportunity yet to develop your love of sailing."

Will went to bed, but he could not sleep. The excitement of a shipping business was more than he had imagined. He whispered under his breath, "I can't believe my good fortune. I have the opportunity to learn to sail a schooner! I will sail to Saint Croix and see my mother and father."

The following morning at breakfast, he had another agenda. He determined to talk to Mr. Forest about Silas's children. He loaded his plate with scrambled eggs and biscuits, poured himself a cup of coffee, and began. "My life changed so much when I learned to read. I mentioned before that Hortense would like to teach Silas's children. She could teach them after their chores are done, one afternoon a week." He watched the melting butter run into the rivulets on the biscuit and added some homemade strawberry jam. "I could see her more often; I wouldn't mind that at all. What do you think?"

Mr. Forest waited to respond, and Will could see he was weighing the effect in his mind. "The law was passed almost one hundred years ago prohibiting slaves to write, although no laws were passed regarding reading, as we want our slaves to read the Bible." He paused, rubbing his chin. "Remember the revolt in Virginia this year? Because of that, new laws were passed prohibiting slaves from receiving education and assembling together. My slaves seem to be content, and I don't fear an insurrection, but it is against the law. You would be breaking the law. Do you understand that, and are you ready to face the consequences? I don't want to give the children a wrong impression or ideas above their station in life." He grew quiet once again while Will waited. "Times are changing. I just don't know how we could manage this big plantation without our slaves, but I will trust you with this decision."

Will listened respectfully until Mr. Forest completed his thoughts. "I am willing to face the cost. I really want to better their lives, and learning to read is one way to open new worlds for them. It is something Hortense and I would like to pursue together. With your permission, I'd like to ride over and see Hortense this afternoon so we can get something started. I will be back in time for supper this evening."

Mr. Forest gave his approval, and after Will completed his work, he saddled his horse and rode to the Marginys'.

He knocked on the door and waited in eager anticipation. When the butler arrived, he said, "I am here to see Hortense. Is she in?"

"Yes, sir, come in, and I will see if she can see you."

Will stepped into the foyer. The beauty and grandeur of the home never failed to impress him. Burgundy velvet covered the small settee with its camelback and wraparound wings that stood to the side. A lamp glowed softly on the round table. Mr. Marginy was a man of great wealth, and Hortense was afforded the finest things, yet she cared about slave children. He loved her all the more.

"Will, I am so happy to see you. I had no idea you were coming today, so I am glad I was not out." She was dressed in a simple muslin gown, and the cream color magnified the delicacy of her fair skin. Someone had told Will she looked like a Dresden china doll, and he agreed. He stood unable to say anything, so overcome with his attraction to her. He reached for her hands. He held them for just a fleeting moment, and she did not protest. She smelled of violets again, a scent he was beginning to love. The butler cleared his throat, and Will reluctantly released her hands, remembering why he had come.

"Now that the cotton harvest is over, I wanted to talk to you about our project." He was careful not to mention reading in front of the butler. "Can we walk in the garden? It is such a beautiful day; I hate to spend the time indoors."

Hortense agreed and gave the butler directions. "Please get my nanny and ask her to bring a light shawl to drape over my shoulders. Tell her she must accompany us on our walk." The nanny arrived with her wrap and followed them at a respectful distance so as not to invade their privacy but still follow the proper rules of decorum.

"Let's walk along the lake. There is a bench there, and we can talk. I have not said anything to my father as I know he will not approve. He is a very kind man but does not want to give the slaves hope of a life they cannot achieve. But I have been going through some of my grammar-school books, and I found a phonetics one that will get them started." She looped her arm through his. The November air was brisk and the lake smooth as glass. A gaggle of geese flew in and settled on the lake, gliding gracefully.

Will put his hand over hers and began, "My uncle said it is against the law to educate slaves, and he asked if I was willing to face the consequences. He also serves in government and on many boards, so I don't want to jeopardize his political position. With the uprising in Virginia, the laws have tightened, but considering it all, I still want to move forward. The children have to get their chores done in the morning. I told him we would not interfere with their work, so they are only free in the afternoons. What day are you available?" he questioned.

Hortense stopped and looked at him. "I don't want to hurt either Mr. Forest or my father, so we will have to be very discreet. I still want to give the children an opportunity to learn to read." She continued walking. "I am free

Tuesday afternoons. The timing is perfect because after I am through tutoring, we could have an early supper and go to the opera in the evening." She laughed and looked at Will out of the corner of her eye, knowing she had been forward in assuming Will wanted to spend time with her.

He laughed, "You think so? What makes you think I want to spend that much time with you?" He squeezed her hand resting on his arm. "Tuesdays are perfect. I will let Mr. Forest know what we are doing and Bella, too, so our supper can be served earlier. The children's names are Moses and Hannah, but I do not know their ages."

As the early evening grew brisker, Hortense pulled her wool wrap tighter, and Will slipped his arm around her waist, drawing her close. She snuggled against him, resting her head on his shoulder. The nanny, following unobtrusively behind them, coughed lightly. The setting sun reflected a fall orange, much like that of the leaves on the trees that lined the shore. They walked in silence, swathed in young love.

Bella was elbow deep in flour and bread dough when Will walked into the kitchen the next day. "My favorite. I love your rolls. Just smelling the fresh-baked bread makes my mouth water." He walked over to the cooling rack, broke one open, topped it with butter, and popped it into his mouth.

Bella wiped the flour from her hands on her already-smudged apron and looked at Will. "What brings you into the kitchen, Mr. Will? I don't sees you in here unless you be lookin' for a piece of my cherry pie. What yo' want this time?" She grinned at him.

"I don't know if Silas mentioned it to you, but my friend Miss Marginy would like to teach Moses and Hannah to read. She has some of her books from grammar school she will use. Would you be willing?"

She threw her arms in the air and then covered her mouth with her hands. "Oh, Mr. Will! I so be wanten' my chillun to get some learnin', but I jus' didn' thin' it would ever happen. Do Mr. Forest say it be OK? I wouldn' do anythin' withou' his say-so."

"Yes, Bella. I wouldn't have asked if Mr. Forest had not given his approval. She can come tomorrow afternoon. They can meet here in the kitchen after they finish their chores. When they are done, Miss Marginy and I would like to have an early supper so we can attend the opera."

"Oh yes, suh! I fix the best meal for you and yo' friend and than' you. Than' you. I bake you a cherry pie." She beamed at him.

Will carried the joy of Bella's response in his heart for the rest of the evening. Later in the library, as he and Mr. Forest sat by the heat of the fire, he told him the news. "Hortense agreed to teach the children on Tuesday afternoons after they finish their chores. I hope it is all right with you if they meet in the kitchen. She has agreed to not say anything. She knows her father would not approve. After the tutoring session, we will have an early supper and then go to the opera."

"I hope this doesn't get me in trouble with the rest of the slave owners. I could be politically and socially ruined if they find out." Mr. Forest reiterated, "It is against the law for slaves to learn to read. You read about Margaret Douglass who was convicted of imprisonment for teaching slaves to read. The fine in Alabama for teaching slaves is between two hundred fifty and five hundred dollars. There is talk about imposing a fine in Louisiana, too. This must be kept very quiet, and I reserve the right to stop the learning at any time. Understood?"

Will nodded. His external demeanor remained calm, but inside he was celebrating. He and Hortense had an opportunity to change lives and to help children the way he was helped.

Hortense arrived late Tuesday afternoon. Will saw her struggling with a big, thick book and ran to help her. It was *Noah Webster's American Dictionary of the American Language.* "I am so eager to use my new dictionary that was just published and these ABC books. I am sure the children will enjoy the pictures." She pulled out a small book with bright-colored pictures and flipped through the pages so Will could see and then slipped them back in her bag. "I also intend to give the children a Christian education so they can eventually read the Bible just like Mr. Webster says in his preface." She patted the dictionary

Will was carrying and then stopped him so she could open to the page and read it to him. "'In my view, the Christian religion is the most important and one of the first things in which all children, under a free government ought to be instructed...No truth is more evident to my mind than that the Christian religion must be the basis of any government intended to secure the rights and privileges of a free people.' Noah Webster."

Will could hear the passion in her voice a she closed the huge book and continued, "This morning, I read an article in the French newspaper *The New Orleans Bee* about the rising discontentment of the slaves. I have heard the discussions of my father and the men of New Orleans, and I have seen their worried looks as the freed slaves impact our way of life. Teaching slave children to read will help them secure the privileges of free people." She stamped her small foot. "This is something I must do even though my father would disagree."

Hannah and Moses, their dark nappy hair damp from a good scrub and their faces shining eagerly, sat waiting at the big wood table in the kitchen, their feet dangling from the bench. Hannah was missing her front teeth, and her shy smile warmed the heart of Hortense. Hortense pulled out the ABC book with the colored pictures. Hannah gasped. "It be so pretty." She ran her fingers over the glossy pictures and turned the pages in awe, her big dark eyes full of wonder.

"I wanna see 'em, too." Moses reached for the book, but Hannah pulled it aside.

Hortense quickly pulled out a second book. "I have one for you, too, Moses. You look at this one." She handed it to him, and he marveled over the colored pictures.

Hortense explained, "See these letters? They are called the alphabet, and we will learn the names of the letters first, and then we will learn to put them together into words."

Hannah clapped her hands in glee, her dark black eyes dancing. Moses smiled from ear to ear. "One afternoon a week, we will practice our letters, but it is our secret. No one must know but your mama and papa. Can you keep a secret?" Both little dark heads nodded vigorously.

Lessons lasted one hour. It was enough for the first time. At supper, Hortense shared the delight of the afternoon. "'Those pictures be real pretty,' Hannah told me, carefully running her fingers over them. She looked at it over and over, turning the pages so slowly. She did not want to put it down. I didn't realize how hungry both were to learn. They will be the first in their family to read." She looked at Will, her smile announcing her pleasure.

"I'm glad it went well." He grinned at her enthusiasm and reached for her hand. "Come on—we don't want to be late for the opera."

CHAPTER 14

When Will returned from the opera, he went immediately to the study. Mr. Forest slumbered in his favorite Queen Anne chair. The fire burned low in the fireplace, and Will stooped to put another log on the smoldering cinders. It crackled into a flame and startled Mr. Forest awake. "How was the opera?" he asked, stifling a yawn with the back of his hand. "I must have dozed; it was so quiet in here. I think I'll go to bed now that you are home." He stood but faltered and fell back into the chair.

Will rushed to his side. "Are you feeling ill?" He stepped back to look at him. All the color had drained from Mr. Forest's face, leaving him blanched, like the cotton fields prior to harvest.

He held up his hand. "Just give me a moment. Lately I have been having these spells, but they always seem to pass if I rest a moment. I don't know what it is. I guess I will have to see the doctor. Will you help me to my room? I would hate to fall down those stairs."

Will knew his uncle was a proud man and stubbornly independent. It took a great amount of effort for Mr. Forest to ask for help. He put his hand under his elbow, just enough to support him if he wavered, and together they climbed the stairs to his bedroom door. "Do you want me to call for Bella?"

"I think I will be fine; if not, I have a bell by my bed that I can ring. You are close enough to hear it." He patted Will's arm. "Thank you. You know I depend on you."

Sleep evaded Will. He tossed and turned, kicked the covers off, and then pulled them back up to his chin. Life was just beginning to fall into a pattern and a pleasant one at that. He enjoyed his evening with Hortense, everything about her appealed to him. It pleased him to see her joy in teaching Silas's children. He understood more about the plantation, and his relationship with Silas was so much better, especially when he wanted to better the lives of his children. He occasionally thought about Saint Croix and his mother, and someday he hoped to go back to see her. If Mr. Forest was seriously ill, he knew that the management of the plantation would rest solely on his young shoulders.

He kicked the blankets off and sat on the edge of his bed. He heard Mr. Forest coughing in his bedroom and wondered if he should check on him. Then everything fell quiet; only the natural creaking of the wooden floors interrupted the silence of the dark. He sipped a drink of the water by his bedside, sighed, and lay down again. The clock on the table read 2:00 a.m.

"Mr. Will! Wake up! Mr. Will!" The pounding on his door jarred him awake. He heard Bella's urgent cry. "I canna' wake Mr. Forest. He don' wanna wake up."

Grabbing his robe, Will opened his door and ran down the hall to Mr. Forest's bedroom. He dropped to his knees beside the bed and listened for life-giving breath. He heard none. There was no movement, no rising and falling of his chest under the blankets. He groped for the pulse on his wrist, but the minute his fingers touched the cool skin, he knew Mr. Forest had given up his tenuous hold on this life. He turned to Bella, tears slipping unheeded down his cheeks. "He's gone. I cannot find a heartbeat. We'd better have one of the men go for a doctor, although it will do no good."

Bella moaned deeply and fell to her knees, covering her face with her hands. "He been my best owner ever. What we gonna do withou' 'im?" Sobs racked her body as she swayed back and forth, wailing.

Will stood utterly helpless, sharing her despair, immobilized. Finally, reaching for her hand, Will helped her to her feet. "We must let the doctor know, and you must be strong to help me. Send Billy to get the doctor, and after he notifies him, tell him to let Hortense know." When Bella left the room, Will knelt beside the bed and let his tears flow unhindered. Mr. Forest had been a father to him, and now he was left alone in a relatively new country with a huge responsibility. The success of the plantation, the lives of the slaves—they all depended on him.

As soon as Hortense heard the news, she arrived in her carriage to see if there was any way she could help.

Will asked her to notify the paper, knowing her ability with words. The following announcement appeared in the newspaper:

November 29, 1828
Communicated: Departed this life, on the 24th instant, Leif Forest, served in government, 42nd year of his age. He was a man of talents and of industrious habits. His deportment was uniformly moral, gentlemanly, and decorous. He was beloved by his companions and respected by all who knew him. His memory will ever remain embalmed in the hearts of his fellow citizens; and, while they deplore the loss of a worthy and valuable friend, the public may regret its sudden deprivation of one who proved an ornament and blessing to his country. His sudden death compels us to exclaim: "Not glowing health, nor youthful years; Not friendship's sighs, nor parents' tears, Can shield us from thy venom sting, thou monster death—thou sateless king." In token of remembrance and respect, wear crape on the left arm for the space of thirty days.

Following the funeral, the solicitor, Judah Benjamin, asked to meet Will at the plantation. "I wish to share the contents of Mr. Forest's last will and testament. Please make sure that his two slaves, Bella and Silas, are present."

The library was cold and the curtains drawn when the solemn group of four gathered. Will found it difficult to even enter the room as his vivid memory of Mr. Forest still lived and breathed within these walls.

"Please have a seat." The solicitor motioned to the burgundy leather chairs positioned in front of the desk. "This will contains some shocking news, so be prepared." He peered over his glasses, looking intently at the three, and with that he began reading the following information:

I, Leif Forest, residing at New Orleans, Louisiana, being of sound mind, do hereby make, publish, and declare this to be my Last Will and Testament and do revoke any and all other Wills and Codicils heretofore made by me.

ARTICLE 1

1.1 - I direct payment of my debts, funeral expenses, and expenses for administration of my estate.

ARTICLE 2

2.1 - I give the rest of my estate to William Leidesdorff with the understanding that Silas, Bella and their five children remain in the care of said person.

2.2 - If any beneficiary shall fail to survive me by 45 days, it shall be deemed that such person shall have pre-deceased me.

2.3 - If William Leidesdorff does not survive me, I direct that the rest of my estate to my brother, Albert Forest, to be executed by my solicitor.

ARTICLE 3

3.1 - I appoint my solicitor Executrix of this will. I direct that no appointee hereunder shall be required to give bond for the faithful performance of the duties of said office.

This Will has been prepared in duplicate, each copy of which has been executed as an original. One of these executed copies is in my possession and the other is deposited for safekeeping with my attorney, Judah Benjamin, 1820 State Street, New Orleans, Louisiana. I, Leif Forest, do hereby declare to the undersigned authority that I am 18 years of age or older, of sound mind, and under no constraint or undue influence willingly sign and execute this instrument as my Last Will and Testament in the presence of the following witnesses, who witnessed and subscribed this will at my request, and in my presence at New Orleans, Louisiana, on this 21 day of October, 1828.
Leif Forest

"There is more." Mr. Benjamin took out a sheaf of papers from his attaché case and read the first one aloud. He continued reading as Silas and Bella listened speechlessly.

Manumission of Silas Goldman
This deed of witness that I, Leif Forest late of New Orleans, Louisiana have hereby mancipated & set free a negro man slave named Silas Goldman, a Black man

aged fourty five about five feet ten inches high hereby releasing the said negro Silas Goldman all claims of livirie as fully & completely as if he had been born free, witness my hand & seal this 7th day of April 1828.

L. Forest
State of Louisiana
Recorded April 5th 1828

"I have six more of these manumissions stating that Bella and all five of their children are hereby set free. Of course, there are some things I would like to go over with you and Mr. Leidesdorff with regard to your well-being." He turned to Will, who stood quietly, overwhelmed with gratitude and feeling the tremendous duty that was to be his. "You have many decisions to make. I encourage you to keep Silas as your overseer until you decide what to do with the estate."

"I plan to keep the plantation and continue working it. I do not want to make any changes for the time being." Will looked pleadingly at Silas and Bella, who sat speechless. "You will stay with me, won't you? I don't think I can manage without you. I will pay wages into an account for you."

Silas nodded. "We won' leave you, Massa Will. You need us mo' than ever. We be right here doin' our job." He reached for Bella's hand. "Where would we go, and what would we do?"

Bella agreed, nodding her head vigorously. "I still do all the cookin', and our chillun can keep on with their meetin'." She looked expectantly at Will, who nodded.

Mr. Benjamin stood and placed the rest of the papers in his case. "You know where to reach me if you need me. I wish you the best, young man." He shook Will's hand, and Bella showed him to the door.

CHAPTER 15

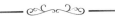

THE STILLNESS OF the house echoed around Will. The emptiness and loss left an open wound that caused him to spend little time at the plantation. Most evenings, he was a guest of the Marginys', and his love for Hortense became more intense each moment he spent with her. Her friend Lynne accepted the hand of one of her suitors and was to marry in the spring. Will began thinking earnestly of asking Hortense to be his wife, but his deceitfulness weighed heavily on his mind; he had not told Hortense of his heritage. He knew her father could not accept him as a son-in-law.

He was keeping secrets: his heritage, the emancipation of Bella and Silas, and the education their children were receiving. The slavery issue was becoming more volatile and intense, so it was best to keep it quiet.

One day, while doing business in New Orleans, he stopped by the Kozyc Jewelry shop to look at wedding rings. Hortense's birthday was in September, and he wanted to get her something special, so he asked to see diamonds set with sapphires. The jeweler brought out a beautiful sapphire just like the color of Hortense's eyes. Its sparkle reminded him of the shine he saw in her eyes when she was teaching the children. He so wanted to purchase it, but he needed to talk to Mr. Marginy and ask for his daughter's hand in marriage first. He asked the jeweler to set it aside for him. "I will be back to purchase it if the young lady accepts my proposal," he said.

When he arrived home, he sought solace in the library. He sat in Mr. Forest's chair, and, for a minute, tears gathered in his eyes. He brushed them aside, got up, and walked to the shelf to peruse the titles. He was looking for the courting book. He found it on the bottom shelf, pulled it out, and went back to the chair by the fireplace. Flipping through the pages, he found the section titled "The Proposal." He read, "Before proposing one must ask the father's permission. This must not be done with a letter but face to face." He was going to supper on Saturday evening; he decided that would be an appropriate time.

When Saturday arrived, Will paced the dining room, not eating until Bella asked him, "What be wrong wit' you today? You got somethin' on yo' mind? Sit down and eat you' breakfast afore it get cold."

He sat down, but the food remained cold on his plate. He wished Mr. Forest was there to encourage him; he had no one who understood him. After his attempt to eat, he went to his room and stood before the mirror. He began, "I have something I want to ask you..."

He stopped and shook his head. *That doesn't sound right. I need to word it differently.* He started again: "I have been courting Hortense for some time, and I would like to ask for her hand in marriage with your permission." He shook his head at that wording and started once more. When he felt ready, he dressed very carefully and called for his horse and carriage.

After the meal, Mr. Marginy invited him to the study to have a glass of wine.

"I'd like to speak to you about something," Will said as he walked to the fireplace. "I have courted Hortense for eight months and would like to ask for her hand in marriage. I am a wealthy man and can provide for her as she is accustomed. I love her and enjoy her companionship. I would like to spend my life with her. Would you give me permission to marry her?" He held his breath and waited. Mr. Marginy said nothing. *He is going to say no,* he thought. *I know it.* He felt the sweat dripping from his forehead and brushed it with the back of his hand.

"I don't know much about you other than that you manage the plantation well for such a young man, and inheriting it was a stamp of approval from Forest. He would not have left it to you if he didn't think you capable. I understand your father is of good breeding and that he remains on the island of Saint Croix?" He raised questioning eyes to William, who averted his eyes and kept his chin down. "I watch Hortense, and I know her heart belongs to you. She speaks only of you." He paced the length of the room and turned to face Will. "If you promise to treat my little girl well, I will say yes. When do you plan to ask her?"

"I am planning a special dinner before the opera, and I will ask her then. I would like you and Mrs. Marginy to come also. I will treat your daughter in a manner worthy of what she deserves." He exhaled a sigh of relief and shook hands with Mr. Marginy. He couldn't wait to find Hortense, who was even more beautiful that night.

Hortense was sitting in the parlor. She wore a blue dress the color of her eyes, and a matching satin ribbon held her auburn curls in place. Her eyes sparkled as she greeted him and reached for his hand. "What have you and my father been talking about?" she asked. "You were in there for so long I thought you both had fallen asleep. Come on—let's play a game before you have to leave."

Will thrilled at the touch of her hand and slipped his arm around her waist; he looked into her eyes and asked, "Will you join me for dinner and the opera on Thursday night? I have something special planned, so I have asked your parents to join us, too."

"That sounds delightful. Just don't let my father know I am teaching the children to read. He would not be pleased about that as he thinks the saves must keep their place. That would not make for a pleasant evening," she cautioned.

CHAPTER 16

WILL CHASED HIS shadows as he waited for Thursday to arrive. He refused to think of the consequences of Mr. Marginy's anger if he became aware of his Negro blood. Instead, he rehearsed his proposal over and over. He wanted the entire evening to be perfect, including the meal.

He found Bella baking in the kitchen; a chocolate cake was cooling on a rack on the table. The wooden spoon moved rhythmically in the bowl as she mixed the chocolate icing. "Ummm, it smells good in here, Bella." He dipped his finger in the frosting and popped it in his mouth. "Tastes good, too. Mr. and Mrs. Marginy and Hortense are coming for supper on Thursday evening, and I would like to have a very nice meal. Use our best silver and china. It is a very special night."

"I do anythin' for you and Miz Hortense. I thin' I'll make beef tenderloin with horseradish cream, some crispy potatoes with fennel, lemon-garlic green beans, and my dinner rolls. Wha' you like for dessert?" A wide grin covered her face. Without waiting for an answer, she continued. "Maybe I make sweet-potato pie, or maybe you like my pecan pie instead?" Her words trailed her broad back as she continued stirring. "I thin' I make you pecan pie."

When Thursday evening arrived, Will opened the french doors to the dining room, handsomely dressed in his finest black suit, white shirt, and red cravat, his unruly hair oiled to perfection. The table was set with the finest linen. The crystal goblets mirrored the glimmer of the candlelight, and the polished silver shone like the stars that dotted the night sky. Red roses, picked from the garden, filled the vases, and their sweet fragrance scented the room.

When his guests arrived, Will seated Hortense to his right and Mr. and Mrs. Marginy directly across from them. Although Will only picked at his meal, he did enjoy the pecan pie, and after he swallowed the last bite, he wiped his mouth with his napkin and turned to face Hortense. "I have asked you and your parents for dinner tonight for a special purpose. You and I have been courting for some time." He pushed his chair back, bent on one knee, and reached for her hand. "You make me laugh, you fill my lonely moments with joy, and you have been a great comfort to me since Mr. Forest passed on. You complete me, and I wholeheartedly love only you." He squeezed her hand, finding it hard to speak without his voice breaking. "Shakespeare said it this way: 'I love you with so much of my heart that none is left to protest.' You occupy my thoughts constantly, and I would like to spend the rest of my life with you. Will you marry me?"

Hortense pushed her chair back, knocking it to the floor, and jumped to her feet. She reached for both of Will's hands as he rose to his feet. "Yes! Yes! I will marry you." She stood on her tiptoes and placed a kiss on his lips before embracing him. The joy of the moment reflected in her eyes, as she turned to her parents. "Did you know? Is that what you both were talking about the other night? Oh, I can't wait to be married!" She gave Will another kiss before sitting down. "We must start planning my wedding right away, Mother. When should we set the date?"

"You and your mother have plenty of time to talk about that. Right now, I think we should leave for the opera so we arrive on time. I have heard Rossini's *The Barber of Seville* is quite good," Mr. Marginy said.

"How shall I sit through an opera when we have a wedding to plan? There are so many things to prepare." Hortense stood and twirled on her toes. "I am so excited to marry you, Will," she said as she danced around the room, her blue dress swishing around her slim ankles and white satin slippers.

The evening was as beautiful as a finely painted portrait with all the colorful period costumes. The rich music filled the air with deep baritones and melodic high sopranos. In the second act, the count and Rosina signed their marriage vows. "That will be us soon," Will whispered into Hortense's ear as he helped her into her father's carriage.

After arriving at the plantation, he lingered in the quiet of the library before going to bed. Bella had left a fire burning in the fireplace, but the evening was warm, and Will let it fade. Troubled, he stared at the dying embers. He knew Mr. Marginy would never agree to the marriage of his daughter to a man with Negro blood. He had wealth, and he was intelligent, respected, and well-read. He could speak five languages, but he was not good enough for Hortense. Yet in his heart he knew Hortense loved him.

Finally, he climbed the stairs to his room, but sleep evaded him. Tossing and turning, he pulled the blankets up around his neck and then later kicked them off. He dreamed of standing at the altar and Mr. Marginy shouting at him in front of all the guests because he had discovered his true lineage. His face a livid purple, he roared, "You can't expect to marry my daughter with that kind of heritage. I won't stand for it!" He grabbed him roughly by the collar. "You are never to see Hortense again!" he bellowed before he shoved him to the ground.

He awoke with a start, his nightshirt damp and clinging to him. Catching a glimpse of himself in the looking glass, he saw dark circles shadowing his eyes. He rubbed at them, relieved the nightmare was over. He dressed in haste, wanting to leave the shadows of the night. He breathed deeply and took in his familiar surroundings. It was a new morning, a new day.

He pulled back the curtains, and the welcomed sun chased away all darkness. Today he had exciting business to attend to. He was going in to New Orleans to meet the manager of the shipping business and to examine *Julia Ann*, a 106-ton schooner that belonged to the company.

When he arrived at the docks, he introduced himself and said, "I'd like to take a look at the schooner *Julia Ann* my uncle told me about." He showed him the papers naming him sole beneficiary.

The water sparkled like shimmering silver in the brightness of the day as they walked to the end of the pier where a wooden vessel with iron bolts and a felt and yellow metal skin was moored to a bollard. Will stood for a minute, admiring it. "It must be seventy-plus feet."

"Yes, it is, and its breadth is at least twenty feet and the depth a little over ten feet. She is rigged as a schooner but sometimes called a brigantine. Isn't she beautiful?" the manager asked.

"She sure is," Will agreed, watching the sun reflect on the golden treasure.

"Originally, the brigantine was a small ship carrying both oars and sails. In the late seventeenth century, the Royal Navy used the term to refer to small two-masted vessels designed to be rowed as well as sailed." The manager pointed to the rigging. "This one is rigged with square rigs on the foremast and fore-and-aft rigging on the mainmast."

Will stepped closer to the boat, touching it reverently, not believing that his dream rested before him in the still waters. "She certainly is beautiful. Can we go aboard? I would like to see the interior."

"Of course. Follow me."

The *Julia Ann* displayed her proud heritage in every inch of the polished brass and woodwork. The teak deck provided seating, and below deck were two berths, perfect for him and Hortense. "I would like to learn to sail her. Is there anyone who could teach me the rudiments of sailing a two-masted ship?" he asked, running his hand over the gleaming brass work. "I'm getting married, so I will not be able to learn until after the wedding, but I would like to arrange a time when we could take her out."

"I will teach you. Let me know a week ahead of time, and I will arrange a time for us to sail the bay," the manager offered.

He completed his trip to New Orleans by stopping at the jewelry store to pick up the wedding ring he had selected earlier. He held it in his hand, inspecting it carefully. He turned it over in his palm, admiring the white gold, diamonds, and sapphires. It was perfect. He rubbed his hand over his eyes. If only the shadows of doubt would disappear.

CHAPTER 17

THE MARGINY HOUSEHOLD was a flurry of wedding arrangements when Will arrived the following day. Hortense flitted around like a butterfly attending to all the details. As soon as he saw her, she reached for his hand and said, "Since we are going to have the ceremony on the shore of Lake Pontchartrain, you must come outside and see the arboretum we have constructed. It is both enchanting and elegant."

Amid the lush green trees, a platform had been constructed and painted white. It was flanked with four white pillars, and on top of the majestic columns were mounds of red roses and white lilies of the valley intertwined with white tulle. A trellis stood in the middle of the platform, also clothed in red roses and lilies of the valley.

"It is just what I pictured for my wedding. The guests will sit on white chairs out there." She gestured to the span of green lawn. "And we will stand under the trellis. I have my dress, too, but you shan't see it before our wedding day." She looked at him under long eyelashes, a taunting look on her face. "We are getting responses to our invitation. So many of my parents' friends will be here, including the governor of Louisiana." She paused, a frown wrinkling the smoothness of her brow. "I wish your family could come. I haven't heard back from your mother although I sent her an invitation. You really haven't told me much about her. I only know about Mr. Forest and his brother in Saint Croix. Will she like me?"

"Of course she will." Will quickly changed the subject. "The wedding arrangements are perfect. It will be the wedding of the season. I hope it doesn't rain."

He pulled her close. "Let me tell you what I did yesterday. I went to New Orleans to see the shipping business my uncle left me, and I saw the most magnificent schooner, named *Julia Ann*. I am going to learn to sail it after the wedding. We can learn together." He lifted her up and swung her around before planting her firmly on the ground. "The day I make you my wife is almost here." Remembering his secret, he grew quiet, the excitement of the moment gone.

Hortense clutched his arm. "What is wrong, darling? You are so somber." She begged again, "You must tell me if something is wrong."

He squeezed her hand but did not look at her. "No, no, everything is just fine. I was just thinking of my mother..." His voice trailed off as they walked in silence.

It was another sleepless night for Will. He argued with himself all through the night. "I can't tell her. Her father would never approve, and I will not be able to marry her.

She is the only woman for me, and I love her so. To lose her would be to lose my life."

Sitting on the edge of the bed, he raked his fingers through his disheveled hair. He stood and paced the length of his bedroom before he sat again. "They do not need to know. But what if we should have a dark-skinned child? Then what? Mr. Marginy is a very proud man. He wouldn't stand for that. Would Hortense be cut off from her family? That would kill her." The accusing thoughts continued in strong pursuit of his sleep. "I must tell them. It is the honest thing to do, and I couldn't live with myself if Hortense was hurt."

As the time grew closer, Will battled with himself each sleepless night. He couldn't go through with it and live with himself. When the evening of the wedding arrived, the late-afternoon sun smiled through the oaks that lined the lake. It was a beautiful evening, but Will was so distraught that he couldn't see the beauty. After arriving at the house, he immediately asked to speak to Mr. Marginy in his study.

"What is it, Will? Are you having second thoughts? I hope not. Hortense would be devastated." He placed a restraining hand on Will's arm.

Will paced up and down the room, tugging at the collar of his shirt. He started to speak, stopped and paced some more

"Out with it! What is bothering you?" Mr. Marginy bellowed. "I have no patience with this behavior. In twenty minutes, you are going to make my daughter your wife."

"There is something I must tell you." Will mopped his forehead with his handkerchief and turned his back to Mr. Marginy as the words spewed out. "I have not told you about my heritage. You think I am the nephew of Mr. Forest. I am not. His brother is my foster father. My birth father is a Danish man, and my mother is a Negress." He turned abruptly to see the reaction of Mr. Marginy, who blanched white before turning an angry red.

"Why did you not tell us earlier?" he thundered. "I would never let my daughter marry a man like you. Whatever made you think I would approve? Leave my home right now and don't return! You may have no more contact with my daughter! Is that understood? Now leave!" Mr. Marginy shoved him toward the door. "What am I going to tell my daughter? What am I going to tell our guests? You have brought great shame on our family."

Will stumbled from the room, tears blinding his eyes. He stood outside the barred door. *Hortense will be devastated,* he thought, *and I can't even explain my love for her. I am not willfully abandoning her. She is my love, my life.* He could hear the five-piece stringed orchestra playing in the background. "It is a funeral dirge," he sobbed, "my funeral dirge."

The darkness engulfed him as he climbed alone into the black carriage, the carriage that was to take him and Hortense on their honeymoon. It became a hearse that would take him away to a life of loneliness, a life devoid of love, a life without his Hortense.

He stared for some time at her window. He watched her pirouette before the mirror, the frothy veil giving her an ethereal look. He saw her father enter the room, his face black with anger. He could watch no more. He did not want to see her heart break before his eyes. "I choose to remember you in the beauty of your wedding dress, my sweet Hortense. I will forever hold you in my heart," he whispered brokenly into the blackness.

The engagement ring was delivered with a letter from her father the following day with strict instructions never to contact Hortense—at the cost of his life.

The community reeled, as it was to be the wedding of the season. The slaves talked about Mr. Will's bride taking to her bed, ill to death they said. On the streets, people turned their heads and whispered behind gloved hands.

Will became a recluse, nursing his pain. In the darkness of night, he drove his carriage past the Marginys' house, hoping to catch a glimpse of Hortense. Her window was darkened, the curtains drawn.

Brokenhearted, his world shattered, within weeks he put the plantation up for sale. He sold everything, including the house on Bourbon Street, but he kept Mr.

Forest's extensive library of books, especially those relating to history and literature. Will did not have the opportunity to speak to or to see Hortense again.

Attending to every detail, he gave the emancipation papers to Silas, Bella, and their children and suggested they go north, where the children could be educated and they could find jobs. "We can't leave you, Massa Will. You be too lonely and brokenhearted," Bella cried.

"I will provide safe passage for you. I have a friend who will travel with you every step of the way and help you find employment. You can stay with him until you are settled. The children can go to school, and you can live together as a free family." He put his arms around Silas and Bella. "You have served me faithfully, but it is too painful here. I must leave."

He was done. He wanted nothing to remind him of the Marginys. From now on, he would proudly bear the name *William Alexander Leidesdorff, Jr.* He would no longer be forced to endure a shroud of secrecy or be imprisoned by a promise. His heart was broken yet free.

CHAPTER 18

1831

SADLY, WILL'S DESIRE to sail the *Julia Ann* was fulfilled much sooner than expected. Within a month, he had moved off the plantation and into New Orleans. He filled his time learning everything about the boat and maneuvering the sea. He gathered a crew and supplies and made ready to sail. Sail anywhere. Maybe to New York, Hawaii, or back to the island of St. Croix. Maybe to London, Paris, or California. Anywhere to escape the pain that plagued him day and night.

On the afternoon prior to his departure, Will was shopping at the general store in New Orleans, buying the last of his supplies, when the storekeeper commented on a funeral procession passing by the storefront. "It must be the young lady I heard about. Her suitor left her at the altar. They say she died of a broken heart."

Will ran to the window in time to see Mr. and Mrs. Marginy, draped in black, walking slowly behind the hearse, heads bowed, shoulders stooped. Red roses and white lilies of the valley draped the casket. Behind them followed the minister, his minister. He looked directly into the store window and caught Will's eye. He shook his head and trudged forward, his eyes downcast again. Next came Mr. and Mrs. Grimes, Louis Canonge, Lynn Quey with her new husband and her parents, and many others, all dressed in black. Wailing and loud weeping shadowed them, keening among the buildings, droning despair. Will dropped to his knees, a low, guttural moan escaping his lips. The wound was ripped open and splayed. His love was gone. Dead. Laid to eternal rest without him. Such loss. Such emptiness.

Later in the evening, he sat alone in the darkness of his rented room. No flickering light warmed the space. As the shadows lengthened, someone tapped lightly on the door. Will ignored it. He did not want to see or speak to anyone, but the person was insistent. Finally, to relieve the annoyance of the knocking, Will opened the door a crack.

The minister stood there. "William?" he questioned.

His face smeared with tears, his hair unkempt, he replied, "Yes. I am not prepared to have guests tonight."

"I have something for you." He reached into the folds of his vestment, took out a tiny gold cross, and placed it in William's hand. "I was with her when she died. Her last words were, 'Tell him I loved him until death.'" With those somber words, he melted into the darkness of the night.

Will closed the door, sat down on the edge of his bed, gripped the small gold cross in his fist, and wept inconsolably. As the gray shades of dawn crept through the window, Will reached for a sturdy gold chain in his bag and replaced the fragile chain. He held it to his lips and then looped it around the thickness of his neck, letting it fall over his heart. "Linked forever, in death and in life," whispered the twenty-one year old man.

CHAPTER 19

1841

TEN YEARS LATER, the *Julia Ann* sailed into San Francisco Bay and landed at the point known as Yerba Buena Cove. William read Richard Dana's book *Two Years before the Mast* aboard the ship in preparation, and the picture before him matched the description completely: a magnificent bay, several good harbors, deep water, and finely wooded and fertile country. Scanning the bay, he saw the presidio about thirty miles from the mouth, on the southeast side. It was diminutive in the distance, but he could see the Mission Dolores where it stood in disrepair. The harbor, called Yerba Buena, berthed few trading vessels, but the newly begun settlement looked promising.

William counted ten to twenty houses and shanties that made up the Mexican pueblo. He heard that the Hudson Bay Company's agents and people completed the entire settlement and the permanent population did not exceed fifty people.

Now thirty-one years of age, his body had thickened, his arms muscled from hoisting ropes and sailing, his thick black hair had grown long and shaggy from months at sea. His skin was darkened by the sun, but he was a wealthy man. In the intervening years, his foster father in Saint Croix passed away and willed his own plantation to Will as well. His broken heart somewhat mended but Hortense not forgotten, William paced the deck in anticipation, fingering the gold cross he wore devotedly at his neck. He called for the third mate to row him in to land.

As Captain William Leidesdorff neared solid ground, he spotted a man standing on the shore. Growing closer, he was able to see the man wore a brown broad-brimmed hat with a gilt band around the crown. His short jacket was of silk and his shirt collar open at the neck. His pantaloons, open at the sides below the knee, were laced with gilded velveteen. White stockings and ornamented dark-brown deerskin shoes covered his feet. Around his ample waist was a brilliant red sash. He waved at Will.

The few Indians present were draped in woven blankets of various colors; a hole cut in the middle of the blanket enabled it to slip over their heads. He was to learn later that the poncho or serape was the mark of the rank and wealth of the owner.

As soon as Will stepped out of the rowboat, the robust man greeted him. "Ahoy. Welcome ashore. My name is William Richardson. I handle all the trade between the Spanish and Mexican ranchers and the East Coast merchants like you who anchor their ships in our bay." He motioned Will to follow him and said in a clipped British accent, "Come with me so we can record your shipment."

He immediately began relaying his story to Will. "I was a mate on the British whaler *Orion* and have been here since '22," Richardson said, sounding very English. "I learned some Spanish, so when the *Orion* sailed into the bay, my captain, Mr. Barney, sent me to explain our visit. I was escorted by soldiers to the presidio where Ignacio Martinez was commander. He promised me the supplies we needed and then invited me to a fiesta, which I accepted. I drank too much and didn't get back to my ship until early dawn, which my captain did not like." He grinned and glanced sideways at Will. "Rather than face his wrath, I decided to just settle here at the presidio. Jolly best thing I ever did." He laughed heartily.

They pushed aside the grass, which had grown tall, and continued to trudge over the rough terrain. "First, I had to go to Monterey and present a petition to Governor Vincente de Sol asking permission to settle in California. I was given approval on the condition that I teach navigation and carpentry to the youth." He stopped, gaining his breath. "Everyone here is Roman Catholic. Mexican, you know. I took religious instruction so I could join the church and become a naturalized Mexican citizen. I eventually married the daughter of Lieutenant Ignacio Martinez." He removed his hat and wiped his perspiring brow. "What about you?" he asked between gasps.

Will answered, "I've been captain of my ship for ten years and sailed into many ports, but this is my first time in Yerba Buena. I have things to trade: tea, coffee, sugar, spices, raisins, molasses, hardware, crockery, tinware, cutlery, and clothing of all kinds." He continued listing the wares aboard: "Shoes, calicoes, cotton, silks, shawls, scarfs, necklaces, jewelry, and combs for the women. In exchange, I hope to get a good amount of hides to take back to Boston."

Richardson shook his head. "Our women don't have much use for fineries. Bloody bad for you. My wife says the women don't wear bonnets like the English ladies; instead they wear large mantles over their heads when they go outside. Inside they wear a scarf or neckerchief. The Spanish women like colors, jewelry, and combs for their long dark hair."

He chuckled, his face reddening in embarrassment. "Too much information about women's style. My wife will have to help you and tell you more. But she only speaks Spanish since this territory first belonged to Spain. She is Spanish nobility, very posh," he said proudly.

"Alta California just won its independence from Spain in 1821. The only difference, my wife tells me, is that the mission can no longer own land, other than the land the church sits on." He turned to Will. "Do you speak Spanish?"

Will nodded. "*Sí hablan algo de español. Es difícil para el comercio de pieles si uno no habla de la lengua.* I also know how to write Spanish."

"Cracking! You will get along well," Richardson responded heartily.

Will wondered how much farther it was to the presidio; his legs were tired. Not much chance for distance walking while aboard ship. Finally, he saw the walls in the distance. Two men were on horses, which seemed a much quicker way to get there.

"I use a couple small vessels that belong to Mission Dolores to move the cargo back and forth from the ships that sail into the bay. As the trade for hides and tallow increased, I saw the need to serve as a liaison between the ranchers we call Californios and the East Coast traders. I guess I'm a self-appointed harbormaster. Someone needed to do the job." Mr. Richardson patted his stomach.

The distant rolling hills, covered with the lush green grass of spring rains, appealed to Will. Christmas berry trees dotted the horizon, and the view of the bay from the surrounding hills was serene. A wind blew off the bay, making it cooler than other areas of California he had read about. Will was tired of ship life and longed to settle down. He could run his shipping business easily from Yerba Buena, and he wished to purchase more ships, own a whole fleet of them. The bay was well protected, perfect for loading and unloading.

After they finished their business at the presidio, Richardson rented two horses for a dollar each. "Horses are cheap here. Ten dollars for a good one and two to three dollars for one not so good. Much easier to see the countryside from the back of a horse—and easier on the legs, too. You'll need a horse."

They rode down the hill from the presidio on the one street thoroughfare. Richardson explained, "Governor Alvarado employed Jean Vioget, a Swiss sailor and surveyor, to survey and lay out this street, called *Calle de la Fundación*. It joins the mission and the presidio."

There were few buildings in the pueblo, but he pointed out one crude shanty and said, "That is where Robert Ridley lives. He is a fine-looking cockney, a tremendous drinker, and very popular with the Indians, Spaniards, and Mexicans. He became naturalized and married Presentación Miranda, the daughter of Juana Miranda, who keeps cows and lives on a ranch on the north part of the beach. If you want milk, you can get it from her. Ridley works for the Hudson Bay Company."

Will tucked away the idea of fresh milk, as he had not had milk for some time, and the thought of it in his coffee was enough to make his mouth water. "I think I would like to settle here and develop my shipping business," he said. "There is still money to be made in the hide and tallow business. Currently, the hides are valued at two dollars, and there is an abundance of them."

Richardson replied, "Yes, this is a cracking port. I have much experience because from 1822 to 1829 I piloted the ships that came into the bay. I sounded it for depth, islands, and shoals, and before long I earned the name Captain among the sailors who arrived here."

Will noticed that whenever Richardson was pleased with himself, he patted his robust stomach.

"Once the ship was in port, the ranchers and local people went aboard and picked out items like the ones you have on your ship and exchanged them for hides and tallow." They stopped and dismounted so they could get a good view of the bay.

"This is one of the best views I have seen, and the weather seems quite agreeable. How does one go about getting land and a place to live?" Will asked.

"Quite. Let me tell you how I received mine. While I was in San Gabriel, I met the governor of California, José Figueroa, when he was on an inspection trip to the mission. We had many discussions about the distribution of land, the promotion of trade, and the colonization of Alta California. For some time, I had been interested in the land north of the entrance to the bay. In fact, three months before I met the governor, I submitted a petition to obtain that tract of land and a lot on which to build my house in Yerba Buena. I have a copy; let me show you." He pulled a worn piece of paper out of the leather bag he carried around his neck and showed it to Will.

It read,

W.A. Richardson, a native of Great Britain and a resident of this place, hereby respectfully represents that he arrived at this port of Yerba Buena on the second day of August last, as mate of a British whale ship, and it

being my intention to remain permanently and become
domiciled in this Province at some place with a suitable
climate, I most humbly pray your Honor to grant me this
privilege and favor.

"With so much trading at Yerba Buena, I thought the government should establish a customhouse and a commercial town. At first, the governor turned down my plans, but eventually he gave me orders to come back here and appointed me official captain of the Yerba Buena Cove. He wished me to lay out a small settlement for the convenience of public offices at the anchorage. I chose a site on a rise above the beach and set up a temporary dwelling made from the materials available to me: ship sails and four redwood posts. It was just a tent."

He chuckled. "One night, a bear put his paw under the tent and carried off one of our roosters. Crikey, scared my children and wife to death. Finally, I built for my family a larger adobe house that I call Casa Grande." He pointed to a large red adobe structure to the north of the road they were traveling.

Next to it stood another adobe building. "It was mighty lonely here until Jacob Leese came in 1836 and built a house not far from mine, but he only stayed two years. In 1838, I was granted the clear title for my land grant of nineteen thousand seven hundred fifty-one acres. I call it Rancho Saucelito. It is the headlands across the water from the presidio." He pointed to a lush green spot on the distant horizon. "Willow trees grow there in the fresh springwater that I sell to the ships. I moved there just this year but come over to the ships when they are in port."

They rode in silence for a while. Will gave his horse its head, and it took off down the dirt road. The pebbles flew as its hooves pounded against the hard pan. It felt good to feel the wind against his face, and he rode some time before he struggled to rein in the unruly horse.

"Crikey! That was some ride," Mr. Richardson said as he trotted up alongside the winded horse. "Must feel good to have a horse under you after so many months of sea legs."

"Yes, it does. I would like to take him on a run down on the beach after we finish our tour."

"There are so many horses about. Take him for a gallop and then let him go. Leave the bridle with one of the Indians, who will catch him and bring him back. Do watch out for rattlesnakes, though," Richardson warned.

CHAPTER 20

WALKING THEIR HORSES in the morning sun, Will and Richardson strolled leisurely along the waterfront. "When Leese came, he and I became partners in providing produce for the foreign ships that came into the bay," Richardson said. "He was here until 1838, and in that time, more than twenty ships a year anchored at this bay and brought in finished goods like shoes, wine, clothing, beads, and knives in exchange for hides, tallow, and fresh produce."

He stopped talking long enough to pick up a shell from the beach and examine it. Tossing it aside, he continued, "As official captain of the bay, I boarded each ship, checked their papers, and recorded the amount of goods brought back with them. No money is exchanged; only goods are bartered. When we get to the customhouse, I will show you the report from 1837. It will help you in your decision to settle here."

After mounting their horses, they left the hardened path and set off south in the tall grasses toward a long rectangular adobe building Will assumed was the customhouse. "Again, be careful of rattlesnakes in the grass. The horses will shy and possibly buck if they hear them."

When they arrived safely, with no mishaps, Mr. Richardson opened the crude wooden door and invited him to come in and have a cup of tea while he showed him the report. He heated the water on a potbellied stove and filled a tin mug with the steaming brew. It smelled pleasing to Will as he sipped the warm liquid and observed his surroundings. The furnishings were sparse and rugged. A barrel with planks laid across the top was his tenuous seat. He sat carefully, knowing that if he moved he could end up on the hard dirt floor. Mr. Richardson sat at a table constructed from redwood poles, he assumed from a ship, possibly the ballast thrown over the side and resurrected from the bay. Rugged planks formed the table surface. He rifled through some papers lying on the table before he handed Will a sheaf of meticulously kept records.

Port of Puerto Buena, Maritime Report of 1837

25 ships entered the port:
  10 from the United States
  5 from Mexico
  5 from the United Kingdom
  2 from Russia
  2 from Ecuador
  1 from Hawaii

California products exported:

    15,928 hides

    12,494 cow horns

    302,654 pounds of suet (inferior beef tallow)

    13,038 pounds of lard

    70,714 pounds of dried meat

    21,714 pounds of potatoes

    14,510 pounds of flour

    111,364 pounds of wool

    2,579 pounds of otter pelts

    270 deerskins

    400 calabashes (a bottle gourd)

    54 live cattle

    100 sheep

    Wheat valued at $4,792.00

    Seeds worth $348.00

    Maize worth $198.00

    Oats worth $35.00

    Beans worth $11.00

Total declared goods exported in 1837: $75,711.00

Being an astute business man, Will was pleased to see the amount of business conducted. He recognized the items needed for a ship to make the return trip around Cape Horn and back to the East Coast with the hides and tallow. It took months, and the crew needed to be fed—hence the live cattle, sheep, flour, dried meat, beans, and potatoes.

He looked for molasses on the list, knowing the sailors looked forward to the treat on Sundays, but didn't see it.

"It's getting late, and you may want to get back to your ship and the crew before night falls. We'll ride down, and I'll take the horses back." He motioned Will ahead of him and closed the door tightly behind him.

When they reached the shoreline at the end of Sacramento Street, Will noticed a raw-brick building, no taller than six feet and no wider than eight feet. "What is that?" he asked, pointing to the structure. Smoke was pouring out of a hole at the top. The entrance looked like the opening of an oven; in fact, the whole building looked like a large kiln. "Is that an oven?"

"No, that is an Indian or Mexican sweathouse, called a temescal. Opposite the small entrance is a furnace of stone or raw bricks in which they build a fire to heat the stones. The bather enters naked and takes with him a pitcher of water, a mat, and a bunch of herbs or leaves of maize. He closes the entrance but leaves the airhole open for a time to let the smoke out. He throws water on the hot stones, which creates steam. After heating himself, he plunges into the waters of Laguna Dulce, where a spring of fresh water flows from under the bank."

Will swung his leg over the horse and jumped down. He winced at his sore muscles and hobbled over to get a better look. "Does it have a good effect on the Indians? Do they heal? I have heard about the Indian remedies."

"The sweating seems to drive out illnesses. The women use it after childbirth and for fevers and stings by poisonous animals like rattlesnakes and for wounds. I have seen Indians recover after a time in the Temazcalli. They have great knowledge of the healing power of herbs. There is no medical doctor, just like on the ship." Richardson turned his horse around and reached for the reins of Will's horse. "I must get back. I would like to see this area established, so if you are interested in settling here, we will talk more." He galloped off, leaving Will to return to his crew and the *Julia Ann.*

CHAPTER 21

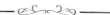

THE NEXT MORNING, Will strolled down the beach, stretching his aching tendons. Excitement welled in him and threatened to spill out, maybe in the form of running, but his muscles reminded him otherwise. The weather was pleasant but cool; the typical gray fog blanketed the land. Unanswered questions assailed him. He needed to find a place to live if he was to make Yerba Buena his home. Could his business thrive here? Could he secure enough dependable manpower to run a business? Would he be able to make a fresh start and put his years at sea behind him? And the big question: Could he love again?

He took off his shoes and let the grainy, damp sand massage his feet. In the distance, below Loma Alta, he could see the rocky promontory known as Clark's Point jut into the bay. It was a convenient landing and perfect place to transport the hides and tallow to the ships. It was in that far distance that he spotted a poop cabin of some condemned ship that had been hauled to shore and made into a livable abode.

In front of him, a Sandwich Island native, a kanaka, sat outside his crude shelter made of an abandoned sail, rigged with driftwood. His tangled black hair was pulled loosely into a ponytail. Almond-shaped dark eyes revealed his Asian heritage. He watched Will approach.

"Cap'in Spear live there with his Mex'can wife," he offered. "We ain't got much to build with, so we use what we find. Wanna sit a spell? I can always use company." He patted the sandy beach beside him.

Will thanked him but refused his offer and continued his stroll, breathing deeply of the salty, moist air. It seemed most men, once they came to this port, married Mexican wives. Who could compare with his Hortense? He fumbled for the cross he wore around his neck, his memorial, his promise never to forget.

Farther on he saw more kanakas seated in front of a rough shanty built from pieces of boards, bits of sailcloth, tarpaulins, beach grass, and boughs of trees. They were passing around a huge clay pipe with a stem not over an inch long. Seeing Will, one of the men asked, "Wanna have a piece of our salmon?" Will looked at the smoked fish lying on a broad leaf on the sand near the hut. "Some Sacramento River Indians who come to trade furs gived it to us. Here, try a piece." He held out a slab of the fish. Will accepted the sample and licked his lips.

"Good, huh? Got anything to trade? We'll give you more if you wanna trade somethin'," the man said.

Reaching inside his pocket, Will brought out a pouch of tobacco. "I'll trade you a handful of tobacco for the fish. It will be a nice change from pilot bread and salted buffalo." He stood for a minute. "Any of you looking for work? I need some men to help me once I get settled."

One of the men with dark skin and no shirt asked, "What kinda work?"

"I'm in the hide and tallow business, but I may need men to construct a building for me. Any of you have experience building?" Will asked.

"Never done that before, but we learn if you teach us," the spokesman responded, stuffing some of the tobacco into the pipe. "We be right here if you need us. What you pay?"

"I also do trading, so I have some things you might like in exchange for labor," Will said.

The men nodded and returned to their pipe. Will sauntered on, eating small bites of the savory fish from the makeshift green leaf plate, leaving his footprints in the damp sand. The sun gradually melted the gray haze away, and the water appeared clothed in brilliant diamonds. Tiny sand crabs scurried beneath his feet, diving into the moist sand. Seagulls feasted on coquina but scattered when he stooped to pick up some of the milky-white shells. This portion of the beach was deserted.

He met no one on his walk until he came to an old adobe building, about a cable length from Clark's Point. When he stopped to look into the open door, he saw what appeared to be a mill for grinding wheat. A dejected mule, connected to a pole, made two revolutions of the ring and then stopped and turned around to see what was going on behind him. A half-Mexican, half-Indian man leaned against the wall; his long black hair was tied with a colorful beaded headband. Whenever the mule stopped, he yelled out in a piercing voice, "*Caramba! Diablo! Amigo! Malo! Vamos!*" The mule dropped his head and promptly fell asleep. The Mexican threw up his hands, rolled a cigarette, struck it with flint and steel, and then squatted down on his heels to smoke. When he saw Will, he asked, "You got any tobacco?"

"What are you grinding?" Will asked as he reached into his pocket, pulled out his dwindling supply, and gave him a handful of the weed. Good thing he had more on the ship.

"When this here lazy mule decides to work, we grind dark sweet flour." He scraped up a handful of loose flour from the grinding floor and handed it to Will, the powder sifting through his fingers. "This mill belongs to Spear—called Spear's Grist Mill. You can trade for the flour at the store."

Amused, Will sat with the man awhile, rolled a cigarette, and lit it with the man's flint. "Any men around here looking for work?" Will asked.

"I dunno." The Indian shrugged. "I got my work if this lazy mule will do his part."

Will left the man and his weary mule. The sun had slipped below the coastal mountains, and the fog reappeared. He hurriedly retraced his steps and returned to his boat, which would take him to the *Julia Ann*. He still had no answers to his questions...

The fog, which he had become accustomed to, swathed his mind as well as the bay the next morning. At least the fog, which settled on Yerba Buena in the morning, burned off by afternoon and allowed the sun to shine clearly. He needed some clear answers. Aware that Yerba Buena did not get as much trade as the other ports, like San Diego, Los Angeles, Monterey, and San Jose, he could still see potential for the future, if he could get workers. He decided to talk it over with Richardson, so he rowed to land, haggled for a horse from an Indian for a dollar, and cantered over to Richardson's adobe. With his sore muscles recovered, the wind in his face was invigorating and the ride enjoyable.

Richardson sat on his veranda, smoking a pipe. He was dressed in a short jacket of black silk, his white shirt under the jacket was open at the neck. He wore black pantaloons. Only his brown hat was missing, but Will spotted it hanging on a wooden peg close to the door. White stockings and brown deerskin shoes covered his feet. Around his robust girth was the ever present splash of a red sash. He pointed to the chair on the veranda. "Have a seat. Feeling better today? I see you took a horse, so you must be."

Will dropped into the leather laced chair and said, "I need some manpower if I am going to run a hide and tallow business."

Richardson nodded and said, "Normally, the Indians from the missions were used to carry the hides to the ship, but since 1834 when Mission Dolores was ordered to secularize its landholdings, the padres no longer manage the ranching of land and livestock, and the Indians drifted away. You saw only a few living at the mission, and they are not dependable. They may or may not show up."

"What about the kanakas living on the beach? I saw some yesterday," Will said.

"Most of them come in on the ships, and some decide to stay. I don't know how dependable they are either. It depends on their need of goods. I guess you could try," Richardson said as he patted his stomach. "What's it take to run a hide and tallow business?" Picking up his pipe, he inhaled, blew out a ring of smoke, and watched it spiral into thin air.

"It's a long process to dry the hides and prepare them to be stored aboard ship. I learned the process while I was at the depot in San Diego. You sure you want to hear?" Will asked.

"Tell me. I have nothing pressing today, so I have time." He settled back in his chair and stretched out his legs in the warm sun.

"Well, when the hide is taken from the bullock, holes are cut near the edge of the hide so it can be staked to dry in the sun and avoid shrinking. After they are dried, the hides are folded with the skin out, loaded on the vessel, and brought to the depot, where they are left in large piles. Then the hide curer begins his work," Will said.

Richardson's wife came out carrying a pitcher of lemonade and some clay mugs. "I made this from the lemons on our tree. Try it." She handed Will a mug and did the same for her husband. Her long black hair hung in one braid down her back. Her movements were graceful and lithe as she served the men the drink. Her long skirt flowed around her slim ankles.

The men sat quietly in the morning sun, enjoying the refreshing drink before Will continued. "The hides are first soaked by carrying them down to the water at low tide and fastening them by small piles and ropes so the water can cover them. I remember each man putting in twenty-five and letting them soak for forty-eight hours. Then, they are taken out, rolled up in wheelbarrows, and thrown into vats containing brine, seawater with great amounts of salt, to soak another forty-eight hours to pickle them."

He stopped and moved his chair into the shade of the veranda as the sun climbed higher in the sky. "Next, they are laid on a platform for twenty-four hours and then spread on the ground, stretched, and staked out with the skin up so they dry smooth. Then the men use their knives to cut off any bad parts, pieces of meat or fat that could infect the whole lot if stowed away on a ship for many months. All this needs to be completed before noon when the hides will be too dry. In the heat of the sun, the grease rises to the surface and needs to be scraped off before the hides are folded with the hair side out and left to dry. Later in the afternoon, they are turned over for the other side to dry."

"Crikey! That's quite a process and time-consuming. You will need plenty of manpower for that operation," Richardson said, scratching his head.

"It is labor-intensive but still profitable. Although I don't imagine the hides will last forever with all the trapping going on." He stood, loosened the reins from the hitching pole, and mounted his horse. "I need to pick up some things from the store. I want to try some of Spear's flour. I stopped by his gristmill yesterday. Tell your wife thanks for the lemonade. It was good." He slapped his horse on the rear and galloped down the hill to the store, where he made his purchases, loaded them in his knapsack, and headed to the water's edge. The mist gently washed his face as he boarded the *Julia Ann*, and the fog enveloped him, cutting off visibility.

CHAPTER 22

MR. RICHARDSON WAS at the customhouse in the morning when Will knocked on the crude door. "I wonder if I might get a horse and do some more exploring today. I would like to find a place to live other than on the ship."

Closing his books, Richardson rose to his feet and said, "I'll come with you. We don't get much trading at this port, and there are no ships in other than yours, so I have time to go with you this morning." He walked outside and whistled to an Indian, who roped two horses and promptly delivered them to the men. "We rode by the Casa Grande yesterday. It is not occupied; you'd be welcome to stay there. I'll take you through it, and you can decide."

They trotted up the hill to the adobe home. Will commented on the red bricks, which seemed to be in abundance. Richardson explained, "The soil here is perfect for making adobe bricks. The Indians lay out forms and mix the clay with sand, water, straw, and dung to make them. The straw works as an adherent, while the dung is a bug repellant. They dry the bricks in the sun."

He pointed to a roof and said, "See? They do the same for the roof but press the clay onto wood forms so the adobe looks like cobs. Wooden slats are the support for the roof, and the mounded bricks are laid over them. The construction works well here as there is plenty of material and the adobe homes remain cool in the hot weather."

As they approached the building, Will could see the different types of bricks used for the walls and the roof. The roof had been extended at one end of the house to create a covered patio area supported by crude wood beams. Three doors faced the road in the long rectangular building. It was much humbler than the plantation he had left behind in New Orleans, so different from the Creole-style homes and the grandeur of his uncle's plantation.

Will had to stoop to enter the low door. The floor consisted of rough-hewn wood planks. A large stone fireplace was situated in the center of the room. Wood beams were inserted in crevices in the wall to create shelves. Gourds left behind lay in abandoned disarray. Although the walls had been whitewashed, the room was dark, as the door and one window were the only light sources. Will felt the coolness in temperature and inhaled the smell, musty from lack of habitation. "This is a castle compared with the rough shanties I saw on the beach yesterday," he nodded, satisfied. "After spending the last ten years on the sea, I could finally make this my home." He ran his fingers over the wood-carved mantel of the fireplace. "I have some fine pieces of furniture aboard the *Julia Ann* that I have collected in my travels. I think they would fit in here perfectly."

"No one has lived here since I moved my family across the bay. You are welcome to use it; the rent will be minimal," Richardson offered generously.

"Thank you. I will take it."

William promoted his first mate to be master of the *Julia Ann* and spent the next six months acquiring hides, tallow, gourds, otter skins, horns, and other items to ship back to the East Coast. He became better acquainted with Richardson, who often invited him to his home in Sausalito. He felt a real kinship with the man and confided in him, shared his dreams with him, but he did not share his love for Hortense with him. He kept that closely guarded in his heart.

The view from Richardson's home was beautiful, and the willows provided lush greenery to the otherwise parched land that saw no rain for an entire six months. Will was also able to purchase fresh water from Richardson until he could dig his own well.

One midmorning on a horse ride with Richardson, they climbed to the top of Telegraph Hill and viewed the entire bay. He could see the islands that dotted the cove, the rocks covered with seafowl and seals, and the low sandy spit that ran out, like a crescent, toward Goat Island. "Why is it called Goat Island?" he asked.

"When the sailors come into port, they are mighty tired of eating salted buffalo and pilot bread, so when Captain Nye sailed the ship *Fama* into port with goats aboard, Nathan Spear purchased them. Since there are no fences in the pueblo, he thought it safe to put them on the island, where they do quite well. Now the island is filled with goats, and we can have goat meat, milk, and cheese." He slapped Will on the back. "Pretty good, eh?"

Richardson pointed to a large adobe house at the base of the entrance into the bay. "That is the ranch of Señora Abarono. She is a wealthy widow and provides cow milk to the sailors and people in the town. That is, if you don't want goat milk." He raised his eyebrows. "You interested in a rich widow?"

Will ignored him, thinking of Hortense.. They rode on in silence until they saw the sand hills. To the south, on the border of a small creek, were the adobe walls of Mission Dolores. "During Spanish rule, the mission was a power in the area, with thousands of Indians and cattle at its disposal, but under Mexican rule, it was stripped of all its influence, and as you see, only a few Indians remain." Part of the roof had fallen in, and the walls were crumbling. Although still a house of prayer, it stood in disrepair, a symbol of bygone days.

On the return ride, Will was contemplative. "I know fur trading is depleting. I will need to pursue other avenues of revenue. I've been thinking this town needs a hotel for the visitors and sailors who dock and trade here. What if I were to build one and call it City Hotel? I have an idea for the perfect parcel for its construction."

Richardson shook his head. "I don't think we have enough people to support it. It is not a good idea. You want to throw your money away?"

"I think that is my business and not yours," Will replied, a bit heatedly. "I will decide about my money and my investments." Talking ceased, and both men rode silently until Will said, "You have done well for yourself. I would like the same."

After the disagreement, the men avoided each other for two weeks. Meanwhile, Will moved his furniture from the ship into the adobe house. When all was in place and the dust had settled from the conflict, he invited Richardson and his wife to his home for supper. There were not too many people to be friends with in the pueblo, after all. Dining on the traditional Mexican fare, Will rolled the beans in a corn tortilla, took a bite, and said, "I think I will apply to the mayor of Yerba Buena for a special brand for the cattle I want to acquire. With all the cattle and horses running wild, I need to identify the animals that are mine. I've sketched it out." He unfolded a piece of paper on which he had written his request and sketched the head of a long-horned steer.

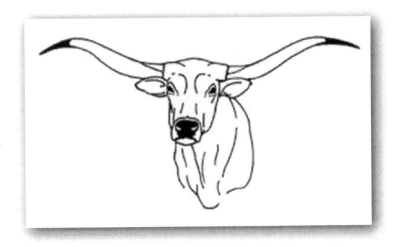

Attention Mayor of _____

Guillermo Leidesdorff naturalized and registered in Mexican Republic, and neighbor of this jurisdiction before and in due form, come and say that being owner of a number of horses and cow I need for their security, the use of iron and sign _____to be marked and be recognized of my legitimate property. My _____ properties and being the one which suits me by _____with other marks and signs of this jurisdiction; the one that propose in the margin, I beg that if there's not the same in the register book, to concede me the corresponding Licenses to use them in the case of no inconvenience, integrating me to the payment of the municipal duty taxed by the decree on the subject.

To Y(our) I ask to provide in accordance to the justice and accept the present in paper _____ not having the corresponding seal, I swear the necessary.

San Francisco de Asis,
July 12th /44[2]

Richardson handed the paper back to Will and nodded his head. "Looks good. I hope you get it."

"I can't acquire land without Mexican citizenship, so I am going to apply for that, too. It will be to my advantage for a number of reasons." He got up from the table, poured Richardson a cup of chicory coffee and set out some churros for dessert, and sat down again. "Every time one of my ships sails into Monterey to pay duties, I end up losing great profit. Custom duties are one hundred percent. On one of my trips, after paying duties, I profited only three hundred thirty-two dollars. After becoming a naturalized citizen, my profit improved greatly."

Richardson nodded his head in agreement. "Well, if you get the Mexican citizenship, you will be able to apply for the land. You always tell me one needs to take hold of opportunities. This is your chance; the land won't be available forever." He took his pipe out of his pocket and lit it, inhaled, and blew the smoke spiraling into the air.

---

2 Gary Palgon. *William Alexander Leidesdorff: First Black Millionaire, American Consul and California Pioneer* (Raleigh: Lulu Press, 2005), 12–13.

CHAPTER 23

WILL HAD APPLIED for and received his Mexican citizenship in 1844. Now he needed to find someone to help with the construction of his hotel. He had met many of the Indians around the pueblo, and one young man caught his eye. He was muscular and well built. His black hair hung down his back in a ponytail like many of the Indians' hair did. He spoke the language of the white man. His friends called him Sam. Will whistled to him as he rode his horse in front of his house and motioned him over. "I need someone to help with the building of a hotel. You look strong. Will you come work for me?"

"Sure, I like that. I be paid?" he smiled a toothy smile and spit tobacco on the dirt.

"Yes, but I will see how well you work first. You will start tomorrow morning. Be here when the sun rises," Will ordered. "If any of your friends want work, I can use them, too."

Sam showed up the next morning with five friends. By the end of the day, Will knew he was a good choice. He followed directions well and was a quick learner. He proved himself a natural leader, as the other Indians responded to his direction.

"How I do?" he asked Will at the end of the day as he wiped the sweat from his forehead. "I listen to what you tell us. We work hard."

"Yes, you did. Come again tomorrow at the same time. Bring your friends," Will said. "We will settle up at the end of the week."

Sam and his friends arrived every morning, even in the rain. Will came to depend on him, and City Hotel was finally completed six months later. The whole community was invited to the grand opening. Will kept the hotel's books the way his father had taught him, ordering supplies from the local butcher and making sure his help was scheduled, but it also granted him a social life to visit with his guests and learn the local gossip. It was there that Richardson often came to talk to him, when he crossed the bay to come to the pueblo.

The fire burned in the large rock fireplace of the hotel's dining room, creating warmth both in temperature and ambiance in the room. Will and Richardson sat at a table close to the fire and ordered flapjacks and some bacon for breakfast.

"I know a man named John Sutter who was given a land grant of forty-eight thousand eight hundred twenty-seven acres along the Sacramento River in '41. I was harbormaster when he arrived on the ship *Clementine*, just a couple years before you," Richardson said. "He applied for Mexican citizenship, just like you, and was given the land grant the following year. He named his settlement New Helvetia, which means New Switzerland, after the country of his birth."

His plate clean, Richardson put his fork down and reached for his ever-present pipe. "He made friends with the Indians, and they helped him construct a building made of adobe bricks and then surrounded it with a high wall for protection. I hear he set up workshops and intends to open a store for the settlers coming west by land. He calls it Sutter's Fort. It is about ninety miles from here in the valley. We should take a trip so you can see the land. There would be plenty of room for your cattle there."

Will agreed immediately. "I received a letter from him asking for some fabric and other items. I occasionally do some trading with him. I can go at the end of the week. We will have to pack our horses for the trip, as it will be quite a journey."

The trip was long and arduous, taking three days to travel by horse. Rolling out their blankets, they slept on the hard-packed ground and listened to the coyotes howl in the night. On the second night, a rustling noise awakened Will. He looked up to see two eyes glistening in the dying embers of the fire. He grabbed the nearest stick, stuck it in the fire until the end glowed, and waved it frantically. The wolf disappeared into the darkness, but Will could not go back to sleep.

On the third night, they gathered grass and sticks and built a huge fire. Sitting in the warmth of the fire, Will told Richardson of his sea travels, his trips to the Sandwich Islands, and the business of hide and tallow trade.

"Ever think of getting married?" Richardson asked as they shared stories.

"Once, but it didn't work out," Will answered abruptly, a flush coloring his cheeks. "I don't care to talk about it, so don't ask." He stood and walked into the brush; all the memories came flooding back as if it were yesterday. He had buried the memories of Hortense in the private recesses of his heart. He walked through the tall grass, pulling at the weeds that got in his way. Lost in the turmoil of resurrected thoughts of Hortense, Will did not return to the campsite until the sun went down.

When he did return, he rolled out his bedroll and stared at the fire. His thoughts continued to wander into that painful place from so long ago. The hurt and loss still buried in his heart, revived itself once again but served as a reminder to him to keep persevering against all odds. He didn't hide from secrets anymore.

When they awoke the next morning, they packed up camp, filled their canteens with clear, fresh water from the Sacramento River, and chewed on salted buffalo. Not far from their destination, they washed the dirt and grime from their travels off in the brisk waters of the Sacramento River. Neither spoke.

They rode in silence until they arrived at the confluence of the Sacramento River and American River called Sutter's Fort. The silence was broken as Will exclaimed, "This is huge. He did all this with the local Indians? That is impressive."

Richardson said, "I'm told the fort encloses an area of four hundred twenty-eight feet by one hundred seventy-eight feet and those walls surrounding it are at least fifteen feet tall. Pretty grand, isn't it?" He paused. "They say the walls are two and a half feet thick. Pretty impregnable."

A full-bodied German guard met them at the entrance. "Vhat is your business, and vhat can I do for you?"

"We are here to see John Sutter," Richardson said. They waited, holding their horses by the reins until a robust man with thinning hair, a full mustache, and strong military bearing met them.

"You must be Richardson." Sutter extended his hand. "It is good to see you. We have been expecting you." He turned to Will. "And this is?"

Stepping forward, Will extended his hand. "William Leidesdorff," he said.

"It is good to meet you both. I like to meet the men I do business with. You bring me my order?" His German accent was strong, his eyes piercing.

"Yes, I did. I am also interested in settling on some land in this area. We wanted to make the trip before the winter rains," Will explained and motioned to the buildings before them. "This is quite an impressive place you have. I understand the Indians helped you with the construction."

"Yes, I couldn't do vithout the manpower of the Indians. Come, let me show you around." He gestured them forward through the gate and pointed to a three-story building in the center of the enclosure. "That is vhere I do all my business: the cattle registered, inventories tallied, and my accounts created. Ve have a large dining hall vhere the residents of the fort eat. Please join us for supper. Ve have a doctor here, too, and his rooms are in that building along with my private office."

"Is that baking bread that I smell?" interrupted Richardson, sniffing the air.

"Ve vill get to that." Sutter said as he turned and pointed to two towers on opposite corners of the enclosed area. "Those are the bastions to protect the fort from attack. They contain two types of cannons: one shoots iron balls to stop attacks from the distance, and the other is like a giant shotgun that shoots bags of musket balls."

He continued walking until they arrived at a beehive structure in the middle of the open area. "There it is. The smell of baking bread comes from that oven, called a *horno*. I employ two men who bake the bread ve eat daily. They build a fire in the oven and heat the adobe bricks. Vhen the bricks are warm enough, they remove the fire, and the bread bakes to perfection. Vait until you try it; it is delicious and a break from all the beef ve eat. Ve vill have some tonight for supper."

General Sutter pointed to a number of smaller rooms along the wall. "Ve have a blacksmith's shop. Smitty is our blacksmith." Although he spoke no English, Smitty, upon hearing his name, stopped what he was doing and smiled a toothless grin at the men. "He makes hinges for the gates, fittings for carriages, shoes for horses, knives for cooking, and lance heads for weapons. He is the most important man ve have here," Sutter said and then pointed to the next room. "That is the gunsmith's shop. Our guns are used for hunting and are often in need of repair, so he stays busy keeping them in order. It is our only means of defense."

He waved his hand, encompassing the other buildings. "Ve also have a general store, a carpenter's shop, and private rooms where you gentlemen can spend the night." He pointed to the far guard tower. "Over there is a jail under that bastion if one gets drunk or involved in a brawl. I am the civil authority around here, so I enforce the laws and mete out the punishment." Someone called his name. "Right now, we have a vaquero locked up who could not hold his liquor and began shooting up the place. I must go, but please walk around and look into the shops. Then come in for supper and have some of that fresh-baked bread. I invite you to use our guest room tonight."

The men thanked Sutter and took him up on his offer, peering into the different rooms. They saw the cooper's shop where barrels were made. They stood for a while and watched him plane planks of wood for a butter churn.

Will was taking mental notes. *Sutter is so successful. He has built himself an empire, and I want to do the same. If he can do it, so can I. Does he pay the Indians, or are they treated as slaves?*

Will and Richardson joined the rest of the residents for supper and ate their fill of the homemade bread, potatoes, and beef. The bread did not disappoint them; it tasted as good as it smelled. After spending the night on mattresses stuffed with feathers, so much better than the hard-packed earth, they rose early and rode farther east to the American River.

Viewing the gentle foothills of the Sierra Mountains and the lazy summer river meandering through the brown countryside, Will commented, "This will work well for my cattle. There is plenty of land for them to graze and a good water supply. The river will provide fresh water for both the cattle and the settlers." Looking around, he continued, "There is an abundance of trees to construct buildings. What kind are those?" He pointed to a grove of trees with great lush canopies.

"They are called blue oaks and survive the long, dry summers. The Maidu or Nisenan Indians who live in this area peel their bark and make their summer shelters from the trees. We may be able to see some of them." He stopped, shielded his eyes from the sun, and scanned the horizon. Not seeing any, he continued, "They also trade with other tribes their acorns for black-oak acorns."

After seeing most of the territory, the men headed back to Yerba Buena with enough food and supplies to see them through the journey. Very satisfied with what he saw, Will applied for a land grant as soon as they arrived home. In August of 1844, he petitioned Governor Micheltorena for land along the American River. He also agreed that he would not prevent the Indians of that neighborhood from cultivation or making use of said land.

To His Excellency the Governor
I, the Citizen, William A. Leidesdorff, a native of Denmark, and naturalized in the Mexican Republics before Your Excellency, with due respect, represent: That being the owner of a large amount of stock, and desiring to obtain a tract of land on which to place them: I

have found such a tract, bounded by the lands of Señor Sutter, as shown by the annexed map: Said land is situated on the banks of the American River and contains eight square leagues, that is, four leagues in length by two leagues in width. Wherefore, I pray, Your Honor to be pleased to grant me said land, in which I will receive favor, Swearing that I this in good faith, and to whatever is necessary.[3]

Each day he waited for the answer. Finally in October, Will received the news and had reason to celebrate. He was given the land grant of thirty-five thousand acres on the left bank of the American River, which he named Rancho de los Americanos. He was ecstatic. The decree confirming the boundary of this tract read as follows:

Beginning at an oak tree on the bank of the American River, marked as a boundary to the land granted to John A. Sutter, and running thence South to the line of Sutter's two leagues, thence easterly by lines parallel to the general direction of the American River and at a distance of as near as maybe two leagues therefrom: Thence along the southerly band of said river and boundary thereon to the place of beginning.

---

3 Palgon, *First Black Millionaire*

Will decided to have an open house, a gala event at City Hotel, now that it was completed, to celebrate his success. He provided the typical Mexican fare of rice, beans, tortillas, and the ever-abundant beef. Richardson and his wife came, bringing some of her lemons, ready to mix up in lemonade. She also made some churros, Will's favorite. Spear brought some bread made from the flour ground at his mill. In all, forty of the seventy residents attended.

Once the guests were settled at the wooden tables, Will raised his glass and proposed a toast. "To the success of the acquisition of my land grant in this land of opportunity, where dreams come true when one perseveres."

Thomas Larkin

WILL HAD HEARD the stories about Thomas Larkin, the US consul to Mexico. Each time one of his ships sailed into Monterey, his goods need to be counted, and Larkin was the man responsible for the counting. He had arrived in California ten years earlier and was responsible for building the wharf and rebuilding the Monterey Customs House. The two-story Spanish colonial whitewashed adobe customhouse housed Mr. Larkin's office. He claimed it was the first two-story house in Monterey and had the original fireplace. Since it was located right on the Monterey Peninsula, he could see the ships from his window.

Upon arrival, all the goods were unloaded from the ship and brought to the counting house to be calculated for tax purposes. The process was long, so Will found Mr. Larkin in his office. The walls were whitewashed, clean and crisp, and the floors laid with wood. A wooden desk and three chairs were the extent of the furniture, although a small potbellied stove heated the room and water for his tea.

After greeting him, Larkin said, "Have a seat," and pointed to a leather-strung chair. He took a seat behind his desk.

Will eyed him with interest. Larkin combed the remains of his gray receding, thinning hair strands forward, Will assumed to improve his appearance. Lamb chops bristled on his cheeks, and a deep cleft marked his chiseled chin.

He didn't look like the romantic kind, but he was rumored to have a romantic past. While aboard ship, coming from Boston to California, it was said he developed an intimate relationship with a married woman who was coming to meet her husband, also a Danish sea captain in California. They traveled together to Monterey and there learned she was carrying Larkin's child. She discreetly moved to Santa Barbara, where she gave birth to their child and waited for the dreaded reunion with her husband. Within a few weeks, she learned her husband had died at sea, so she was able to return to Larkin and marry him.

"Would you like a cup of tea?" Larkin asked, breaking the silence and Will's thoughts.

"Yes, thank you. That sounds good. There is a brisk wind out there today; I'm chilled to the bone," Will responded, shivering.

Larkin poured the hot water over the loose tea leaves and handed the cup to Will, who clutched the mug with both hands. "This will warm my hands." He took a drink of the steaming liquid and let it burn down his throat.

"I have news for you," Will said. "I have just become a land baron. I have acquired thirty-five thousand acres along the American River. It is prime land, and I am going to commission Sutter's Indians to build me an adobe on the land. I intend to raise cattle there."

"Congratulations. You must have applied for Mexican citizenship." Will nodded, and Larkin explained, "You know, I never wanted to become a Catholic, so I never applied for Mexican citizenship. Of course, I have to renew my visa annually to maintain legal status." He took a sip of his tea. "Nonetheless, I have obtained land grants in the names of my children, since they were born here and are naturalized Mexican citizens, so I do have land, and so will they one day."

He stroked his lamb chops, although Will could not see that it tamed the bristles in anyway. They reminded him of his own unruly hair.

"Being involved in politics in a distant province of an unstable nation is a difficult thing," Larkin said as he smoothed his remaining hair forward. "Although I support Governor Juan Bautista Alvarado, I chose not to become tangled in the group of American and European immigrants who led a coup against Governor Gutierrez in 1836. Graham and his men wanted Alvarado to be governor. Eventually he was, but later he turned against the men who had worked to overthrow his predecessor and had about one hundred foreigners arrested."

He exhaled, a look of relief on his face. "It is a good thing I did not support the coup, or I could have ended up in a Mexican prison. It became a diplomatic crisis that involved Mexico, the United States, and the United Kingdom. Did you hear about it?"

Will shook his head, and Larkin continued. "They called it the Graham Affair." He walked over to the window and looked out on the Pacific Ocean, sparkling in the winter sun. He stood in the warmth of the light, rubbing his hands together, and continued, "A lawyer by the name of Farnham arrived and defended the group, so they were eventually released. I find it is best not to get involved, especially when one is uncertain of the outcome. I am convinced that we will eventually become part of the United States."

Will joined him at the window. He could see his ship anchored at the wharf. Just like with the slavery issue in Louisiana, this country was facing a crisis, too. The European immigrants were changing the face of Alta California.

"I read about the annexation of Texas and how it was admitted to the Union as the twenty-eighth state," Will said. "You know President Polk is a strong supporter of territorial expansion. I hear there is talk of Alta California being annexed. I certainly hope it doesn't mean war. Loss of life is a terrible thing."

Mr. Larkin agreed vigorously and said, "There are two groups of immigrants coming to California." He pointed at Will. "You represent one of the groups, a man from the East Coast coming for economic reasons and trading. The other is represented by rough trappers and mountain men who come from the Border States and over the mountains. Graham was one of those and did things by brute force." He poured himself another cup of hot water from the teakettle heating on the stove. He turned to Will. "Would you like another cup?"

Will accepted the cup of the steaming brew, which he sipped in silence.

Larkin continued, "I don't know if you heard about US Commodore Jones who landed his marines when John Tyler was president. He was on a mission to take over Monterey because he heard that war had broken out between Mexico and the United States. I worked with Hartnell to smooth over that situation. I had Jones write a letter of apology to the Mexican officials, as they were very angry. He withdrew his troops, but things were pretty tense for a while."

He shook his head and went on. "This job is not for the faint of heart. That situation caught the attention of Washington and President Tyler. That's when I was appointed to be the first American consul to Alta California. The next year, the British tried to acquire California, but we were able to thwart that attempt, too. All this was happening while I was trying to help the Mexican government build a smallpox hospital here."

He stopped and focused his attention on Will. "How about you? Do you have any aspirations of being involved in politics? You have your own shipping company. I hear you have had experience managing a plantation and a crew, and now you are a land baron."

Flattered, Will responded, "I haven't thought about politics, but I would consider it since I am now a citizen of Mexico and own land along the American River. I received a brand for my cattle, too. I recently built a hotel in Yerba Buena called City Hotel. You will have to come and stay there. Of course, we are not as settled as Monterey. We do not have the shipping traffic you have."

A knock sounded at the door. It was one of the men employed by the customhouse.

"We have finished the counting of the Leidesdorff ship, and it is sealed and ready to depart." Larkin thanked him and shook hands with Will as he left for his ship, thinking that politics might indeed interest him.

Communication was slow between Washington and the US consul, but as Alta California continued to grow, Mr. Larkin, after observing William's flair for management and politics, appointed him to be vice-consul under the jurisdiction of Commodore Stockton, the military governor of California. Since cross-country communication was sluggish, this appointment was never officially confirmed by the State Department in Washington, DC, or formally accepted by the government of the Republic of Mexico in Mexico City. Yet William accepted the position with civic pride and duty.

CHAPTER 25

WHALE OIL LAMPS stood on the wooden tables of City Hotel. A fire blazed in the stone fireplace. The guests stood with drinks in hand, and some sat at the rough-hewn wood tables. Will, known for his generous and lavish hospitality, was hosting a supper. The guests included Mr. Forbes, the vice-consul to California from Britain, along with Richardson, Sutter, Nathan Spear, William Hinckley, and other leading men in the community. Will smoothed his thick black hair, brushed some lint off his trousers, and walked over to Mr. Forbes, who was talking with Sutter, and introduced himself. "Good evening. I am William Leidesdorff, the vice-consul for California. I understand that you are the vice-consul for the British government."

Mr. Forbes, erect and tall with stiff British bearing and accent, eyed Will from his six-foot-two height and said, "I am pleased to meet you, but I have no knowledge or communication from my country or from the supreme government of Mexico as to your position. Nor have I received any from the Department of California. Therefore, I cannot acknowledge your position." He turned and walked away.

Will stepped backward, feeling like he had been slapped in the face. He was speechless. His face burned, and his heart beat rapidly. He braced himself. This was not the place or time to explode. He struggled to hold on to his self-control, something he had been working on. *Who does he think he is?* he thought. *I am an esteemed man in this community. I will not be treated like that in my own hotel.*

Clenching his fists, he walked to the bar and ordered a drink. He downed it in one gulp and motioned to Richardson, who came right over. "I have been snubbed by that pompous British snob." He pointed toward Forbes. "I do not want to see him the rest of the night, or I may not be responsible for my actions. Will you take over as host? I need to take care of some business."

He went straight to his room and wrote Mr. Larkin, asking him for an official notice. He dispatched it by Mr. Mellus directly. In a few days, Will received a reply that did not soothe his pride.

Consulate of the United States of America

Monterey, California, November 25, 1845

Sir:

Your communication by Mr. Mellus was rec'd last night. You place to[o] much importance respecting the non-acknowledgement of your office by Mr. Forbes. As to his saying he has not received any notice from the Supreme

Government of México, or from this Department of California, respecting your appointment, that's nothing. I do not expect he ever will. Excepting seeing my name in a Mexican paper naming my appointment, he has not other information of my commission. The same respecting his knowledge of the French Consulship of this country—I shall by no means give Mr. Forbes official Notice of your appointment. By Section 7, page 22 & 23 in your Book of Instructions, you will see the power given US Consul to appoint Vice Consuls. That I am US Consul of California, by authority of President Tyler, my commission will show, and the Mexican & California Governments are well-informed on the subject. It will ten or twelve months before I have answers to my letters to Washington relative to your appointment, and as the power of appointing you is invested in me, the appointment will in time be confirmed by the State Department at Washington.

Again, it's a matter only of politeness and good feeling and Neighborliness between you two what Mr. Forbes may say or think on the subject. The Authorities of your place know you as U.S. Vice Consul. All our Commanders of Ships of War or privates ships will acknowledge you as such, and you must wait a[n] eight or ten months for full acknowledgement. Whatever your Neighbor may tell you about his correspondence with the Departments in London, you may believe his correspondence goes four days; you will send them at my expense as cheap as possible. Read the papers and without having them go out of yr [your] hands, carefully enclose them again. As I have no time to write this letter over or any other you will show it to Mr. Howard and Capt. Vince.

There is every appearance of war with Mexico, none with Eng. Her Gov't is confused by the passing of the Corn Laws. Peale was out ten days, had to be recalled. Mr. Packingham was two or three times offered Mr. Buchanan to settle the Origon [Oregon] question (which our President refuses) by arbitration. The opening for grain is to be much importance to the States who now ought to modify our Tariff for the benefit on Engl. If you are selling and Real Estate, hold on a time, and see if it may not bring more in '47.

By John H. Everett' letters of Dec' 12, it appears at over 1,000 Mormons are coming. I have no letters for or about Mr. Howard's business of a new ship.

I am inclined to think some of the great ones here are preparing for the coming change. If so, I hope the[y] will not allow their followers to entirely be in the dark. And after all, these reports may prove but squalls/ Yet the pear is near ripe for the falling.

Yrs. in haste

Thomas O. Larkin

Send me yr a/c
Dr. & Cr.[4]

Will read the letter hastily, pulled his desk drawer open, and stuffed in the letter. So much for being recognized officially as vice-consul.

---

4   Palgon, *First Black Millionaire*

CHAPTER 26

1845

BY THE END of 1845, fifty buildings and fifty people inhabited the pueblo of Yerba Buena. Will moved from Richardson's house to a cottage that he built facing the waterfront on the corner of California and Montgomery Streets. He also built a hide house a block away from his cottage, on the same block as the temescal, or sweathouse. His trading business had grown big enough for him to purchase two more ships for a fleet of twelve.

Americans were coming by sea and overland. John Sutter's New Helvetia provided services for the overland immigrants who arrived in greater numbers. Will's business interactions with Sutter increased. Sutter sent him a letter, asking him to send bolts of brown fabric so the Indians could be clothed. It read, "It doesn't look good for the Indians to be without clothing when the people from the East come." Will in return asked him to send ten of his Indians to help out with his ranch and with housekeeping for both him and the hotel. Sutter was able to pay his debt to Will by charging him for the Indians. When Will saw the charge, it struck a chord deep in his heart. Wasn't that slavery? Hadn't he left all that behind? Did this new land practice slavery, too?

City Hotel provided meals, a private room, and a place to meet other people. Will often dined there in the evenings to hear the local news. On this particular evening, when Will entered the room, his attention was drawn to a confident young man with a full head of wavy brown hair and a beard that matched. A group of men had gathered around him as he spoke animatedly, "I am a strong supporter of the Manifest Destiny, an expansionist movement." He brushed his hair off his forehead and continued, "My father-in-law, Mr. Benton, and I have pushed Congress to give us money to survey the Oregon Trail and the Oregon Territory so people in the East will feel comfortable moving out here to the West. After we received the funds, we explored Nevada country and then crossed the Sierra Nevada Mountains to Sutter's Fort. The reports have created great interest in the East because it gives people a picture of the Wild West."

Will walked over to meet the young man, who introduced himself as John Frémont. He was staying at the hotel and eating his meals there. Later that evening, Will noticed him having a bowl of bean soup, ham hocks, and corn bread, so Will asked, "May I join you for supper?"

"Sure, have a seat. I like company." He motioned to the chair across from him.

"I heard you talking about the expansion, and I'd like to know more about it and you. I am interested in the development of our country," Will said as he pulled out the chair and sat down.

"Well," John smiled, "I taught mathematics before I joined the Army Topographical Engineers Corps. I became part of a party led by Nicollet and surveyed and mapped the territory between the Mississippi and Missouri Rivers. We surveyed the Des Moines River in 1841 and, in the next year, mapped most of the Oregon Trail."

He stopped for a moment and sopped up his soup with the corn bread. "Kit Carson was my guide into the Laramie Mountains and then crossing the Rocky Mountains until we finally reached the Great Salt Lake." He stopped long enough to ask Will, "You've heard of him, haven't you? He's making quite a name for himself. Yes, sir, I've seen a good part of this great country. This year I explored the Great Basin and the Pacific coast and now have just been appointed to the rank of major in the United States Army." He frowned and shook his head. "I can tell you things have been heating up with Mexico since we annexed Texas. There could be war."

There it is again, he thought. *The possibility of war. I hear it everywhere.* Will leaned forward in his chair, listening intently. The man had seen a great deal of this new land for being so young.

When Frémont finished speaking, Will said, "I find history and your exploration very interesting, especially since I think California is on the cusp of being annexed to the United States. The question is, when and where will it all start? I sure hope for a peaceful annexation without bloodshed or the loss of lives."

Almost every day, Will walked by the store that belonged to Jacob Leese on Montgomery Street. Jacob had moved up from Los Angeles and entered a mercantile partnership with his friends, Nathan Spear and William Hinckley, before Will moved to the area. He did business mainly with the large ranches and the ships seeking hides and tallow. Jacob met the sister of General Vallejo, Rosalia Vallejo, fell in love, and married her. They lived in an adobe house on the corner of Grant Avenue and Clay Street. Will had opportunity to speak to her on many occasions. He thought she was lovely and realized his often-ignored desire for female companionship.

Most of the European men were married to Mexican women. He fingered the gold cross that hung on a chain near his heart before tucking it away, out of sight. The loss of Hortense still pained him, and although he wished to marry, he had not met a woman who stirred his heart. His hide and tallow business kept him busy. His mind was occupied, but not his heart.

CHAPTER 27

IN THE QUEST to find more pelts for his hide and tallow business, William often boarded one of his ships to Sitka, Alaska. While dining at a hotel he frequented, a lovely half-Russian and half-Alaskan waitress attracted his attention—a half-caste just like him. Each time he ate a meal, he noticed the gracious way she served her customers. She was petite with smooth olive skin and dark-brown eyes. Her thick black hair hung in a single braid down her back, reaching almost to her waist. Will wanted to touch it, to caress the softness of her skin.

Sadness seemed to envelop her countenance, and when he asked how she came to be a waitress, she responded, "I used to live with very cruel and mean husband, and when I take it no longer, I move to Sitka and get this job. It support me." She did not make eye contact and spoke without emotion, although she did linger at his table, fingering the silverware. Moments later, she shifted her gaze to Will, and he identified with the pain he saw in her eyes.

Although he had told no one of losing Hortense, he surprised himself by responding, "I have been hurt in love too, it is a pain that never goes away." He reached for her hand, wanting to connect in some way. In despair, she gripped his hand, like one on a sinking ship.

"What is your name?" Will asked gently.

"My family call me Moon because I was born under a full moon." She released his hand and tucked hers in her apron pocket.

"It is nice to meet you, Moon." A thought flashed through his mind. He took a deep breath and spoke aloud. "I am sailing to Yerba Buena tomorrow, and I need a hostess and a manager for my hotel. The weather is much friendlier there than the harsh Alaskan winters are. It could be a new beginning for you. My ship, the *Julia Ann*, is leaving tomorrow morning, and if you want to go, be at the dock at seven o'clock."

She took her hands out of her pocket and wrung them together. "I don't know," she said. "I have not traveled away from my home. I think about it."

The next morning when Will went up on deck, he was surprised to see her waiting on the wharf with a small faded valise, which he assumed contained all her belongings. His heart went out to her, as she looked so forlorn, so lonely, yet so very lovely.

She saw him and lifted an uncertain hand. He dispatched one of the crew to help her board and settled her into one of the small private cabins before she changed her mind. The water was smooth and the sailing uneventful. Will did not see Moon through the day, but as the supper hour arrived, he invited her to dine with him. "Why did you decide to come?" he asked. "I didn't think I would see you this morning."

In a subdued voice, she said, "I tell you I leave my abusive husband, and that is true, but he do not leave me alone. He come often to the hotel and tell my boss lies about me. I afraid of him. I decide this be new beginning. It seem like right thing to do." Her eyes remained downcast and her voice flat. She fingered the handkerchief lying in her lap, twisting the corners.

In the following days, as she dined with Will in the evenings, he learned that she was soft-spoken but intelligent and a quick learner. She listened intently as he told her about the hide and tallow business and City Hotel, his life in Yerba Buena. A shadow of sadness seemed to envelop her when no one was looking. Will hoped that would be replaced with happiness in time, in a different environment.

When they arrived at Yerba Buena, she said, "This be so different from Sitka. I think I like it here. The hills be so beautiful and the trees so green." She smiled at Will and picked up her faded valise, exposing her arm.

The big purple bruise on her upper arm alarmed Will. It was the size of a tomato and ugly. When she saw his face, she quickly lowered her arm and pulled her sleeve over the welt.

Sensing her embarrassment and her desire not to draw attention, Will reached for her valise and said, "Let me show you City Hotel. There is a room waiting there for you. I think you will find it very comfortable."

On the walk to the hotel, Will pointed out his home, the temescal, and the hide house.

Some Indians were selling colorful woven blankets by the pier. Moon walked up and fingered the bright blankets. She lifted one up and wrapped it around herself, hugging it close. She sighed, folded it up, and put it back on the ground with the others. They continued on to the hotel. Will showed her the room that would be her new, safe home. It was small, containing only a single bed, a nightstand, a chair, and a window that looked out on the bay.

A big smile lightened her face. "This be perfect," she exclaimed as she walked over to the window and looked out at the water. "Thank you for giving me fresh start on life. This is nicest room I ever have." Tears welled in her eyes, and she brushed at them. She recovered and said, "I am going to buy colored blankets I see Indians weave. It add pretty color to my room." She walked over to the nightstand and ran her fingers over the surface before sitting down. She folded her hands in her lap and looked up at Will. "You tell me what I do at City Hotel."

"I have a man that cooks the meals; I do the ordering and take care of the books. I would like you to help with the menus and give me a list of what we need to purchase. I also want you to be the hostess and greet the guests." He paused, trying to read her reaction. "You may

have to help with waitressing, too, like you were doing in Sitka."

"It be pleasure to work for you." She bowed her head to Will. "Thank you for opportunity."

There was so much that needed to be done in this raw, unsettled land Will called home. His friends and business acquaintances agreed. Henry Mellus was a sailor like him who had returned to Yerba Buena aboard the ship *Pilgrim*. He became a successful merchant. Just recently, he and William Howard formed the commercial business of Mellus and Howard. He told William, "I don't think the Hudson Bay Company is doing well. I anticipate they will sell out and move with the hide and tallow business declining. If so, I want to purchase the building."

Two weeks later, Mellus stopped by City Hotel and said, "I just heard Hudson Bay is disposing their property and moving from here, just like we thought. It will be sad to see them go, but the trading business is not what it used to be with the hides getting harder to acquire. Howard and I are going to purchase the business."

"Congratulations," Will said and shook hands with Mellus, pleased that Yerba Buena was developing. It made business good for him. "You have time for a cup of coffee? I have some great churros that go well with coffee."

Mellus sat down at one of the tables, and Will motioned Moon to bring them some churros and coffee. Mellus sipped his hot coffee and took a bite of the churro. He brushed the cinnamon and sugar off his mustache and said, "I hear things are heating up between Mexico and the United States. It's a time of change, and it seems inevitable that California will become a part of the United States."

Will nodded, a frown on his face. "I just hope it is a peaceful annexation. I don't want to see everything we have worked so hard to build here destroyed. I recently received a letter from Larkin saying there is every appearance of war with Mexico and none with England. I think we should prepare ourselves for what seems inevitable, war."

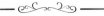

CHAPTER 28

1846

THE WINTER AND spring of 1846 ushered in the much-needed rain to the parched brown mountains. The rolling hills turned green, and the lemon, orange, and plum trees, which grew so cheerfully in the climate of Yerba Buena, blossomed. The air was scented by the blooms, but the pleasantness stopped there: rumors of war were escalating, and a letter from Larkin had confirmed them.

News arrived by men traveling on horse or ship as they sailed into ports along the coast. Receiving a letter from Sutter, Will learned that American army officer and explorer John Frémont arrived at Sutter's Fort with a small corps of soldiers. Supposedly, they were conducting a scientific survey, but Sutter wrote, "Frémont is convincing the settlers and some of the trappers to form a militia in preparation for a rebellion against Mexico. I don't know where this will take us."

A short time late, a letter arrived from General Vallejo stating,

Fréeemont, Ide, and Merritt arrived with a party of approximately thirty to forty Americans wearing mostly buckskins and surrounded my home. They told me I was a prisoner of war which surprised me as I am a supporter of the annexation. I invited the men in so I could explain my position. We had some drinks, and I thought things were going to transition smoothly until Ide arrested me and my family. As I write this, I am sitting in Sutter's parlor for lack of a more suitable prison. It is a large room on the second story of his two two-story adobe house. The room only has one door which is guarded by a sentinel. I hear they have raised a new flag on which Ide and his men painted a grizzly bear and a lone red star and the words "'California Republic.'" I perceive they are now on their way to Yerba Buena. Take caution.[5]

After reading the letter, Will paced up and down his small office. He reread the letter and paced some more, running frustrated hands through his hair. *We must do something about this. We must be prepared.*

After contacting Richardson, he and some of the other known American sympathizers began meeting secretly in

---

5 *Magazine of American History with Notes and Queries.* https://books.google.com/books?id=ze4OAAAAYAAJ. 1891. United States. March 16, 2016.

the back room of City Hotel to discuss the US orders to take action in case of a war with Mexico. In the midst of all the tension, ex-governor Alvarado asked Will if his hotel could host a grand ball. Not wanting to alarm the Mexican authority, or to give them wind of the rebellion brewing, Will agreed. He asked Moon to be the hostess for the evening and told her to have a gown made with some of the rich magenta damask fabric one of his ships had just delivered. She would be a beautiful distraction to the men.

On the eve of the ball, the dining room was transformed under Moon's capable hand. The crude tables were set with white linen cloth, and the candles on the tables waved small beacons of peace, light, and warmth. Moon wore her dark hair wrapped around her shapely head, and the magenta coloring of the gown was gorgeous against her olive skin as she flitted around the room, a beautiful butterfly making everyone comfortable. A pig had been slaughtered for the night. Pork roast with baked apples, sweet potatoes, and corn were just part of the evening menu.

Will was dressed formally in his black suit, his hair greased to perfection. He enjoyed hosting these political events and was a charming host as he circulated among the guests, greeting them and making small talk. A young American named Lieutenant Gillespie was one of the visitors. Will introduced himself, and they were talking for some time about the pueblo when the lieutenant asked if he could speak privately with Will.

Will led him to a corner of the room, and behind a gloved hand, the lieutenant whispered, "I hear you are an American sympathizer." He waited for Will's affirmative response before he went on. "I am a confidential agent of the United States government. It is very important that my identity not be exposed. War is inevitable, and I am here to gather information."

Will looked around the room. No one seemed to notice them in the corner. "I am a sympathizer and I will do all I can to help you and to keep your identity a secret," he pledged. "Your life may be in danger if you are exposed so be careful." He began to walk away, "Let's join the others before anyone notices our seclusion. We don't want to draw attention"

Suddenly, Will's world changed. He became aware of each person in the room and watched them all with close intensity. Were there other spies in the crowd? He singled out the *comandante* general Castro of the Mexican Army, the most powerful man in the room. He watched as one of the Mexican lieutenants pulled him aside and whispered something in his ear. General Castro was immediately on the alert, scoping the room.

Watching the interchange, Will sensed the identity of Lieutenant Gillespe was exposed. He maneuvered his way through the crowd until he reached Gillespie. "Come with me," he whispered. "I think your identity has been revealed." He ushered him into the kitchen and then led him to the larder, a small cool room used to store food.

He closed the door and said, "You will be safe here until we can get you out. Your life is in danger."

"I cannot accomplish my mission with my identity being exposed. I must leave. Can you find me a boat so I can make my escape?" Gillespie asked, his eyes showing alarm.

"I know the harbormaster, who has access to a boat that can get you out tonight. I will tell the guests that you are in ill health and must leave. Meet me at the waterfront, and the boat will be ready. I will have Moon give you warm clothes, as the nights on the water are cold," Will said.

Richardson was enjoying his pumpkin pie and coffee when Will found him at one of the tables. "Come quickly. I need your help, but do not show any fear." He followed him into the kitchen, where he explained the situation.

Richardson responded immediately, "I will go right now and get the boat ready. I will make sure he gets to Monterey, where he will be safe."

Much later that evening, there was a scratching noise at Will's office window. He opened the door to Richardson, his hair wet and his slicker glued to him. He was shivering from the cold.

"Come in out of the cold and sit by the fire. Give me your slicker. I will hang it here so it can dry." He hung the oilskin on a hook and walked over to toss another log on the fire. It blazed into warmth, and Richardson rubbed his hands, heating them in the glow of the fire. "How did it go?" Will asked.

"We were able to get to the boat before anyone realized we were gone. I don't think anyone followed us. It's pretty windy out there tonight, and the water is choppy; fortunately, the harbormaster took matters into his own hands and found a seaworthy boat and man who could get him to Monterey," Richardson said, covering a yawn with his hand.

"Good. Why don't you sleep on my couch tonight? It is too late for you to get a boat and cross the bay to your house. I'll get some blankets and a pillow," Will said.

The warmth of the fire and coziness of the room were too much for Richardson to resist. He stretched out on the couch in the shadows of the fire and slept soundly.

After a breakfast of eggs and toast, Richardson left for home, and Will went to his office and immediately wrote a letter to Larkin to inform him of the latest development.

W. A. Leidesdorff to T. O. Larkin
United States Consul, Monterey, California
Yerba Buena June 17th 1846

Sir

This is to inform you of what has taken place in Sonoma, it appears that on the 14th instant about forty men, said to be Americans, entered the town of Sonoma and took charge of the arsenal (if it may be so cald [called]) a person by the

name of Ive [probably Ide] is in command, they
have taken as prisoners Dr. G. Vallejo, L. Vallejo,
V. Prudon, and I.P. Leese, it appears very strange
to me, that they should take Mr. Leese prisoner
when he is known to be an American and a Friend,
I suppose that there is something found on that
we know nothing of, as Captain Montgomery
has written you, I shall not say anything about
what message he has received, and what answer
he made, we are now in a critical situation, and
if the Portsmouth was not here I am sure things
would not on as easy as they do, you must think it
strange that you have not received this news from
me sooner, but it is not my fault ever since the
news came here I have been trying to get someone to take you a letter, but without success until
my backary returned here who takes a pass port
form this place for Santa Cruz, so that he may not
be waylaid. Weather [sic] I am Justifiable in sending you this courier I do not know, but if such
news is not of enough account to send one, you
will oblige me by informing me, it is not my fault
everyone that I have tried to get, have refused, for,
or in fear of being prest [impressed] by I. Castro,
and made soldiers of, I have agreed to pay the boy
$30. And have already paid him in part, he will
return by way of Santa Cruze [Santa Cruz], unless
you wish him to return direct, Mr. Gillespie left

here a few days since with supplies for Captain Freemont and according to what he said when he left ought to be back in three or four days, I was told today that Dr. Jose Castro is at Santa Clara preparing to go up to Sacramiento [Sacramento] to put things to rights, it is a great pitty [pity] for the Mexican nation that they have not got some more such patriotic officers as Captain Hinckley pretends to be. I called on him yesterday at the request of Captain Montgomery to pay him a visit which Captain M wished to make, in the course of conversation, he mentioned the Californians were fools if they did not emidaitely [immediately] take as many Americans, prisons [prisoners] as were taken in Sonoma by the Americans, and keep them until the others were given up, I then mentioned, that I thought he would have some difficulty to find so many, real Americans in the place, he then answered that they might possible take me for one to commence with, and so on, Captain Montgomery, merely told [him] that he should be verry [very] sorry to se[e] any thing of the kind take place, for it would only be putting him to some trouble, the answer however was to the point and captain H[inkley] haled in again, I really wish that Captain Hinckleys office would be taken from him, he only does all the injury he can here, and is the greatest enemy that

Americans have in this country, he is continu-
ally making disputes between those that arrive
here and the authorities, yesterday there was Mr.
Lasaras Everheart who applied to the Alcade for a
passport to Monterey and was refused, he emidi-
ately [immediately] caled [called] on me to assist
him in getting one, I caled [called] on the Alcade
and he said that as he had come from Monterey
without one that he might return without one
and that as Sanches's farm there were men placed
to se[e] that no one passed, so he had better not
attempt to go without one, he wishes you to get
him the form Monterey so that he may return, I
am sure that it is from Hinckley's advice that he
was refused for I heard him say that he thought
that he was one of the same gang at Sonoma.
About the knife you wrote, I send you one and
wish you to accept it, I have picked it out, and it
is one I would carry myself. No more at present,
hoping to hear from you soon

I remain Your Obt Servt [Obedient Servant]
Wm A. Leidesdorff
Yerba Buena June 18/46[6]

---

6 Palgon, *First Black Millionaire*

CHAPTER 29

THE REVOLT WAS official in Sonoma, a bloodless victory. The participants declared independence from Mexico and acknowledged California an independent republic. With a cotton sheet and some red paint, the men constructed a makeshift flag with a crude drawing of a grizzly bear, a lone red star, and the words *California Republic* on the bottom. From then on it was known as the Bear Flag Revolt.

Frémont then advanced to San Solito (Sausalito), the home of Richardson. He launched an assault on the undefended Castillo de San Joaquin, a fort constructed on the south side of the entrance of the bay. He spiked the seven cannons stationed at the *castillo* to prevent them from being used. He also dispatched a small group of men to patrol the narrows of the bay to prevent any communication or passage of Mexican forces. He named the entrance to the bay Chrysoplylae, or "Golden Gate." It was another bloodless victory.

On June 18, 1846, Dr. Robert Semple, the ferryman at Benicia, arrived and arrested Bob Ridley, who was the Mexican official at the time. He was marched off to prison at Sutter's Fort.

In the midst of the confusion and the anticipation of becoming part of the United States, Will continued business with his friend Larkin and ordered a consignment of goods.

Wm A. Leidesdorff to T.O. Larkin

Yerba Buena June 21st 1846

T.O. Larkin

Dear Sir

Yours of the 19th inst [sic] came duly to hand this morning. I emidately [immediately] dispatched a boat to Capt. Montgomery, who has written a letter to Com[modore] Stockton which I forward to you, you say that I don't give you information enough ro as much as the Capt: [sic] fave you, the fact is that I waited for Captain to write first and then wrote my letter in a hurry. I have had a long one ready for you for 3 days I have not been able to get a courier either for love, or money, one man asked me $50 cash and so on, I now send you the letter I have had ready for some days. Sutter has joined the rebels, (so called) which you will see by a copy of Capt Montgomery's letter to me, I am told that some of the Californians has driven all their horses of[f] to the sea co[a]st so that Castro wile [will] not get them—

If you will sell me some of your goods, cheap, as you say on time I will take them, but not to be paid this year for I fear that there will be verry [very] small collections, on account of the affair.

You mention for me to say what I will pay, it is impossible for me to put the prices down, as I have not seen the goods. However, I will leave it to your generosity to put the prices, send me 1 or 2 bales of wide brown cotton, One of white cotton, one of blue prints one of fancy prints, one of blue drill one of blue cotton & [one] or 2 dozen chairs. If the prices don't suit me, you will losse [lose] nothing. I will pay the freight, and it will allways [always] sell here, although I would prefer purchasing, send them p[e]r firs operunity [opportunity] and I will not make any purchase until I hear from you,

I remain your Obt Servt [Obedient Servant] Wm. Leidesdorff[7]

Although a republic was formed, no functional provisional government was established, so the "republic" never existed under any real authority and was not recognized by the nation. At the end of the twenty-six-day revolt, the US Army arrived and claimed the area for the United

7   Palgon, *First Black Millionaire*. 35.

States, at which point the "republic" disbanded and supported the US effort to annex Alta California.

The following morning, Will meandered through his flower garden, admiring the beauty of the purple hydrangeas and the abundance of golden orange poppies. It was the only flower garden in all of Yerba Buena. Not one of his prize vegetables had been uprooted during the rebellion, in fact nothing was harmed.. He stooped to pluck a carrot from the rich dark soil, brushed it off on his trousers and took a bite.

The sky was a vivid blue and the water sparkled brilliantly in the sun. He gazed with pride at the largest and most impressive home in Yerba Buena, his home. He called to Moon, "Moon come out here, I need to talk to you."

Wiping her corn meal covered hands on the gunny sack apron she wore, she stepped out on the veranda, "Yes?" she asked.

"I want to celebrate our independence! I would like to host a party on July fourth for all our neighbors, the first Independence Day as part of the United States. I will invite Richardson, Mellus, Howard, and their families and any other people of prominence." He strolled through the garden, occasionally stooping to pull a weed. "I want to invite Juan Fuller, the butcher, and his family. He often provides meat for my hotel."

Moon replied, "You offer finest foods and wines and most lavish entertainment in the pueblo. Your home is decorated like no other with its carpets, mirrors, Broadwood piano and the French furniture you bought in Paris. The important people you entertain enjoy luxury of your home. Everyone does." She smiled proudly at Will. "I think it grand idea and you be the perfect one to host it."

Will, who was in the habit of correcting her English, did not say a word but returned the smile, looking like a proud fluffed turkey.

The following days, Moon bustled to prepare the food while Will invited the guests. It was a beautiful day and after enjoying a typical Mexican meal of beans, rice, tortillas, and beef, Will asked them all to find a place to sit on the lawn, and he took the center position. "As a proud supporter of the United States, I have asked Captain Montgomery, an officer of the United States Navy, to read the Declaration of Independence to you on this day of celebration." Captain Montgomery stood and in a commanding voice began to read,

When in the Course of Human events, it becomes necessary for one people to dissolve the political bands which have connected them with another, and to assume among the powers of the earth, the separate and equal station to which the laws of Nature and of Nature's God entitle them, a decent respect to the opinions of mankind requires that they should declare the causes which impel them to the separation.

> We hold these truths to be self-evident, that all men are created equal, that they are endowed by their Creator with certain unalienable Rights, that among these are Life, Liberty and the pursuit of happiness...

Overcome by emotion, Will took out a handkerchief and blew his nose profusely. As a Saint Croix boy of Negro blood, he was guaranteed equal rights in this growing country. He had prospered and was a respected man in his community. By hard work and perseverance, he had achieved much. He looked around at his friends who had accepted him. He wiped away the grateful tears that blurred his vision and held his head high, listening closely to every word of the reading of the document. There was a deafening silence as all sat respectful and did not interrupt until the very end. Will took off his hat and threw it high in the air, yelling, "Three cheers for America!" The whole crowd broke into clapping, hooting, and hollering, joining him.

"Now, for the best part," Will announced when the cheering subsided. "I have grown watermelon in my garden, and there is plenty for all." Moon arrived carrying big trays of the sliced green melon, revealing the red sweetness.

Richardson's son was the first to take a piece. The juices dripped down his face and onto his shirt. He ignored it and gulped it down, reaching for a second piece before his mother grabbed him by his shirt collar and said, "Not another piece until all have had a chance to have some."

When the last of the people left, Richardson stopped to thank William and to tell him some news. "I hear two hundred Mormons are planning to arrive by ship in just a few days. That will certainly change things around here."

"Our population will more than triple at that rate, considering there are only about fifty people in Yerba Buena currently," Will said, thinking about his hotel and the need to house two hundred people. He would have to get more supplies and make sure he had enough food to feed them all—that is, if they chose to stay at the City Hotel.

On July 7, a few days later, Will heard that US Navy commodore John D. Sloat claimed California for the United States during the Mexican-American War. Two days later, US Navy captain John Montgomery and US Marine second lieutenant Henry Bulls Watson of the US *Portsmouth*, which floated in the bay, claimed Yerba Buena by raising the flag over the town plaza, which was renamed Portsmouth Square in honor of the ship.

The news traveled quickly in the little pueblo. The City Hotel was bustling with people sharing the news when Lieutenant Washington Allen Bartlett arrived and announced, "I have just been appointed the first American Alcade. I will be the mayor with judicial power." The guests gathered around, slapping him on the back and congratulating him. "I will be ratified later, when you all have a chance to vote for me." He swept the group with a toothy smile.

Captain Montgomery was present and sat at one of the tables. He pushed his chair back and stood. In a booming voice, he announced, "Since we are all celebrating, let me add another first." He paused and waited until the crowd silenced. "We will have our first Protestant worship service on Sunday. This has been a Catholic community, but now that we are Americans, we can worship as we please." Another burst of cheering issued forth.

Will stood quietly, thinking about his childhood, his baptism in the Protestant Lutheran church of his father, and his attendance at the Methodist church in New Orleans with his uncle. He had stopped attending church, but maybe he would go again.

And he did. On the following Sunday, Captain Montgomery conducted the first Protestant worship service in the Catholic community. Will attended with Moon.

C H A P T E R   3 0

AT THE END of the month, July 31, 1846, the ship *Brooklyn* sailed into Yerba Buena after spending six months navigating around South America. The group was led by a twenty-six-year-old New York printer named Samuel Brannan. There were seventy men, sixty-eight women, and one hundred children aboard.

US marines and navy sailors from the USS sloop *Portsmouth* were still in port, so a boat of uniformed men rowed out to the *Brooklyn* and boarded. After greeting the group, the officer in command said in a loud tone, "Ladies and gentlemen, I have the honor to inform you that you are in the United States of America." Three hearty cheers erupted.

After arriving ashore, Sam, an energetic, handsome six-foot-tall young man with blond wavy hair that obeyed no one, went to City Hotel to get a meal, something to eat other than ship fare. He sat down at one of the wooden tables and ordered the Mexican supper. Will joined him.

After introducing himself, Sam explained, "I have just arrived on the *Brooklyn*, and I need to get information about housing, supplies, and things our families need."

Will was immediately interested, as he realized more people meant an increase in business. "Tell me what some of your needs are, and I will see if I can help you. I would also like to hear about your journey. How was the trip?"

In between swallowing bites, Sam shared snippets of their arduous journey. "We spent six rough months at sea. It was hard. We buried twelve of our party at sea due to scarlet fever when we rounded Cape Horn. Their deaths caused great mourning and sadness as some lost children and their spouses. We lost much of our will during that difficult time."

He stopped, blew his nose, and wiped his eyes before he continued. "There were two hundred thirty-eight of us confined to an area of about twenty-five hundred square feet that pitched and rolled with every movement of the ship. The ship was outfitted with a long table that extended the full length of the ship." He swept the length of the dining room with his arm, demonstrating the enormous length. "We did school at that table, held our council meetings, dined, and worshipped on our Sabbath. Life happened at that table. The quarters were cramped, and the men could not stand up below. A hurricane blew for three days, but we were sure God would protect us."

He brushed the unruly hair off his forehead and smiled for the first time since beginning his story. "On a good note, we did have two babies born on the trip, and both survived—one on the Atlantic side and one on the Pacific side. Each was named after the respective oceans.

After all that, our people are ready to settle down in this new land."

He took another bite of the tortilla and reached for some more beans. "A third of our cargo is plows, plow irons, scythes, sawmill irons, and nails. We also included seeds for planting and textbooks for a school. Now, we just need to find help with housing. Some of our families will push on to Utah, where the rest of the Mormons are located." He swept the plate clean with the last of the tortilla and patted his stomach, satisfied.

He pushed the empty plate to the edge of the table, and Will motioned Moon to bring some corn bread. While listening to the young man's story, Will had been thinking of the hardships the people had endured to reach Yerba Buena, and now they needed places to live. He wanted to help. "The hide and tallow business has dwindled, so the customhouse is not as busy. I will talk to my friend Richardson, but I think some of you can stay there. You may have noticed the crude huts built along the beach. You are free to move into any of them or the vacant adobe huts the Indians have built and abandoned." Will stopped speaking and scratched his head for a moment, trying to think of other places. "The military barracks may have some empty rooms, although with the Bear Flag Revolt, there is more of a military presence. Also, Smith's adobe is available to rent." He leaned back in his chair. "We have makeshift housing all over. You may have noticed that some people will even set up tents using abandoned ships' sails."

Moon arrived at the table with some rich yellow corn bread, some native honey, and a cup of milk. Will thanked her and continued, "Of course, I have a few rooms at my hotel, but there is a cost to stay there, and I hear your people do not have much money."

"That is true. These people could not afford to purchase wagons and horses to travel overland like some of the Mormons heading to Utah. It was much cheaper for them to book passageway on the *Brooklyn*. We did stop at the Sandwich Islands because we carried merchandise and supplies for them, which helped with the cost of the voyage." He took a sip of the milk and smiled in satisfaction. "It's been a long time since I have had a glass of milk. It tastes mighty good." He continued, "I brought a printing press and a flour mill with me. Since my experience is in the printing business, I am hoping to establish a newspaper—if there isn't one in Yerba Buena?" he queried.

"No, we do not have a newspaper, although there is talk of one being published in Monterey. The only news we get here is by letters or word of mouth, and it is always late. We like when a ship comes in so we can hear what is going on in the rest of the country."

"I will have to solve that problem, as people need to be informed," Sam replied.

Will sensed the young man's energy and ambition, especially when Sam asked next, "Do you have any schools in the area? With our one hundred children, we need to make sure they are learning. Did I mention we brought about one hundred eighty textbooks with us? It is a beginning."

Will shook his head. "No, sadly, we don't have any formal schools, so the few children we have learn at home. I was fortunate to study abroad, and I would like to see our children have an opportunity to go to school. Education is important. I have land. I could see about donating some of it for a school."

Sam nodded and finished the last of the corn bread. As he stood, he reached into his pocket for some coins to pay for his meal when a folded, worn paper fluttered to the floor. He picked it up and said, "Agusta Crocheron, one of our passengers, wrote this about our journey. I asked her if I could publish it in our first newspaper. Read it." He handed the paper to Will, who read quietly.

As for the pleasure of the trip, we met disappointment, for we once lay becalmed in the tropics, and at another time we were "hatched below" during a terrific storm. Women and children were at night lashed to their berths, for in no other way could they keep in. Furniture rolled back and forth endangering limb and life. The waves swept the deck and even reached the staterooms... Children's voices were crying in the darkness, mothers' voices soothing or scolding. Men's voices rising above others, all mingled with the distressing groans and cries of the sick for help, and above all, the roaring of the wind and howling of the tempest made a scene and feeling indescribable.

Will folded the paper up and handed it back to Sam, who put it back in his pocket. Will reached to shake his hand. "I am grateful you have arrived safely and your horrendous journey is over. We will do everything we can to help you settle into your new land." Sam thanked him and went back to his people still aboard the *Brooklyn*.

New competition for Will arose in Yerba Buena as a man by the name of Brown decided to open his own hotel called Portsmouth Hotel, and hire Mormons to help set it up and run it. Disturbed by the competition, Will hired Indians to paint the front of City Hotel and had Moon order fabric to make new tablecloths and coverings for the windows. He offered a lunch special and posted signs about town.

Still the Portsmouth House flourished. Richardson reported to Will that the officer in charge of the marines who guarded the town secretly visited Brown each night to have his flask filled with whiskey. "I hear he taps on John Brown's window twice and whispers the code, 'The Spaniards are in the brush.' Well, one night, Brown, who was sleeping soundly, did not hear the knocking at his window, but one of the other officers who had been drinking heard it and fired off one of his pistols. He yelled at the top of his voice, 'The Spaniards are in the brush!'" Here Richardson was laughing so hard he could hardly get the words out. "An alarm sounded at the barracks, and the Mormon Saints and the townspeople got up to furnish what service they could with their arms and ammunition. Several shots were fired in the distance, but in the light of dawn, they discovered not dead bodies but scrub oaks filled with bullet holes." He clapped Will on the back. "Great story, don't you think?"[8]

Because of the increase in population, City Hotel did well in spite of the competition. And with its success and the capital acquired from it, Will followed his mantra of perseverance and purchased more land and buildings. Before the Bear Flag Revolt, Will had acquired land on the waterfront and built a warehouse, which he now leased to the new US government. Wanting more room to entertain, and since his businesses were flourishing, Will decided to buy the house that was located on the corner of Montgomery and California Streets. The house was fifty-five feet back and stood diagonally like Richardson's Casa Grande. It was a low one-story bungalow of adobe with a long piazza facing the bay.

He immediately asked his Scottish gardener to transplant the flowers from his previous home and develop a new garden even more beautiful than the previous one.

---

8   Brown Hotel Story. November 11, 2015. http://californiapioneer.org/ heritage-brochures/san-francisco-walking-tour.

He moved his piano and his French furniture in and asked Moon to come help him arrange it. Although the bungalow had windows facing the bay, Moon suggested, "Why don't you whitewash the walls? It make it much lighter in here." She stood gazing out the window at the water. Her silhouette bathed in the morning sun.

Will watched her. She was such a good friend, not the love of his life, not like Hortense, but a good friend. "I like that idea. Ask Sam to come in and help us," he said.

With Sam's muscle, and under Moon's direction, they were able to get the painting completed and move the furniture in place. When they were finished, Will stepped back to admire the completed project. "I like the settee facing the window. It gives a good view of the bay. The piano fits well against the inside wall, and there is plenty of room to entertain guests. This suits me well." He stepped back to admire it again, fondling the gold cross at his neck.

CHAPTER 31

THE LEAVES FROM the birches and willows turned a golden yellow and orange and puddled on the ground. The evenings and mornings cooled as fall moved into the growing pueblo. The children needed an education, and one of the Mormons, Angeline Lovett, took it upon herself to set up a temporary school in the old Franciscan Dolores Mission. The rooms were cool in the summer when the temperatures reached the high eighties. In the winter, the students brought warm serapes to drape over their shoulders as they studied their letters. It was the first English-language school in California, and twenty children, both from the Mormon community and the pueblo, arrived the first day and used the books brought by the Mormons.

On Monday morning, Will stood in the back of the schoolroom and observed the students recite their numbers and letters. He watched a young boy named Charles go to the slate board at the front of the room and write his multiplication facts. He noticed the makeshift desks and tables and crude benches. The room was cold—not a great environment for children to learn. As he mounted his horse to return home, he seriously considered which piece of land and location would be best to donate for a school.

Besides a school building, an alcade needed to be officially elected. Although many of the saints had moved on to Utah, the customhouse referred to as "Old Adobe" still housed some of them. Bartlett was appointed as alcade, but he needed to be officially elected, so it was decided the first municipal alcade election would be held at Old Adobe on September 15. The main room was cleared of any items used by the saints, all of it crated and stacked in the adjoining rooms so the polls could officially open at 11:00 a.m. The morning mist lifted, and the sun shone brilliantly.

Will was the first in line. As a patriot and a strong supporter for the United States, he wanted to be the first to cast his ballot for Lieutenant Bartlett. The doors closed at 2:00 p.m. after ninety-six citizens had voted. After the votes were counted, Lieutenant Bartlett was declared the victor and the new official alcade.

As soon as he heard the results, Will decided to host a postelection party at his new home to celebrate. The table was laid with the finest white linen, and the crystal stemware and china from his travels to Europe graced the table. He chose not to serve the original Mexican fare of beans and rice but something very English and American instead. He discussed the menu with Moon and decided to serve a beef roast with potatoes and carrots grown in his garden.

Moon asked the cook to make gravy from the juices of the roast. They would serve yorkshire pudding with the meat and gravy. For dessert, apple pie. Will discovered the land and climate along the American River was perfect for growing apple trees, and he ordered the trees be brought on one of his ships returning from the East Coast.

When the guests arrived, the table sparkled with soft candlelight that reflected off the whitewashed adobe walls. His fine French furniture was highly polished, and his home looked ethereal compared to the dry brown grass outside the door and the rough adobe buildings. The guests were awed. Lieutenant Bartlett and his wife were seated to Will's right, and Moon sat on his left, as Will wanted her by his side. She wore a dress of deep emerald and a necklace of shells with bits of turquoise made by the Indians. Will marveled at her ability to look so exquisite with so little.

As Lieutenant Bartlett and his wife said their farewells, he commented to Will, "I have heard that you have the urbanity of a seasoned diplomat and the persuasiveness of a politician and a man who knows how to handle his affairs. I can see those rumors are true. Thank you for hosting a fine celebration dinner for me. I am sure we will see much of each other in the future."

Will thanked him, grateful his dinner had been a success.

The next morning Will woke with an intense headache and a sore throat. Later in the afternoon, his temperature soared. He tossed and turned on his bed, pulling the covers around his neck when chilled and kicking them off when burning hot. He was miserable. Moon brought him simmering beef broth and swathed his brow with a rag bathed in cool water, but the temperature did not break. "Try Indians' treatment. Go into temescal. Steam drives out infection," he murmured.

Moon, along with Sam the Indian, helped him mount his horse so he could make the short trip to the temescal. The smoke was pouring out the chimney when they arrived. Sam took the woven mat and crawled through the narrow opening into the sweathouse, followed by Will. Sam dropped the mat on the dirt floor, and Will lay down and allowed the intense heat of the steam to do its work. He began to sweat profusely. Sam continued to pour water over the sizzling rocks, causing the small room to grow heavy with hot, moist air. Will inhaled deeply and then exhaled. He continued until he could take the steaming room no longer. "I have to get out," he said to Sam and crawled out.

Normally, the Indians would jump into the frigid waters of the nearby Laguna Dulce, but Will could not bear the idea, and Moon bundled him into a warm serape. He mounted his horse with the help of Sam and arrived at his home moments later. He climbed into bed and slept soundly, and when he awoke, his temperature was gone. He felt so much better; he sat on the piazza, watching the fading sunlight catch the waves of the bay and listening to the water rhythmically slap the shore.

He slept peacefully through the night and rose with the sun the next morning just in time to see Richardson racing across the beach toward his adobe. Waving a rolled-up paper in his hand, like a beacon of light, he yelled, "Will! I want you to be the first to see this!" He spurred his horse on vehemently, and a burst of dust settled to the ground as he came to an abrupt halt and leaped off his horse. "I have it! The first newspaper published in Alta California. It just came in from Monterey, half in English and half in Spanish." He took a deep breath and continued. "Reverend Walter Colton, a chaplain in the US Navy, and Dr. Robert Semple are the editors. They are calling it the *Californian*." He stabbed at the title with his index finger. "Here, read this: 'This press shall be free and independent; unawed by power and untrammeled by party. The use of its columns shall be denied to no one, who have suggestions to make, promotive of the public…We shall lay before our readers the freshest domestic intelligence and the earliest foreign news.'"

Will picked up the paper and looked at the date. "This was published a month ago, August 15, 1846. Better to get news late than not at all. Wait until Sam Brannan sees this. He wants to publish a paper for Yerba Buena. You need to show this to him, too."

Together, they sat down on the piazza in the sun and read through the small sheet. Although it was mostly about shipping, they discussed each point, as news was sparse and hard to get.

A few months later, Sam Brannan set up his antiquated printing press in an abandoned adobe house between Clay and Washington Streets, close to the house Brannan rented from the Smiths. Although the adobe was dark, he placed the press under a window to get good light and printed the first crude edition of the *California Star* all in English. Dr. Elbert P. Jones was the editor.

The STAR will be an independent paper uninfluenced by those in power or the fear of the abuse of power, or of patronage or favor. The paper is designed to be permanent, and as soon as circumstances will permit will be enlarged, so as to be in point of size not inferior to most of the weekly papers in the United States. It will be published weekly on a Royal sheet at six dollars per annum. As soon as a suitable person can be employed, all articles of general interest will be published in Spanish as well as English. S. BRANNAN

Will received one of the first free editions and read through it from top to bottom.

CHAPTER 32

"FALL IN YERBA Buena is the best time of year. The days are warm and sunny, and the nights are mild and clear. The rain hasn't started, and the fog has cleared," declared Will as he sat with Richardson over a cup of tea at City Hotel. "When I lived on the East Coast, we celebrated Thanksgiving in November. Now that California is part of the United States, I think we need to adopt the customs of our country. I'd like us to officially celebrate a day of Thanksgiving on November 16. I think I will host a dinner at my house and invite the community. Just like the first Thanksgiving, I will ask everyone to bring something to share, and we will have time to acknowledge the providence of Almighty God."

Will went to his office and came back to the table with a yellowed book bound in brown leather. "See this? I have George Washington's proclamation he made on October 3, 1789, over fifty years ago, designating the first Thanksgiving Day by the national government of the United States of America. My uncle had an extensive library in New Orleans. Although I sold many of the

225

books, I kept most of the history and literature books."
He opened it to the page and handed it to Richardson
to read:

Whereas it is the duty of all Nations to acknowledge the providence of Almighty God, to obey his
will, to be grateful for his benefits, and humbly
to implore his protection and favor, and whereas
both Houses of Congress have by their joint
Committee requested me "to recommend to the
People of the United States a day of public thanksgiving and prayer to be observed by acknowledging with grateful hearts the many signal favors
of Almighty God especially by affording them an
opportunity peaceably to establish a form of government for their safety and happiness."

Now therefore I do recommend and assign
Thursday the 26th day of November next to be
devoted by the People of these States to the service of that great and glorious Being, who is the
beneficent Author of all the good that was, that is,
or that will be. That we may then all unite in ren-
dering unto him our sincere and humble thanks,
for his kind care and protection of the People
of this Country previous to their becoming a
Nation, for the signal and manifold mercies, and
the favorable interpositions of his providence,

which we experienced in the course and conclusion of the late war, for the great degree of tranquility, union, and plenty, which we have since enjoyed, for the peaceable and rational manner, in which we have been enabled to establish constitutions of government for our safety and happiness, and particularly the national One now lately instituted, for the civil and religious liberty with which we are blessed; and the means we have of acquiring and diffusing useful knowledge; and in general for all the great and various favors which he hath been pleased to confer upon us.

And also that we may then unite in most humbly offering our prayers and supplications to the great Lord and Ruler of Nations and beseech him to pardon our national and other transgressions, to enable us all, whether in public or private stations, to perform our several and relative duties properly and punctually, to render our national government a blessing to all the people, by constantly being a Government of wise, just, and constitutional laws, discreetly and faithfully executed and obeyed, to protect and guide all Sovereigns and Nations (especially such as have shown kindness unto us) and to bless them with good government, peace, and concord. To promote the knowledge and practice of true religion and virtue, and the encrease of science among them and Us, and generally to grant unto all Mankind such a degree of temporal prosperity as he alone knows to be best.

Given under my hand at the City of New York the third day of October in the year of our Lord 1789.[9]

The sun dawned gloriously on November 16, and by noon, Will, Sam, and his Indian vaqueros had constructed wooden tables by arranging long planks on crude sawhorses in his garden. They did the same with benches so the guests would have a place to sit. The orange and yellow mums, the golden marigolds, the purple alyssums, and the tall waving sunflowers were ablaze with color. Moon collected orange, red, and golden leaves from the fall foliage and placed them down the center of the table. Little orange pumpkins and squash from the garden were arranged artistically in the leaves. Moon and her Indian help baked pumpkin pies and cooled them on one of the long tables, filling the air with their scent. Wild turkeys roamed the

9 George Washington's Thanksgiving Proclamation. November 20, 2015. http://en.wikipeia.org/wiki/Thanksgiving_(UnitedA_States).

hillsides in abundance, and the vaqueros brought home enough to feed the pueblo. The ears of corn lay shucked and ready to roast over the fire.

As the guests arrived, Moon directed them to set their food on the table. Mrs. Richardson brought corn bread and corn pudding. The Ridleys, released from confinement and back in the pueblo, brought grapes from their own vineyards. Others brought vegetables of cabbage, carrots, spinach, and beans. They were going to have cranberries, too, boiled in sugar. Will's mouth watered in anticipation as he strolled along the bountiful tables, thinking that perhaps they had become civilized after all.

When all had arrived, he welcomed them and said, "As we are now part of the United States, like George Washington, our first president, said when proclaiming a day of public Thanksgiving and prayer, 'We are to observe this day by acknowledging with grateful hearts the many favors of Almighty God especially by affording you an opportunity peaceably to establish a form of government for your safety and happiness…'" He looked around at his friends and acquaintances and continued, "We have survived the Bear Flag Revolt without bloodshed or loss to our pueblo. We have increased in population because of the addition of our Mormon friends." He nodded to Sam Brannan, who was standing with his family. He gestured to the table laden with food. "Look at the abundance. We are blessed by God; let us bow our heads and give thanks." The men, women, and children bowed their heads as Will thanked God for His blessing. When he finished, he said, "Now please enjoy the bounty."

The adults filled their plates and then the children. As soon as the children finished eating, they rushed to play blind man's bluff, one of their favorite games, and the adults visited in the warmth of the fall afternoon.

As the sun dropped in the sky and the weather cooled, people began leaving. I. F. Popoff was one of the guests at the feast whose ship lay moored in the bay. He was a short man with light sandy hair and a full beard. He appeared disheveled and distraught. As he approached Will, he clutched the hand of a boy who appeared to be about ten years of age. Another younger boy was clinging to his pant leg, making it difficult for him to walk. "Thank you for inviting us to this feast. My wife has just passed away, and my two sons are devastated by the death of their mum." At his words, the youngest of the boys burst into sobs and clung more tightly to his father, who patted his head, trying to console him. "My ship leaves tomorrow, and I am at a loss as to what to do with my oldest son. My youngest can stay with my brother in Monterey, but he has no room for Serege here." He nodded toward the older boy. "I would like him to get an education. I can pay for his room and board. I know you are a man of generosity and given to hospitality. Would you be willing to board Serege until I can return?"

The boy stood quietly by his father, his eyes downcast, while this interaction took place. When his father ceased talking, he stole a shy glance at Will. Will looked thoughtfully at him.

"Yes, I can do that. When I was a child, someone provided me the ability to get a good education. I would like to return that favor. Does he have a trunk and clothing? Sam, my Indian, can come with you and get his belongings. I will have Moon prepare a room for him." He smiled at Serege, who dropped his eyes.

With haste, Moon prepared the spare room. She spread a brightly woven red and blue compass striped Indian blanket on the bed and placed an oil lamp on the table that stood next to the bed. After setting a wooden chair in the corner of the room, she laid a woven rug on the floor to warm his feet. "This should do. Any little boy would like this." She stood quietly by the window that provided light during the day but cast soft shadows on the whitewashed walls at night. The changing surf pounded the shore below.

Hearing a slight tap on the door, Moon hurried to open the heavy wood door. Serege stood there with Sam, a worn carpetbag valise clutched in his hands. His jacket hung loosely on his thin shoulders, and his brown hair fell limp and long on his collar. Sam held a small trunk on one shoulder. "We're here, Moon. This is all he has. Mighty small boy."

Moon took his hand and said, "It is late. We have time tomorrow to talk. I show you to your room. You tired?" She looked at him, but he did not return the look or speak. He followed her into the small room. "Put valise there for the night, and tomorrow we get you settled in." She pointed to the wooden chair in the corner.

Serege dropped his valise on the chair and sat on the edge of the bed; he cradled his face in his hands and wept silently. His thin shoulders shook, but no sound was emitted. Moon sat down beside him and placed a comforting arm around his shoulder. "I know it hard to lose a loved one. It painful but get better. You like Yerba Buena. Sun shines most afternoons, and you collect shells on the beach. Boys love to ride horseback, and you ride, too." The intense sobbing softened, but the thin shoulders continued to shake sporadically. "I leave you now. Go to bed. If need me, you call."

Will was sitting at the kitchen table when she came out. "How is our boy? He is mighty little to lose his mama. Do you think you would be willing to move from the hotel to take the spare bedroom here? I think Serege will need more attention and care than I can give him. He needs a woman's touch."

"Yes. I do that. My heart hurt for him, his broken heart. I sorry he lose his mother. Yes, I get my things and bring them here until Serege returns to Father. I do that tomorrow afternoon."

"Thank you," Will responded humbly. "I will take him around tomorrow so he gets acquainted with the other boys. One time in my life, a man took me in and helped me." He stopped. He had not shared that part of his life with Moon, nor did he wish to expose his love and loss of Hortense to her.

Serege appeared quietly at the breakfast table the following morning in the same clothes he wore the day before. His hair stood at odd angles to his head. He brushed at it with his hand but to no avail.

"I hope you slept well, Serege. After you eat breakfast, I am going to take you on a ride around Yerba Buena. Do you know how to ride horseback?" Will asked.

He nodded and pulled out a chair, his long hair flying in all directions. He ravenously ate the eggs and beans set before him. Soon his plate was wiped clean. "More eggs and beans for the boy, Moon. He is hungry this morning, a good sign," Will said. "When you are finished, I have horses out front for you and me. We are going to take a ride around this fine country of ours."

They spent the morning riding around the mission, the presidio, and down on the beach. Serege had a natural seat and rode as one with the horse. It gave Will an idea. Near Mission Dolores was a wide-open meadow, perfect for staging horse races. He would advertise a race for the younger boys and then one for the older men, the first competition in the pueblo. Maybe Serege would win.

CHAPTER 33

"It is time for you to earn your keep and learn a trade," Will said to Serege one morning at breakfast. "I will teach you how to run a business, place orders, and keep the books, just like my father taught me." He picked up the *California Star* lying on the table and said, "I placed an ad in this paper; let me read it to you." He read, "'William Leidesdorff has made arrangements for supplying the Town with *Lumber*, persons wishing any kind of lumber can have their orders executed by leaving them at his Store.'"[10] He looked at Serege. "The orders are coming in slowly but steadily, and you can help me."

"I don't know my numbers very well, and I can read some. My mum taught me before she died. But what if I can't do it?" Serege asked, his eyes downcast.

"Until we have a school, I will teach you in the evenings," Will said, standing. He pushed in his chair and patted Serege on the head. "Don't you worry; you are a smart boy. Now come on, we have work to do."

---

10 *California Star,* "Lumber Ad". September,22,1947.http://cdnc.ucr. edu/cgi-bin/cdnc.

Will was reminded again of the need to establish a good public school in the pueblo, one that all children could attend. He seriously contemplated which of his landholdings would make the best location for a school. He eventually decided on a plot at the intersection of Kearny and Washington Streets, a location easily accessible by all. Establishing the school board, which consisted of three men, he authorized an expenditure of $1,000 and began ordering the materials and paying for labor:

Paint for the school house	$8.00
Wm Davis lumber for the school house	$450.00
Mr. Hauck, for hauling brick for the school	$4.00
Silas Hearris for work on the street	$4.50
Mr. Clark for school house	$300.00[11]

The construction began, but before the building was completed, however, construction came to a halt as winter rains arrived in torrents. The wind blew off the water, chilling the pueblo. Will burned wood and cow dung in their fireplace, and Serege huddled next to it to keep warm. Moon added extra blankets to the beds and began baking for Christmas.

Having a child in the house made all the difference once Serege adapted to his new surroundings and gradually began to talk. Together, he and Moon shelled pecans

11   *California Star.*"School Expenses" November 10, 2015. http://cdnc. ucr.edu/cgi-bin/cdnc?a=d&d=C18470922.2.7&srpos.

for pie, and Sam went hunting for more wild turkey so they could have stuffed turkey for Christmas dinner.

Serege had his first experience of plucking feathers. "How do I do this?" he asked, holding the turkey by its neck. "I've never done this before." He held the turkey at arm's length and wrinkled his nose in distaste. "It smells awful."

"I show you, and we save feathers to make you nice feather pillow. You like that?" Moon asked as she dipped the turkey in scalding-hot water. She held it in the water for one minute and then pulled it out and flopped it on brown paper spread out on the wooden table. "Come help me," she instructed as she began plucking the feathers and dropping them into a bucket. "We clean these feathers and dry them before we make pillow. Goose down makes best pillows, so if we get goose, we mix the feathers of the turkey and the goose."

Serege joined her reluctantly, but eventually a contest developed as to who could pick the most feathers the quickest. In no time, the bird was ready to be stuffed, trussed, and then tied over the open fire so it could bake slowly.

Earlier, they had dug up potatoes from the garden, and now they added sweet potatoes to the embers to roast for the feast. In the afternoon, they strung popcorn and cranberries and draped them around the cedar tree Will had chopped down, which now stood in the corner next to the piano spilling its fragrance everywhere.

Perseverance

On Christmas morning, a blazing fire warmed the room, and the fresh smell of cedar greeted Serege as he awakened. Will read Luke 2:6–7 from the Bible about the birth of the Christ child. "While they were there [Bethlehem] the time came for the baby to be born, and she gave birth to her firstborn, a son. She wrapped him in cloths and placed him in a manger, because there was no room for them in the inn." Together they sang "Silent Night," "Deck the Halls," and "Joy to the World." Holly hung from the mantel, and red Christmas berries added sparks of color.

Will handed Serege a small package wrapped in burlap and tied with a string. As he ripped opened the gift, he exclaimed, "My very own knife!" He turned it over and over in his hand, opening the blade and closing it again and again before putting it into his pocket.

Moon received some lovely pink silk fabric to make a new dress, and she, in return, gave Will a new book, *The Christmas Carol*, written by English author Charles Dickens in 1843 and bound in red leather with gold print. "My father used to order us new books and first editions. This is a very special gift," he said, holding it close to his chest.

After they finished breakfast, they carried their hot apple cider in by the fireplace, and Will opened his new book and read the story of Ebenezer Scrooge and Tiny Tim out loud to them. "A good lesson to be learned from that book," he said when he finished. "What is the lesson, Serege?" he asked.

"Don't be stingy but be generous, especially to those who are poor." He looked at Will. "Just like you. You let me live here with you and Moon."

Will's heart was touched by the simple comment of the boy, and he treasured it away, always mindful of the kindness given him in life. Later in the afternoon, Mr. Richardson and his family came by and shared some pecan pie with them. Although the temperature was cool, the rain stopped, and Serege and Richardson's two boys played outside until it was time for them to go home.

The following day, December 26, a package was delivered to Will from one of the ships that sailed into the bay. It was from Serege's father, and he was eager to see what it contained. "Serege, come here," he called. "Your father has sent us a package. Come see what it is." Serege came running, and so did Moon. He handed the boy the smallest brown-wrapped package.

Packages did not arrive often, and Serege took and held it, turning it around and upside down and then shaking it. He carefully untied the string holding it together, and when the brown paper fell away, he saw something none of them had seen before. "What do you think it is?" he asked. He held it to his nose and sniffed it. "It looks like something we can eat, and it smells good." He broke off a piece and put it in his mouth. "It is sweetmeat like I have never tasted before. Here, try some." He broke off two pieces and gave them to Moon and Will.

Will said, "I heard of a Joseph Fry in Bristol who learned how to mix melted cacao butter with sugar so it would create a paste that could be pressed into a mold. This must be it. I think they call it a candy bar or a chocolate bar." Will savored the chocolate in his mouth. "Mmmm, it tastes wonderful." He licked his lips, not wanting to lose any of the sweetness. "We'd better put that away and save this as a special treat." He took the bar from Serege and handed it to Moon, who retied the string and set it aside.

The next package was a box. Will held it to his nose. "Smells like tobacco." He opened the box to discover Spanish cigars. He counted the first layer: one, two, three...thirteen. He lifted the top layer off and counted the bottom layer. "Twelve cigars in the bottom. Twenty-five cigars altogether. I can't wait to enjoy one of these." He tucked one in his shirt pocket before he closed the box. "I'll smoke that later...outside," he said, knowing Moon did not like the smell of tobacco in the house.

He handed Moon the last tin, and when she opened it, she said, "Fish. Smoked salmon I think. Try a bite." She gave a small piece to Will and to Serege, who smiled and smacked in approval. "We have some for supper tonight," she said and closed the tin.

"That was very thoughtful of your father to send us gifts. I must write him a thank-you letter and tell him how you are doing, too." William stopped, grew quiet, and looked at Will. He had grown to love the boy like his own son. "Do you want to go back to your father? Are you missing him and your brother?"

"I do miss them, but I like it here in Yerba Buena and don't mind staying here," Serege said, smiling, and gave both of them a rare hug. His hair was combed neatly, and his clothing fit him so much better. He was becoming quite a handsome young man.

CHAPTER 34

NEW YEAR'S DAY, 1847, was birthed in strong gales and rainstorms, causing the snow to pile high in the Sierras. Will was shocked and horrified to learn of the wagon train of eighty-one pioneers trapped in the snows of the Sierra Nevada Mountains as they tried to come west. He learned in a letter from Sutter that Charles Stanton, a member of the party, had arrived at Sutter's Fort to get supplies to bring to the stranded emigrants. Stanton loaded seven mules with provisions and took two Indian guides with him as he headed back up the mountains.

Sutter wrote later that Reed and McCutchen, two men from the party, also arrived and attempted to take provisions back to the settlers but were unable to, so they returned to the fort.

Warning the people of New Helvetia that the women and children would all die without assistance, Sutter challenged someone, anyone, to take on the dangerous mission, but no one was willing. Finally, John Sutter and Captain Edward Kern, the fort's temporary commander, offered three dollars a day to anyone who would join the rescue party.

Two weeks passed before any person consented to go. Daniel Rhodes, one of the men at the fort, wrote in his diary in February: "We concluded that we would go die trying, for not to make any attempt to save them would be a disgrace to us and California as long as time lasted."

In Yerba Buena, the news took on an alarming note. On February 3, Alcade Bartlett called a public meeting that Will attended. He stood in the back and listened to Bartlett's plea for help. "We must raise funds for these poor starving people. They must be rescued. If you are willing to join the party to help rescue them, see me afterward." His piercing eyes swept the room, challenging any able-bodied man to say no. "Think of your wives and children starving in the snow. If you cannot go, we must collect supplies and food for them. Bring your warmest blankets, clothes, and especially food."

Will was deeply moved. He felt the need to help and called for Sam. "Help me gather salt beef and pork from my supply. Include some of the potatoes and carrots from the garden. Moon and Serege can help you dig them." After filling burlap bags, they carted them down to the ship. Sam helped Will pile a large sack of beans on his horse that he took down to the ship under the command of Selim Woodworth, who was also in charge of the relief operations.

"We're heading out today to sail for Sutter's Fort," Woodworth said as he helped Will unload the food. "James Reed is heading across the bay and will recruit men and horses from Sonoma and Napa." He took his hat off and wiped his brow. "I just hope we are not too late."

Eleven days later, Woodworth's launch arrived at Sutter's Fort. The wind and the strong current of the swollen Sacramento River had hindered his travel. Not wanting to waste more time, he left the same day for Johnson's Ranch, which was the staging point of the rescue party. Will heard no more news until April.

On the way to the store the next morning, Will stopped to read a poster that had been nailed to his door. He read, "Beginning today, all stray hogs in Yerba Buena must be securely penned, or the hogs will be confiscated. The owner will also be fined five dollars." Will laughed. That would put an end to the hogs that ran freely and loved to root in his garden. No amount of chasing them with a broom kept them out. In a temper, he had threatened to sue Juan Fuller for allowing his hogs to uproot his prized carrots. Now he could be fined. "Aha! Serves him right!"

In the cold evenings, when the winter sun went to bed early, he and Serege sat by the blazing fire and studied Spanish in the same way that Will sat and read with Mr. Forest in the library in New Orleans.

Serege had grown tall and lean. His pants no longer covered his ankles, and he cut the toes off his boots so his toes were free to wiggle. An active boy, he loved the outdoors, so it was difficult for him to sit still and practice Spanish vocabulary by rote. "Repeat after me: *hola. Hola* means *hello. Adiós. Adiós* means *good-bye. Cómo estás?* That means *how are you?*" Will instructed.

After restating the phrases numerous times, Will asked him to repeat them once again. Serege jumped to his feet, shook his head, and said, "I do not want to speak Spanish tonight. Don't make me. I am going to my room." He stomped out, slammed the door, and spent the rest of the night in his bedroom.

Moon had been listening from the kitchen, and as soon as she heard the door slam, she entered the room. "I know that not respectful of him, but he a good boy and works hard to please you." She walked next to him and placed a hand on his shoulder. He looked up at her. "He work hard today, and I think he tired. He be himself in the morning." She patted Will's shoulder before going back to the kitchen. "Maybe he practice ride his horse for the race and get outside more. Too much learning."

The next morning, Serege came sheepishly to breakfast. "I am sorry I behaved badly last night. Please forgive me. I will try to do better tonight."

Will said nothing and continued eating. He was seeing more of Serege's stubbornness; just yesterday, he refused to count boards. Mr. Larkin had recently placed a big order of lumber with him, and he needed to fill it. He asked Serege to go with him to count the boards that would be loaded on a ship and sent to Monterey, but he declined, saying he had other things to do. Next time Will wrote to Serege's father, he would mention the stubbornness.

Richardson appeared at the hotel the next morning. Once again, he was delivering the latest news. Just once Will wanted to hear it first so he could be the one to inform Richardson. "We are no longer called Yerba Buena. We have been renamed San Francisco. It is in the paper and posted on the storefronts. Here, read this." He handed Will a newspaper and pointed to the headlines.

AN ORDINANCE WHEREAS, the local name of Yerba Buena, as applied to the settlement or town of San Francisco, is unknown beyond the district; and has been applied from the local name of the cove, on which the town is built: Therefore, to prevent confusion and mistakes in public documents, and that the town may have the advantage of the name given on the public map;

IT IS HERE BY ORDAINED, that the name of SAN FRANCISCO shall hereafter be used in all official communication and public documents, or records, appertaining to the town.-Washington Bartlett, Chief Magistrate January 30, 1847.[12]

---

12 *California Star." "Yerba Buena Name Changed to San Francisco". January 30,1847.* http://cdnc.ucr.edu/cgi-bin/cdnc?a=d&d=C18470922.2.7&srpos.

"Chief Magistrate Barlett wants to bring order to the official town of San Francisco, so he had the records of the previous alcades transferred to him and posted another declaration for the public to see," Will processed as he read on.

> *San Francisco, Feb. 22, 1847. "I hereby certify that this plan of the Town of San Francisco is the plan by which titles have been given by the Alcalde from the first location of the town, and the numbers and names of lots and streets correspond with records transferred by me.*
> *Washn. A. Bartlett,*
> *Chief Magistrate."*

"There is going to be a meeting for the citizens of San Francisco on the corner of Portsmouth Square, opposite the Portsmouth House, for the purpose of the disposition of the public beaches," Richardson said. "We should make sure we attend."

They did attend, and Mr. Clark was appointed chairman at the meeting and Hugh Reed, Esq., secretary. The *California Star*, volume 1, number 7, of February 20, 1847, recorded the following resolution: "Resolved—That we will use every effort to induce the governor and council to divide the beach lands in front of the town into convenient business lots and to sell them for the benefit of the town, or the territorial government."

After the meeting, Will and Richardson walked back to City Hotel. "I like the changes being made in our little pueblo. Alcade Barlett is bringing order." He stirred some sugar into his coffee. "Soon, we'll be as sophisticated as Monterey and see more ship traffic, which means increased business in our newly named town. I'm glad I voted for the man."

CHAPTER 35

DETERMINED THAT SEREGE learn, Will continued his lessons but included some fun. The anticipation in the town was building as the news of the upcoming horse race at Mission Dolores spread. Will went to Sam Brannan's printshop and asked, "Will you make me some hardboard to put about the town advertising the race? I'd like a picture of a black horse running in the wind. Can you do it?" He waited for Sam to respond.

"I think I can do that for you. I'll look for a picture. How many do you want?" he asked.

"I'd like at least five. That ought to do it." He smiled in satisfaction, nodding to affirm his choice.

"Do you want me to include it in the *Star* as well?" asked Sam.

"That would be good. I want as much publicity as I can get. The whole town needs to come to this first horse race. The purse is growing." He patted the bulging pouch hanging from his belt.

The day of the race, fifty people showed up at the meadow at Mission Dolores. Most brought brightly colored woven blankets to spread on the ground so they could sit. When walking among the crowd, Will observed families enjoying beans and tortillas. It was a sunny day and a great day for a picnic. Serege ran up to him and pulled on his jacket. "Is it time yet? When do we start? Do you think I'm going to win?"

"Do your best. Always do your best. I am sure you will do fine. When the gun goes off, you know to hit it. A good start means a good finish." Will patted his shoulder reassuringly.

The course was marked off on the meadow at Mission Dolores, and Will had his pistol ready to fire the start. A man of speculation, he placed a wager of five dollars on Serege and said, "If you win the race, I will give you the winnings from my bets."

They rode the course three times. Serege's friend Juan passed him in the second lap. "Come on, Serege, you win!" Moon yelled from the sideline. She clutched Will's arm. "I want him to win; he need it."

"Faster! Faster!" Will yelled as Serege passed around again, neck and neck with Juan. Not until the final lap was Serege able to push his horse forward and win the race. Moon ran to the finish line and threw her arms around Serege, "You did it! I know you can do it!" Moon said, giving him a big hug.

Will slapped him on the back. "You did it. I knew you could. I promised you the winnings and here they are." He handed Serege the pouch of coins. "Now you can buy your own horse if you wish, but know that you will be fully responsible for him."

Serege could not conceal the smile that played about his mouth. "Thanks, Mr. Will. I promise to take real good care of my horse. Will you help me find a good one?"

"I think Richardson has some nice horses at his place. We will go look. Now run along." Will watched him run off and considered the situation. *That young lad has turned out quite well, although he still has to work on his attitude,* he thought. *I will write to the boy's father and thank him for the gifts. I wouldn't mind his brother coming to stay with us.*

Back at the adobe, he sat down at his desk, took his knife out of his pocket, and sharpened the quill. He dipped the pen in the ink, and with the afternoon sun shining on the water below him, he wrote,

Yerba Buena
Feb 26 1847
    Mr. I.F. Popoff

Dear Sir
    Your kind favour dated 26 Dcebr [December] 1846 came duly to hand as also the fish, segars [cigars] and sweet meats. I return to you many

thanks. I am only sorry I have nothing to send in return. I only send a barrel of beef which please to accept of, next time the vessel comes I shall be able to send you some fruit, please to send me next year all the small smoke fish you can get and will pay you whatever you say, the shoes you mention about is a good article, if not invoiced to high, Serege is getting to be a smart boy, speaks English and Spanish, the only fault he has, is, a little bad disposition, but that will ware off with age, if you like to send me your other son you can do so, as this will be a great sea port town, and after learning a little all boys will be able to maintain themselves by their wages, if Serege stops with me, I shall give him a small salary to commence with this year & next year more. I have inquired of him if he wishes to go home and he says no, he prefers living here, give my compliments to your lady and all the rest of the family. Say to them that I am sorry not to be personally acquainted with them, if you can procure me any more of those Spanish segars [cigars] you sent me called silva purchase me all you can get and send them in the next vessel, they are much better than the manila... Having no more to say at present remain yours truly.[13]

W.A. L

---

13 Palgon, *First Black Millionaire,44*

William sent the letter off, eager to see if Serege's brother would be sent to live with him. In the meantime, Will practiced his Spanish, often speaking the language in his home so that Serege became fluent as well.

Will's ability to both read and write the Spanish language, along with his aptitude and perseverance, made him a successful businessman. He continued to receive orders, and the newly established United States government ordered from him, too. The ship USS *Columbus*, under the command of Commodore James Biddle, was called to California at the outbreak of the Mexican-American War and arrived in Monterey, but it was too large to be used in the California operations and was ordered to return to Norfolk. Hard bread kept on the ships for a long time and was most often made of whole-meal rye flour, salt, and water. Will made the trip to Monterey to sign the contract to sell the ship some bread for its return; the contract read as follows:

One hundred thousand pounds of hard bread of the best quality at ten dollars per one hundred pounds the thousand pounds to be delivered in quantities of not less than twenty five thousand pounds...commencing on the 20th day of March 1847 free of all costs and changed to the United States and subject to such inspection as the Commanding U.S. Naval Officer at San Francisco may direct; the contract to be completed in four months.

Payments to be made on the delivery of the bread. Proved however that in the event of the U.S. Naval Forces being withdrawn from California before the completion of the contract and before all the bread or any part thereof is ready for delivery the said William A. Leidesdorff is at liberty to furnish flour in lieu of bread at the rate of fifteen dollars per barrel, one barrel of flour to be finished in lieu of every one hundred and sixty pounds of bread, unless the Commanding U.S. Naval Officer at San Francisco shall require all the bread do be furnished in which case the said William A. Leidesdorff shall go on and complete the contract.

Witness our hand and seal, on board the United States Ship Columbus, Harbor of Monterey the eleventh day of March in the year of our Lord one thousand eight hundred and forty seven.

The words "the bread" were underlined before signing of this contract and are in full force. Signed in duplicate.

Edward T. Dunn

William A. Leidesdorff[14]

---

14 Palgon, *First Balck Millionaire, 48.*

On the long journey back from Monterey to San Francisco, Will's thoughts returned to the emigrants who had been stuck in the mountains, and he wondered how they fared. News was slow in arriving in San Francisco, and he had not heard anything. Not until April 17 did he learn of the Donner Party's arrival at Sutter's Fort. The *California Star* reported,

> There were 87 emigrants in the Donner Party, plus Luis and Salvador, two Californian Indians who joined them in Nevada, for a total of 89 people. Of the 89, only 81 were trapped in the mountains because there had been additions to and subtractions from the group along the way. Of the total 89 people, 41 died and 48 survived; of the original 87 emigrants, 39 died and 48 survived; of the 81 people trapped in the mountains, 36 died and 45 survived. About two-thirds of the women and children survived while about two-thirds of the men died. All four Donner adults (the couples George and Tamsen Donner and Jacob and Elizabeth Donner) died; most of the Reeds and Breens survived.[15]

After reading the account, Will set the paper aside for a moment and sat quietly as he mourned the loss of the

---

15 *California Star." Donner Party". April17,1847.* http://cdnc.ucr.edu/cgi-bin/cdnc.

people he never met and the death of their dreams. With a heavy heart, he recognized it as a very dark moment in the westward expansion and one that would not soon be forgotten.

CHAPTER 36

WILL STORMED OUT the door of his office, his face red with anger. Moon was in the kitchen preparing supper. "Listen to this, will you?" He threw a letter down on the table and then picked it up again. "I just received this letter from Larkin, and he's telling me the wood boards Serege and I counted out were not delivered." He paced around the kitchen table. "You know the fences Sam, Serege, and I put around his lots? He's saying he doesn't want those either. It's a little late since it is already done. Who is going to pay for that?" He stalked across the floor to his office and turned abruptly. He held the letter in his hand and struck it with the other. "He also says he paid me for his child's funeral expenses, and I received nothing for that. This is the last time I do business with him." He wadded up the letter and threw it on the floor.

When he was gone, Moon picked up the letter and read it also.

Later, during supper, Moon asked Will, "What are you going to do about the letter?"

"I am not going to pay it. I was acting as his agent while he was in Monterey, and he does this to me?" He strode up and down the kitchen, agitated. "I will write him a letter and then cut off any business with him. I will not be responsible for his debts."

He went to his desk, pulled out paper, and slapped it down. He jerked his knife out of his pocket.

Moon looked at him in alarm. "What you do with that knife?"

"I am going to sharpen this quill so I can respond to the thief." He whittled away at the plume until the end was sharp to his finger. He dipped it in the ink and began scratching ferociously. When he finished, he said, "Listen to this. I'll read it to you. I have tried to behave like a gentleman, although Larkin has not.

Oct14 1847
San Francisco

Tho O Larkin
    Monterey
Dr Sir
    I am indeed surprised at the tone of your last and suppose that this is the thanks that I am to receive for acting as your agent and making many enemies in defending your property. You're a/c [account] was made out in full exactly as it stands on my Ledger and is right. The last time you were

here you acknowledged it to be so. The only money I even see from Ths [Thomas] Larkin was ninety dollars for which you will find a credit on the a/c. The reason the amount of Lt. Gillespie was there was to give you and a/c in full as our wrote for. Mr. West came to me an [and] informed me that your agent would pay him so much and that you ought to have been here as he said you promised him either to be here yourself or leave and agent here to pay him and that you told him I was your agent which was the reason I paid him as how would he have know[n] I was your agent with out your telling him. As regards to Benito Dias if you had not written me that you was indebted to him and that my amt might be included with yours against him, I would not have charged. You saw this in my ledger before and never made any objection.

I thank you for fencing in the Lots of Mr Green and mine and hiring out the House on Forbes Lot. Are the words of your former letter and now you say that you do not want the fencing of the two lots for Mr Green and yourself and that you will not pay for them. Now let me inform you that most all my payments for you have been Hard dollars not effects for these lots I paid Hard dollars and to Mr West part was Cash and part was Hides a 12/- and most every other payment I have made for you has been cash.

I am glad you are so candid but have to assure you that Mr Sherman holds a note of mine for

$400 in your favor, which is one thing that shall not be paid until I am convinced that I will receive from you that amt you justly owe me. Moreover I now must respectfully decline acting as you agent my business is such that it will not accommodate me in throwing away time and money on the peoples affairs. Your house on the Beach was only kept by Mr Rop for two thirds of a month. Consequently it is now empty.

Very Respy [Respectfully] Yours Signed WA Leidesdorff[16]

After he finished reading, Moon said, "It good thing you keep letters so you prove you right." Moon stopped and repeated herself carefully, "It is a good thing that you keep the letters so you prove you are right. Did I say that right? I am learning to speak correctly. I listen to you teach Serege."

"Yes, you did that well," Will said absently, too agitated to listen closely. He shook his head and walked over to the window. "How can Larkin deny what is so obvious?"

Will put the letter in an envelope and sealed it. He sent it off immediately to Monterey with a carrier. Making the break clean, he resigned from his duties as vice-consul of California. Will did no more business with Larkin, and the relationship ended abruptly.

---

16   Palgon, *The First Black Millionaire,* 38.

CHAPTER 37

It was a brisk September morning. The air was crisp and the sky clear, a perfect morning for a ride along the waterfront. Will waved to Richardson galloping his golden palomino at full speed down the beach.

Will kicked his black stallion into a gallop and soon caught up with him. They slowed their panting horses to a casual canter, and Will said, "Did you read the article in the *California Star* about organizing a town council?" He waited for Richardson's acknowledgment before pursuing the topic. "There is going to be a meeting on Thursday evening at the alcade's office. Our city is growing, and I want to have a voice in its development. I think I will attend."

Richardson replied, "I think that is a good idea. Your experience as vice-consul gave you knowledge of politics beyond our little town. If I weren't so busy with my cattle and land, I would attend."

On a Thursday evening, September 16, 1847, Will was the first to arrive to the meeting. Dressed in his black tailed jacket and a cravat at his neck, he looked quite official. Will stood outside the office of Judge Hyde, the newly elected alcade of San Francisco. The building there was made of adobe, and the red tile roof looked like the other Spanish roofs in town.

He rapped on the door and entered the barren room. Only a wooden table and eight chairs occupied the room. A lantern stood in the center of the table, casting soft shadows. Judge Hyde motioned to one of the chairs and said, "Sit down. The other men will be joining us soon." He no sooner finished speaking than Will heard voices outside the door. Judge Hyde opened the door, and E. P. Jones, Robert Parker, W. Howard, William Glover, and William Clark stepped into the room all dressed very much like Will. He stood as they entered, and the men shook hands.

"Let's get right down to business," Hyde said in his terse manner. He placed a worn black Bible in the center of the table and turned to Will. "Place your hand on the Bible and repeat after me, 'I do solemnly swear that I will faithfully execute the office of the city council of the town of San Francisco and will to the best of my ability preserve, protect, and defend our town.'"

Will repeated the words and passed the Bible to Jones, Parker, and the rest of the men until all were sworn in. "I now declare the town council of San Francisco organized," Hyde stated and sat down at the head of the table.

Dr. Jones asked to speak. "I make a motion that a committee of three be appointed to form a code of laws for the regulation of the affairs of the town and that said committee report at the next meeting of the council."

"All in favor, say aye," Judge Hyde responded, and the men chorused in agreement. "I appoint Howard, Dr. Jones, and Clark to serve on that committee." All the heads nodded in consent before he proceeded. "We must have a treasurer." He looked at Will. "You have experience in keeping books and running a business. I appoint you as treasurer of San Francisco City Council. Do you accept?" Will nodded, proud to be named to such an honorable position. After some discussion, the council agreed that Will be required to give bonds in the amount of $10,000.

The men then discussed the position of secretary, as minutes needed to be taken at each meeting. Judge Hyde suggested, "The clerk of the alcade's office may certainly act as secretary of the council, too. We will compensate him since he is also paid for the alcade duty."

The men again agreed, and the meeting moved on to the problem of seamen who deserted their ships when arriving in San Francisco. After further discussion, they passed an ordinance to prevent the desertion of seamen. With that, the meeting was adjourned until the following Tuesday evening.

When Will arrived home after the meeting, Moon was waiting for him. She sat with her feet tucked under a blanket and a fire burning in the fireplace. Her thick black hair, normally fixed in a knot on her head, lay loose on her shoulders, falling in spiraling ringlets. The room was softly lit by candles.

"Standing before you is the town treasurer of San Francisco. What do you think?" Will strutted around the chair where she was sitting, like the male turkeys at breeding time, his feathers fully plumed.

She laughed at his behavior before she said, "You be perfect for the job." Once again she stopped and repeated, "You are perfect for the job. You have a good business head; you are quick-tempered but honest." She pointed to the chair across from her and said, "Sit down. Tell me about responsibilities." She corrected herself, "your responsibilities."

Will pulled the chair closer to the fire. "I will write the checks for the town and keep track of the books. We will be meeting on Monday evenings at seven. I am also responsible for giving bonds for ten thousand dollars." He slipped out of his black jacket with the tails and let it fall to the back of his chair. "The population of San Francisco is currently four hundred fifty-seven people, enough to do some improvements to our town. The mayor, Judge Hyde, will receive a salary of fifty dollars a month. We are going to read the proceedings of the previous meeting each time we meet and correct any mistakes before moving forward."

He took a paper out of his pocket and read it to her. "Every motion, resolution, or other proposition shall be put in writing and be distinctly read before any discussion will be allowed. After sufficient time has been allowed for deliberation, the vote shall be taken by the alcade, viva voce, which means'by word of mouth' until further directed by a majority of the members in council." He folded the paper and put it back in his pocket.

"We will meet one evening a week, but now that I am no longer vice-consul, I will have time." He stopped and listened. "It is so quiet; where is Serege? Has he gone to bed?"

"Yes, he had a cup of hot chocolate and complained of a sore throat, so I sent him to bed. He be—no, I mean *is*—eager to hear about the new town treasurer. He will be proud." She stood, folded the blanket, and said, "Now that you are home, I will go to bed." She patted his shoulder and smiled. "I am happy for you. Good night."

As the weeks progressed, Will, true to form, kept accurate and articulate records of the town's expenses. He had learned his lesson from Larkin: he would not be accused of cheating.

Amount of cash paid for town	
Ab. F. Watkin Hawling	36.00
Wm. A. Leidesdorff for lumber	1000.00
Staff office	37.40
Leidesdorff bill for two months rent	60.00
Wm. A. Leidesdorff bill for nails	88.00

A few months later, at a Monday-evening town meeting, a disagreement occurred. While the council members sat at the wooden table in the home of Mayor Judge Hyde, he picked up Will's statement of cash paid for the town and frowned. He pointed to the line item "Wm. A. Leidesdorff for lumber" and said, "One thousand dollars for sidewalk lumber seems a great amount for the city to pay. Along with that, you have charged the city eighty-eight dollars for nails. None of the other items are that expensive." He scowled at Will while the rest of the men sat silently, watching. "That is a conflict of interest, Mr. Leidesdorff. You cannot make a profit at the expense of the city, especially when you are keeping the books. What have you to say for yourself?"

Will's face flushed with anger. He pushed back his chair, jumped to his feet, and slammed his hand on the table. "I sold that to the city for a fair market price, I have not cheated my city. Am I to donate my wood? How shall I make a living that way?"

Mayor Judge Hyde stood and faced him head-on, his eyes narrowed. He pointed a finger at him. "I charge you with a conflict of interest."

Just as Larkin had accused him of injustice, now the mayor accused him of the same. His blood boiled, but he did not let it show. His temper under control, he gathered his papers and said, "Very well. We shall see what happens." He turned to the rest of the men at the table and said, "Good evening, gentlemen. I trust you do not share our mayor's thoughts." He exited the room and closed the door behind him.

The very next day, Will pressed charges against Mayor Hyde. The *California Star* reported Will as saying, "The town is in disgraceful disorder, and Hyde prevents reform."

An investigation followed, and the mayor was dismissed. All charges were dropped against Will.

C H A P T E R   3 8

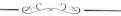

WHILE WALKING HOME from the store on a balmy April afternoon, Will stopped to watch Serege and his friends playing blindman's bluff in the dirt streets, oblivious to the horses, carts, and dust. Serege stood in the center of the circle with a rag tied around his eyes. The children circled him until he yelled, "Stop!" He then called one of the youngsters into the circle and tried to identify the child.

Before long, a scuffle broke out between two of the boys as to who should be next. The bigger boy threw a punch, and a fight started. Will strode into the mix and grabbed both boys by their collars. "You boys cool down and go home. No fighting in the streets." He urged the two on their way, and the game continued for the others. Will stepped back to the sidelines and counted about forty children that needed to be in school before they became delinquents and a bigger problem.

His desire to see the school completed rekindled, he called a school-board meeting and asked the other two men, Mr. Eddy and Mr. Davis, to meet at his house on Tuesday evening. When they arrived, he met them at the door and invited them in. "Take a seat at the table, and I will ask Moon to get us something to drink." The April evening was unusually warm, so Moon opened the windows to allow the sea breeze to cool the room before serving homemade lemonade.

Will began speaking passionately. "I counted a least forty children playing in the street last week on my way home from the store. I know there are at least twenty more in the pueblo. It is time we get that school building completed. The rains are over now; the weather will be warmer and dryer. It is time."

"Yes! Yes!" the other two men chorused in agreement, nodding their heads vigorously. "I have four children at home that need to be in school," Mr. Eddy said and turned to Mr. Davis. "You have six school-age children, don't you?"

Mr. Davis set down his glass and responded, "Yes, and both my wife and I would like to see them get a good education. They need to be doing more than playing in the street." He looked at Will and said, "Thanks for sending my Tommy home. He told me all about the scuffle. It won't happen again."

"I needed to stop the boys so no one would get hurt," Will said as he cleared his throat and continued with the business at hand. "I think we can get it completed for a thousand dollars. I priced out the lumber. Here is the quote."

He handed the men a piece of paper, and as they looked it over, they nodded their agreement. "I will order the timber needed and have it delivered to the site." And so the building began, and a year later, the first public school opened on April 3, 1848, on the southwest corner of Portsmouth Square, just as the citrus trees were beginning to blossom. The *California Star* printed the following announcement:

> The school to be kept at the public school use of San Francisco, will commence on Monday the third of April next, under the superintendence of Mr. Thomas DOUGLASS, a graduate of Yale College, Connecticut. Mr. D, has had more than ten years' experience in the instruction of Academies and High Schools in the States, and has in his possession testimonials from the Trustees of those Institutions, which speak of him as a skilled and successful teacher, and as well qualified for the business of his profession. The undersigned Trustees, therefore, cheerfully commend his school to the patronage of the citizens of this Town and vicinity, confident that he will do all in his power to impart a thorough education to the pupils committed to his care. The terms of tuition will be as follows: For instruction in Reading, Writing, Spelling and Defining, and Geography, $5 per quarter...

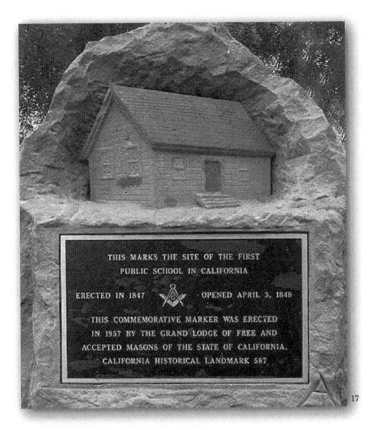

THIS MARKS THE SITE OF THE FIRST
PUBLIC SCHOOL IN CALIFORNIA

ERECTED IN 1847   OPENED APRIL 3, 1848

THIS COMMEMORATIVE MARKER WAS ERECTED
IN 1957 BY THE GRAND LODGE OF FREE AND
ACCEPTED MASONS OF THE STATE OF CALIFORNIA.
CALIFORNIA HISTORICAL LANDMARK 587

On the first morning of school, Serege arrived at the breakfast table with his brown hair sleeked down. His gray plaid knickers were held up by suspenders attached to loops on his pants. He wore a white long-sleeve buttoned

---

17 Monument to Site of First School, November 25, 2015. http://eres. ca.gov/geo_area/counties/San_Francisco/landmarks.html. http://www.nochill.com/sf/landmarks/ca10857.asp.

shirt with a black bow tie at the neck. Will purchased a new pair of black laced ankle boots for his first day, and he wore them proudly. "I couldn't get to sleep last night. I think I was too excited and nervous about school." He mumbled between bites of corn bread and eggs.

"You look nice," Moon said. "Everything will be fine. Remember all the students are anxious." She poured a glass of milk for him and then set a tin box on the table. "I packed you a lunch of dried beef and corn bread with an apple. Go now so you are not late." She swooshed him out the door.

"Thanks for the lunch. I'll tell you all about it tonight." He waved and ran down the gravel road to catch up with his friends.

At supper that evening, Serege could not stop talking. He carried his McGuffey reader to the table and wanted to show Moon and Will the pictures. "Hold on," Will said. "We'll have a proper discussion and a look at your book after we finish eating. Put it away until then."

Serege put the book in the sitting room and sat down at the table. "Can I tell you about my day?" he asked.

"Of course you can. I am eager to hear." Will smiled at Serege as he scooped potatoes onto his plate and asked, "How was your schoolmaster?"

"Oh, he was nice but very strict. We are not allowed to talk out and have to raise our hands to get permission to speak. He is very smart," Serege said.

"Good. There must be discipline and order for children to learn. Do you know you are attending the first public school in all of California? You are a fortunate boy."

After supper, Will built a fire in the fireplace to take the chill off the evening. Serege set the kerosene lamp on a nearby table and plopped down on the brocade-covered horsehair settee between Moon and Will so they could see the pictures in his reader. "I am in the fourth reader because of you, Will." He looked up at him. "Most of the boys have to start in the second or third reader but not me. It is written for the highest levels in grammar school, our teacher told me."

Serege opened the pages of the book and leafed through them. "We get to read *Robinson Crusoe's House* and *The Wreck of the Hesperus*." He pointed to the drawing of Crusoe's house.

"I read *Robinson Crusoe* when I was a young man in New Orleans. It is a very good book," Will said. He sat quietly for a minute, ignoring Serege's chatter as he remembered his years with both his father and his uncle and the rich opportunities they provided him. He hoped to do the same for Serege.

"I have to bring a Bible to school, too. I will bring the one you gave me when I came to live with you." Exciting as all this was, Serege looked at Moon. "Can we have some popcorn now? I'm hungry."

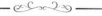

CHAPTER 39

THE HIDE AND tallow trade pushed Will's trapping business farther north up the coast, as fewer animals were available on the California coast. That meant taking numerous trips to Sitka, Alaska, Moon's home. "It is the most beautiful island on west side of Baranof Island," she told Will. Majestic snowcapped mountains flanked its east side, and the Pacific Ocean guarded the west.

On one trip, Will spotted a thirty-seven-foot steamer bobbing in the frigid water. He immediately took an interest and asked one of the men with whom he was trading, "Whom does that little boat belong to?"

The man tugged his fur cap down over his ears and replied, "That little lady was built by an American at Sitka as a pleasure boat for the officers of the Russian Fur Company." It was obvious to Will that he had knowledge of the boat, especially as he continued. "Its bow breadth is about nine feet and the depth about three and a half feet, drawing eighteen inches of water. It uses a small piston and cylinder from a railroad engine to move the side wheels. Quite a little boat."

Will was fascinated; he could not take his eyes off the boat. "Is it for sale?" he asked. He looked around to see whom he could speak to about purchasing it. He had been thinking of ways to efficiently transport goods to Sutter's Fort on the Sacramento River. This little vessel could handle the narrow and shallow passes. It would be perfect.

The man pointed his gloved finger up the snow-laden street to the Russian Fur Company building. "Someone in there should be able to direct you to the right person. They own it, but it hasn't been used much."

Will thanked him, plucked his wool hat down over his ears, pulled the hood of his jacket over his head, and walked the short distance to the building. Picking his way carefully over the icy path, he marveled at the influence of the Russian architecture surrounding him. All the structures were of logs and painted a dull yellow. The metal roofs were red and steeply pitched, standing out in contrast to the dark green of the nearby wooded hills. The logs of the business buildings were hewn so they left no crevices.

Pulling open the heavy wooden door, Will entered the warm room. He pushed the hood off his head and snatched off his hat. He ran his fingers through his thick dark hair, attempting to smooth it flat. He pulled off his calfskin gloves and rubbed his hands together, trying to get feeling in them once again. It felt good to get out of the cold.

Perseverance

A black potbellied stove bravely burned wood in its attempt to thwart the freezing outdoor temperatures. Judging by the smell and the gray haze in the room, it must have been smoking recently. When his eyes adjusted, Will noticed the closely hewn log walls, the logs so close they could be painted or papered. The tongue-and-groove planked floor was a warm golden color, like honey. Glancing at the ceiling, he noticed a thick layer of sand supported by canvas that was stretched across the joists and nailed into place. He was impressed with the efficiency of using sand for insulation.

Walking over to a lanky man behind the counter, he asked, "Can you tell me who owns that little boat bobbing in the bay? I am interested in purchasing it."

The man closed the journal that he was writing in and studied Will. His coarse black hair was long and tied in a ponytail at the base of his neck. He wore a red plaid wool shirt, as did the other men in the store. When he talked, Will guessed he was a native Alaskan. "It made for us by American. We use it some, but I think we sell it. Talk price." The two men dickered back and forth before finding a reasonable price.

"I have a shipping business out of San Francisco. I don't imagine it could make the trip in this weather, being the middle of winter. Are any large ships leaving that could bring it down?" Will asked.

"*Nosledrick* leaving in few days. They may take it." The clerk rested his hands on the wood counter. "I talk to captain. He come in here once a day."

275

Will paid the agreed amount and asked the man to make the arrangements to have it sent to San Francisco. He figured it would arrive in October.

The days were long as Will waited in anticipation for his new arrival, just like Serege at Christmas. Each day, he scanned the horizon for the *Nosledrick*, and finally, on a crisp October morning, he awakened to the site of the ship anchored in the bay. He banged on Serege's door. "Wake up! My boat has come in, and I want you to go with me to see it. Get dressed; we are leaving now."

Serege pulled on his trousers and grabbed a warm wool shirt from the hook in his room. He met Will at the door, and together they ran down the hill to the waiting ship. They watched as the men attached ropes, hoisted the smaller boat overboard, and dropped it into the San Francisco Bay.

Will asked one of the Indians to row them to the boat in a dinghy, and they clambered aboard the *Sitka* in great eagerness. It took some time for Will to figure out how to get it ashore, but eventually he succeeded in landing it.

Will spent days learning to maneuver the boat. He first planned a short maiden trip to Santa Clara at the end of the bay. He finally decided it was ready to make the trip to Sacramento on November 28. He hired a four-man crew, consisting of a cook, a deckhand, a fireman, and an Indian pilot from Sutter's Fort.

After hearing about the trip, a dozen passengers signed up for the historic journey, including George McKinstry and L. W. Hastings, who went as far as Montezuma. Mrs. Greyson and her baby were also on board. The trip was about one hundred miles long and took six days and seven hours. The progress of the *Sitka* was so slow that one of the impatient passengers said, "I can walk faster than this to Sutter's Fort. Let me off." Sure enough, when they finally reached the fort, the same passenger had arrived a number of hours before the steamer.

Although the report was not good when it reached San Francisco, Will and the crew intended to make it a success. The *California Star* reported,

> Several violent northers visited this port. A most furious gale of wind visited our harbor, continuing with unabated violence until the evening of the same day...Little Sitka had as much as she could do to keep her head above the water long enough to say her prayers. She tossed and tumbled and to the bottom went. The only evidence of her whereabouts was the plain view of part of her smoke pipe above water.

Disappointed, Will had *Sitka* raised and hauled inland by a team of oxen and worked to have it restored into a schooner that he christened *Rainbow*. "Maybe someday she will make the trip successfully," he said, again not willing to give up.

CHAPTER 40

JOHN MARSHALL, A man who served under Fremont during the Bear Flag Revolt, lodged at City Hotel one night and spent the evening dining and talking with Will, "When I returned to my ranch on the north side of Butte Creek after the revolt, I found all my cattle had either strayed or been stolen."

Will shook his head in disbelief, "I'm so sorry to hear that. You lost your livelihood."

"I did. I had no way to support myself so I met with Sutter, who agreed to hire me to assist with the building of a sawmill. In return, I was to receive a portion of the lumber. After scouting the area for a suitable location, I decided on Coloma, about forty miles upstream from Sutter's Fort. You been there?" Marshall asked.

"Yes, I was given a land grant in that area so I own 35,000 acres along the American River." Will replied.

"You will be pleased with the news you are about to learn," Marshall said and took another bite of his fried chicken. After he finished eating his chicken and rice, his stomach satisfied and the saloon warm, he pulled a small leather pouch from his pocket. He shook the contents onto the table and said, "I'm here to have this tested."

Will picked up one of the shiny nuggets and studied it, holding it to the candlelight.

Marshall continued, "I think it's gold, but I wanna make sure, and I don't want the news to get out yet, so don't say anything." He swept up the gold and dropped it back into the pouch. He pulled the drawstring tight and put it away. When he finished, he patted the pocket. "This may make us rich."

Will sat in stunned silence. The discovery of gold would shake his world far more than the California earthquakes that occasionally erupted.

"How did you come about discovering gold?" Will asked once he regained his composure.

"Let me tell you the story," Marshall said and leaned back in his chair. He took a pouch of tobacco from his pocket, loaded his pipe and then lit it. "I'll start at the beginning. It was a cold January day. The Indians and veterans from the Mormon Battalion who made up my crew were freezing in the morning rain, clutching their cowhide coats around them. They sought shelter under the nearby oak trees as I examined the results of the previous night's excavation. It was then that I noticed and said, 'The ditch that drains water away from the waterwheel is too narrow and shallow. We will never get the volume of water needed to operate the saw.'"

Marshall inhaled and then exhaled sending a puff of smoke into the air. I told them, "We are going to have to divert the river to use the force of the water to excavate and enlarge the tailrace. We will do that tonight. Safer that way."

Will sensed that Marshall enjoyed story telling and this story could take quite some time. He motioned to Moon to bring more black coffee. "Please continue," encouraged Will.

'Well, when I returned to the site the next morning, I examined the excavation done the previous night. What I saw made me stop dead in my tracks. I bent down and picked up one or two pieces and examined them carefully." Marshall stopped long enough to take a drink of his coffee. "I have some general knowledge of minerals, but I could not call to mind more than two which resembled this, sulphuret of iron which is very bright and brittle; and gold, which is malleable. I then tried it between two rocks and found that it could be beaten into a different shape but not broken. I then collected four or five pieces and went up to Mr. Scott who was working at the carpenter's bench making the mill wheel. With the pieces in my hand I said, 'I have found gold!'" He patted the gold pouch in his pocket, a broad smile spread across his face. "That's why I am in San Francisco. I am here with James Bennet to have it tested."

Just then, the door opened and James Bennet and another man walked into the hotel. Marshall waved him over to the table where he and Will were sitting. Both men stood and Marshall introduced Will to Bennet.

"This is Isaac Humphrey," Bennet said referring to his guest. "He is a gold miner from Georgia here to authenticate the gold."

"Let's go into the back room," Will said, "I do not think this information should be public."

Will lit a candle in the darkened room that smelled heavily of frying bacon and onion. He set it on the table and motioned to the men to sit on wooden chairs with cowhide woven seats. Silence hung in the air.

Marshall reached into his pocket and pulled out his bag. He let the contents tumble out onto the table. Catching the light from the flame, the nuggets sparkled incandescently.

Humphrey picked up a nugget and held it to the flame of the candle, turning it around and around and studying it for some time, The men sat silent. Next, he bit down on it and leaned back in his chair. "Yep," he said, "this is gold. You have found the real thing."

Bennet and Marshall leaped to their feet and pounded one another on the back. "We're rich! We're rich!" they crowed in unison.

"Gentlemen, I think we need to keep this quiet for your safety. Please keep you're your discovery to your-selves," Will said, calming them.

Knowing that his land was in the same vicinity, Will rode with the men to Sutter's Fort the following day. When they arrived, he followed Marshall to Sutter's pri-vate room and waited while Marshall knocked on the door. "Come in," Sutter invited. He sat at a small black table on which rested a quill pen and ink, a candleholder and snuffer, and some papers. A thick woven blanket was neatly pulled up on his bed, and another blanket lay at the foot. He acknowledged both men with a nod.

"I've come to give you the news," Marshall said as he sat on the only other chair in the room while Will stood aside. "Humphrey confirmed exactly what you thought. It is gold." He couldn't restrain the grin that almost lay hidden under his full beard and mustache.

"I thought as much. That is good news." Sutter sat silently for a moment. "If this news gets out, we could have bedlam on our hands. I want to keep this a secret." He stood and wandered to the window overlooking the compound he had built. "Instruct the men not to say a word to anyone."

Will returned home with the possibility that his land contained gold too. In February, Marshall went down the American River to Mormon Island and found scales of gold on the rocks of Will's land. A month later, in March, Sutter wrote to Will asking him if he was interested in investing in a company to mine for gold.

New Helvetia March 25, 1848

WA. Leidesdorff Esq

Dear Sir!

The launch "Dicemi Nan" arrived here on the 17th inst evening. My wagons has all been in the Mountains then, and I thought it would be best to send her up to my farm "Hock," as the house is right on the river bank. I furnished the Canaea's immediately with a good pilot and crew to take them up likewise plenty of provisions.

We had last Sunday, and several other day's in this week, very bad stormy weather, that had to lay by, and one day they lost themselves in company with their countrymen. I furnish them again with provision for which I charge nothing. The Launch have 180 fanegas of Wheat. To complet [complete] the 1500 fanegas for the Russians, I have to send 416 1/2 fanegas more.

My Launch has not arrived yet, but I hope she will be in the river.

My Sawmill in the Mountains is now completed. She cuts 2000 feet of planks in 12 hours. The Grist mill is advancing.

> We intend to form a company for working the Gold mines, which prove to be very rich. Would you not take a share in it? So soon as if it would not pay well, we could stop it at any time.
>
> I have the honor to be Your
>
> > Obedient Servant
> > J A Sutter[18]

After reading it, Will carried the letter in to Moon, who was in the kitchen preparing the evening meal. He smelled the frying onions that she would add to the beef. "Sure smells good in here, Moon. Wait until I read you this letter! Can you sit a minute?"

He sat down on one of the hard-backed chairs, and Moon pulled out another. Will read aloud the letter he had just received from Sutter. "He wants me to invest in gold mining, and he thinks there might be some on my land, too. Wouldn't that be something? I'd be rich!" He smacked the table and jumped to his feet. "I have to tell Richardson. I will be the first with the news."

18 Palgon, *The First Black Millionaire.* 61.

News was beginning to leak, and other landowners initiated looking for gold on their properties. P. B. Reading was one of those men. A prominent and wealthy citizen of California, he owned a large ranch on the western bank of the Sacramento River. After making a trip to Coloma, he went back to the hills near his ranch and, in a few weeks, reported that he had found diggings near Clear Creek, at the head of the Sacramento Valley.

He wrote to Will in April, as Mormon Island was part of his land grant.

New Helvetia April 29th 1848

Capt W. A. Leidesdorff
My Dear Sir

Enclosed please find a letter from Co J.C. Freemont to your address, also one for Mr. Abel Stearns and another for Mr. John Roland, which please have the goodness to forward by first opportunity. I also send to your care a letter for Major Snyder who is residing at Santa Cruz.

Some more recent discoveries on the upper part of your ranch prove that the gold washing could be pursued with much profit. Tomorrow I

shall leave for the upper part of the Valley. On my
return will write you the news.

I am, Very truly
Your Obdt Svt.
P. B. Reading[19]

Marshall did succeed in keeping his discovery of gold
quiet for a time. Not until March 18, 1848, did the
California Star give account of the discovery:

> We were informed a few days since that a very
> valuable silver-mine was situated in the vicinity of
> the place, and, again, that its locality was known.
> Mines of quicksilver are being found all over the
> country. Gold has been discovered in the north-
> ern Sacramento districts, about forty miles above
> Sutter's Fort. Rich mines of copper are said to
> exist north of these bays.

At first, not much importance was attached to the discovery, although on March 25 the *California Star* recorded,
"So great is the quantity of gold taken from the new mine
recently found at New Helvetia that it has become an article of traffic in that vicinity."

---

19 Palgon, *The First Black Millionaire,* 62.

CHAPTER 41

On May 13, Will sat at his desk, recording, adding, and subtracting the expenses for the city council. His window gave him a spectacular view of the undulating bay. He watched the sunlight dance on the fluid blue water. He fingered the cross at his neck and leaned back in his chair. His mind drifted to Hortense and lost love. *I wish she could see me now. Would she like this wild country with its untamed beauty? Would she be pleased about the new school and my continued desire to provide education for children? I think yes. I continue to persevere and hold to my roots and the ideals that shaped her life as well as mine. It is a memorial to you, Hortense, my one true love.*

He massaged his temple. The headache he had awakencd with did not seem to be lessening. He pivoted his neck. It felt stiff. In fact, the room was spinning slightly, making him feel nauseated, and the sunlight, instead of warming him, hurt his eyes. He called, "Moon, come here. I am not feeling well, and I think I need to lie down. Please bring me a drink of water."

Moon arrived at the door, a cup of water in her hand. He saw the concern in her eyes as she handed the drink to him and then reached to gently touch his forehead. "You are very hot. I think you have a fever. Drink this water. Fluids will help."

Will drained the mug and asked for more. Moon quickly fetched another cup of water, and he downed that one, too. "I think I'd better lay down for a while. Maybe this will pass." He stood to his feet, wavered, and immediately fell back into his chair. His face blanched white. "I think you are going to have to help me. I am very dizzy." He reached for Moon, who linked his arm in hers. Together, they walked slowly to Will's bed, and he dropped on the mattress ticking. Moon covered him with an Indian blanket as he shuddered with the chills.

"More b-b-blankets. I am so c-c-c-cold. I cannot stop sh-sh-shaking," he stuttered between chattering teeth.

Moon returned with more of the thick bright-colored woven blankets and piled them on Will. She closed the shutters to darken the room and sat down on the hard-backed chair to keep vigil. Soon Will settled into a restless sleep. As day turned to night, Moon kept watch, giving him sips of water whenever he awakened. His temperature did not diminish, and in the morning she sent Serege for Sam.

When Sam arrived, Moon cried, "Will woke up confused. He could not sit on the edge of the bed—had to lie down. I'm worried. He tells me his head throbs and he cannot move his neck." Moon paced up and down outside the bedroom door wringing her hands. "I think you need to get Richardson right away. Maybe he will know what to do."

The door slammed, and the hooves of Sam's horse pounded the dirt-packed path as he rushed to get Richardson. Moon went back into the darkened room and continued to bathe Will's forehead with a cool, damp cloth, urging him to take frequent sips of water. She tried to give him chicken broth, but he brushed it aside, spilling the contents on his white night shirt. Finally, the welcome sound of the returning horses' hooves echoed outside.

Richardson burst through the door, his hair tousled and his face red. "How is he? Can I see him?" He didn't wait for an answer but pushed through to Will, who lay listlessly on his bed. Richardson leaned over and touched his fingers to his forehead. "He is burning up. How long has he been like this? Have you been giving him fluids?" He pummeled Moon with questions, and she nodded vigorously to each of the hurled darts. "He is too weak to move, and I don't think the temescal would help him, although we could give it a try," he said.

Moon shook her head in opposition to that idea, knowing he was far too weak to mount a horse and take the trip. "He doesn't eat. He has no strength. I made broth, but he did not touch it." She tried to suppress a yawn.

Richardson said, "You look like you've had a hard night. Have you been sitting with him all night? Why don't you go lie down? I will sit with him for a while." He patted her shoulder.

"Yes, it has been a long night. I tried to doze in the chair, but it is too hard." The chair, brought from Paris, was elaborately carved and beautiful, but with its stiff upright wood back, it was not made for sleeping. "I want to be near him in case he cries out for me. His sleep is so troubled." Moon stood to her feet, covering another yawn. "Wake me in hour. I do not want to be away from him long."

Richardson sat quietly on the hard-backed chair and watched his friend's labored breathing. They had been through so much together, and Will had certainly brought life and adventure to him. He smiled briefly at the memory of the river trip to New Helvetia and Will's dream of making it a regular occurrence. Sam came in once and asked, "I bring you anything, Mr. Richardson? You want something to eat? Tea or coffee?"

Richardson declined and tried to doze in the chair. Moon was right. Sleeping did not work. When Will moved, Richardson was right there with another sip of water. Although Will occasionally opened his eyes, the light was too uncomfortable for him. He did mumble, "Thanks for coming to sit with me. I feel miserable. My neck is so stiff, and my head pounds."

When Moon awoke and came into the room, Richardson said, "I feel so helpless. What can I do for my friend? He is in misery. Who can I send for? I don't know a doctor." His face showed the impotence he felt, and his shoulders drooped as he paced the rough wood floor of the small room.

Moon shrugged her shoulders. "I know exactly how you feel. I pray for him." She touched his forehead again. The temperature had not lessened. She took the damp cloth, dipped it in the cool water in the basin, and gently wiped his face. She lifted his head and held the cup of water to his lips. It took effort, but he did swallow a few sips.

"Here. You sit here." Richardson motioned to the chair. "I will leave you, but I will be back tomorrow. You have Sam with you, so if you need anything or there are any changes, send for me." He patted her on the back and quietly left the sick man's room, his hat held in his hands.

The next morning, nothing had changed. Will woke less and seemed to be slipping in and out of consciousness. When Richardson arrived, Moon said, "Will is not a practicing Catholic, but I cannot watch him die without last rites. He is a good man and must go to heaven. I will send Sam for the bishop. He will anoint him and pray for him, and then he can be buried at the mission." She held her catechism book in her hand and pointed to an open page for Richardson to read.

"The anointing of the sick is not a sacrament for those only who are at the point of death. Hence, as soon as any-one of the faithful begins to be in danger of death from sickness or old age, the fitting time for him to receive this sacrament has certainly already arrived." He closed the book and handed it back to her. She sat down in the chair, cradled her face in her hands, and wept quietly. "I do not want him to die; he is only thirty-eight years old. What will Serege and I do without him?"

Richardson, a strong Catholic who practiced his faith and belief in God, agreed. "Yes, we must send for the Bishop. Nothing can save him now except God." He dropped to his knees at the edge of the bed and whispered a prayer.

Moon left him and tiptoed out of the room to fetch Sam, who was sitting at the kitchen table, his head cradled in his hands. When he raised his eyes to her, she saw the trace of tears on his weathered brown cheeks. "Go quickly to the mission and bring the Bishop. Will is not getting better." She placed her hand on his shoulder, and for just a moment they were both silent. "He must go to heaven. He needs the prayer and blessing of a Bishop. Hurry!"

Sam grabbed his hat and rushed out. The sound of galloping hooves receded in the distance, and Moon returned to Will's bedroom. Without making a noise, she dusted the wooden table by the bed and straightened the bedsheets. She pulled the blankets up around Will's neck. Next, she arrived with a glass of water for Richardson, who accepted it without a word.

What seemed like hours later, Bishop Alemany from the mission arrived in his full vestment and was ushered into the room. A large jeweled cross hung at his neck on a woven cord. He carried his prayer book in his hand.

Only Moon and Richardson remained in the room with the bishop. He first gave the sacrament of penance, absolving all his sins. He then took a vial of oil from his pocket and anointed Will's forehead in the form of a cross. He repeated in a quiet tone, "Through this holy anointing, may the Lord in his love and mercy help you with the grace of the Holy Spirit." Next, he placed drops of oil on Will's hands and said, "May the Lord, who frees you from sin, save you and raise you up."

Moon stood, her head bowed, her lips moving in silent prayer, as the tears flowed gently down her smooth olive cheeks. She pulled a handkerchief out of her apron pocket and wiped her nose, blowing softly. Will did not open his eyes or move, although she could see the movement of his chest as he struggled to breathe.

Before the day was done, the news of William's illness had spread throughout San Francisco, and a steady stream of friends began to visit. Sam Brannan arrived at the same time Ridley showed up. They crowded into the small room and sat in the straight-backed chairs Sam carried into the room.

Will opened his eyes briefly and gave a slight nod. They sat hushed, not knowing what to say but wanting their friend to know they cared. When he was leaving, Brannan turned to Moon. "Do you want Serege to come and stay with me? It has to be hard on the young lad; I know he cares deeply for Will. He is a father figure to him."

Moon thanked him and said, "Yes, I think that is a good idea. I have no time to fix meals. I want to spend all my time with Will." She called for Serege and said, "I want you to pack your valise and spend a few days with Brannans. If Will gets worse, I will let you know; now it is better if you stay with them."

"But I want to be here with Will. I don't want him to die. He will get better, won't he?" He clung to Moon's hand. For such a young boy, he had already experienced much of the pain and horror of death. He knew about the emptiness and the vast hole left behind by his mother's death and separation from his father and brother, and now the man he loved like a father lay deathly ill. "Will can't die." He burst into heart-wrenching sobs. Moon held him tightly. She knew his hurt; she had loved and lost, too. To lose Will would have a deep effect on both of them.

Moon held him close and stroked his hair. "I hope he will get better. I do not know. We will pray for him. You will be fine with Mr. Brannan; you can play with his children, and when Will gets better, I send for you." After Moon held him and spoke comforting words, he reluctantly departed with Sam Brannan.

As they were saying their good-byes, Juan Fuller and his wife came with a basket of tortillas, beans, and rice. They sat for thirty minutes in the hushed room before leaving just as Dr. Jones, the editor of the *California Star*, arrived.

The Bishop, who had been sitting, quietly praying, motioned Moon to follow him into the other room. When the others gathered around, he said, "All we can do now is pray and hope the Lord choses to save him. I am sorry to see him so ill. He is a good man and has done much for our community." The close circle nodded in agreement, but no one had words to say.

Moon did not leave his side but kept a constant vigil along with Richardson, who gave her occasional breaks. Both were sitting in his room on the evening of May 18, a week after his illness struck him. He slipped into a coma late in the afternoon, and both knew it would not be long until he breathed his last breath. At one o'clock in the morning, Moon heard the rattle of his breathing and saw that he had lost the ability to swallow. Moon let out a muffled sob knowing the time had come. The blankets covering his chest lay deathly still, as did Will. Richardson gently pulled the blanket up, covering his face, and told Moon to go to bed. They would deal with the coroner in the morning.

Moon nodded, exhausted, but she kept her vigil all through the night over the man who had been so kind to her.

CHAPTER 42

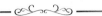

Moon

THE LARGEST AND finest adobe house in San Francisco sat cold and silent. The heart of the home was gone. Moon sat deadly still in the straight-backed chair in Will's room. She had not moved since they had carried his body away. Through the blackness of the night, memories assailed her: her first meeting with Will in the restaurant in Sitka, his kindness and offer of a new home and a new beginning, her job as hostess to dignitaries both at the adobe and the hotel.

After the arrangements were made, the day of the funeral arrived with a chill in the air, which added to the coldness of Moon's heart. She heard noises outside the open window and stood to look out on the bay. All the flags on the ships were flying at half-mast. The city was beginning to awaken. Knowing she was expected to be part of the funeral, she dressed in black satin and tied a veiled black hat over her long dark hair, which she tucked in a bun.

Richardson was coming for her and Sam. Mr. Brannan was bringing Serege to walk with her and the rest of the city mourners. She knew she should eat some-thing, but she felt no desire for food. Instead, she drank a strong cup of black coffee and waited.

When Sam Brannan arrived with the boy, Serege broke into a run and clung to her. He was dressed in black trousers and a black jacket. "I am so sad. I have cried and cried. I didn't want Will to die. Why did he have to die?" Moon wrapped her arms around him and held him.

"Come," she said quietly, "we will walk together to the mission, Will's final resting place." She took his hand and led him out the door. Sam followed with Richardson and Sam Brannan close behind them.

Moon kept her head down, keeping her emotions in check. She did not want to wail aloud or alarm Serege. Slowly, she heard the people gathering and falling in behind her. She peered beneath her veil. Every business they passed, even the saloons and gambling halls, had a sign in the window saying *Closed*. As they walked through Portsmouth Square, she saw all the flags were hanging at half-mast from the military barracks as well as the ships in the port. The abrupt crack of a gunshot startled her. "Who would fire a gun on this most sad day?" she asked.

Richardson whispered in her ear. "The guns at the presidio will be fired during the procession. You will hear minute guns, too, but don't be alarmed. They are to honor William." He patted her arm and smiled reassuringly.

She turned to look at the crowd that gathered behind her. She could not see the end of the procession, but she did recognize many of the faces. It seemed the whole city had turned out to mourn William's passing.

Serege tugged at her sleeve and whispered, "What will happen to me now that Will is gone?" The young man wiped away the tears that trickled down his cheeks, leaving gray smudge marks.

"I will write to your father so he knows the change. He will want you to live with him. You are almost a man." She smiled at him and squeezed his hand. "Until that time, you will stay with Sam and me at the house."

Serege said quietly, "Thank you, Moon. We will miss him terribly, won't we?"

"Very much." And a sob escaped from under her veil and cut through the heaviness of the air, joining the lament of the four hundred other mourners. Slowly the procession lumbered its way through the winding streets to Mission Dolores.

Moon climbed the steps and entered the cathedral through the open front doors. She failed to notice the decorated redwood ceiling beams carved by the Indians and the wooden columns painted to resemble Italian marble. With her head bowed, she walked the long aisle to the front of the mission chapel and sat down between Richardson and Serege. It was then she noticed the abundance of flowers that banked the altar. Wild flowers gathered in full arrangements of golden-orange California poppies, yellow pansies, and purple irises, and tucked among the vivid colors were sprigs of delicate white cow parsnips and blue flaxes. Their fragrance infused the air with hope.

The bishop was speaking, but her thoughts were elsewhere. She did not want to believe the body that lay embalmed in front of her was that of her beloved William. She reminisced over the years they had together. *William saw something in me no one else saw...Maybe he was hurt in love, too. He thought I was beautiful, me, a half-breed. He was proud of me, and let me help him entertain dignitaries and important political people from all over the world. I most liked our quiet evenings at home where Serege, he, and I made a family.* She buried her face in her hands and wept silent, despairing tears.

Serege looked up at her contorted face. This time, he did the consoling. He slipped his arm through hers and patted her hand.

When the service was over, Moon stood at the edge of the grave excavated in the floor of the mission. Even though Will was not a Catholic, the bishop had given him last rites, and he would be the only Protestant buried inside the mission chapel.

Serege huddled close to Moon's side. She sensed his grief, he who had already watched his mother die and now was watching his father figure being lowered into the cold, impersonal ground. He did not look up but kept his eyes on the cold, tiled floor. This time she draped her arm over his young shoulders, wanting to give him so much more than comfort, as Will's body was lowered into the deep dark hole. Together, they stepped to the edge of the cavern and dropped golden California poppies that Richardson handed to them on the closed casket, their blooms fitting for the discovery of gold Will would never recognize. His investments lay in the people gathered around him.

After the priest finished the last prayer, all gathered around and prayed the Lord's Prayer in one accord.

Our Father, which art in heaven,
Hallowed be thy Name.
Thy Kingdom come.
Thy will be done in earth
As it is in heaven.
Give us the day our daily bread.
And forgive us our trespasses,
As we forgive them that trespass against us.
And lead us not into temptation,
But deliver us from evil.
For thine is the kingdom,
The power and the glory,
For ever and ever.
Amen

The bishop blessed the grave, and William was laid to his eternal rest.

Two days later, on May 20, 1848, William's obituary appeared in the *California Star*.

Died in his own residence, in this place at one o'clock, A.M. on the 18th inst., after an illness of seven days, of a fever, William A. Leidesdorff, Esq. late U.S. Vice Consul for this port. Having received the consolations of the Catholic religion during his illness, he was buried yesterday, at 3 o'clock, after the appropriate ceremonies, in the Mission Church of Dolores, near San Francisco. One of the largest and most respectable assemblages ever witnessed in this place, followed the deceased from his late residence to the place of interment, and everything was done on the part of the community to evince its deep feeling for the loss it has sustained. All places of business and public entertainment were closed, the flags of the garrison and the shipping were flying at half-mast, and minute guns were discharged from the barracks and the shipping as the procession moved from town.

It is not our intention to comment upon the history or merits of the deceased; a few brief remarks for affirmation of strangers will suffice. Captain Leidesdorff was of Danish parentage, but was a native of the West Indies, and is supposed to have been about thirty-eight years of age at the time of his death. He was formerly well known as a merchant captain in the ports of New Orleans and New York, but for the last

---

seven years he has been in business on the coast, where he has gained high character for integrity, enterprise, and activity. In private life he as social, liberal, and hospitable to an eminent degree, and in his attachment he was warm, cordial and confiding even to a fault. As a merchant and a citizen, he was prosperous, enterprising, and public-spirited and his name infinitely identified with the growth and prosperity of San Francisco. It is no injustice to the living, or unmeaning praise for the dead, to say that the town has lost its most valuable resident, and the feeling evinced by the community is an involuntary tribute to this merchant and a citizen. His energy of character and business enterprises have so blended his history with the start of San Francisco, that all classes deplore his death as a great public calamity. While many mourn the various social virtues in Captain Leidesdorff all class of the community and the poor have lost a magnificent patron and a generous man.

Papers in New York, Philadelphia, and New Orleans are requested to notice.[20]

After arriving at the empty house, Moon, Serege, and Sam sat silently at the kitchen table. No candles illuminated the dark space that shrouded them. The sun

20 Palgon, *The First Black Millionaire,* 59.

dipped below the bay, and the moon spread soft shadows over the forlorn trio.

"Should I fix you something to eat?" Moon offered. Both Sam and Serege shook their heads in one accord. "We will talk tomorrow. I will write the letter to your father, Serege. He will be eager to hear." She walked over to his chair and placed both her hands on his shoulders before going to the window. "Go to bed now. Try to sleep."

Serege stood for a moment before pushing in his chair. "It has been a long time since I have seen my father and my brother. I am sure my brother is big now. Maybe I can teach him how to ride a horse. He doesn't know I won the race." He went to his room.

Moon watched him leave the kitchen. *He is a young man, all grown up,* she thought. *Will taught him how to be fine man.*

"What about you, Moon? What you do, and where you go?" Sam asked.

"I will not go back to Sitka and my old life. The weather is much more agreeable in California then Alaska. Maybe I will continue to work at City Hotel." She paused as though uncertain to share more. "I have always wanted to be teacher. Maybe I could help at school with Mr. Douglass and the small children." She smiled for the first time in days. "I learned much watching Will teach Serege. I can now read and write, too. I liked his knowledge of books. He spoke at least five different languages—such a smart man. He cared so much about children learning too." She turned to go to her room but stopped and said simply, "I will carry on his dream. He would like that."

Portsmouth Square in 1851, looking north

In 1848, the school census showed a population of 575 males, 177 females, and 60 children, with a total population of 812. The buildings numbered two hundred. There were two hotels, boardinghouses, saloons, and ten-pin alleys. Twelve mercantile houses were established, two more wharves were in the course of construction, the townspeople were hopeful, and the prospects of the city were good. On April 3, 1848, the first public school was opened.

Bibliography

Bancroft, Hubert Howe, *History of California*. San Francisco: The History Company,1884-90.

Bryant, Edwin. *What I Saw in California.* Lincoln: University of Nebraska Press, 1985.

Fossier, Albert E., M.A., M.D., *New Orleans, the Glamour Period, 1800-1840.*Gretna: Pelican Publishing Company, Inc. 1998.

Palgon, Gary. *William Alexander Leidesdorff: First Black Millionaire, American Consul and California Pioneer. Raleigh*: Lulu Press, 2005.

Thomes, William H. *On Land and Sea.* Chicago: Laird & Lee, Publishers, 1883.

Vella, Christina. *Intimate Enemies.* Baton Rouge: Louisiana State University Press, 1997.

Catholic Church. Compendium of the Catechism of the Catholic Church. Rome: Liberia Editrice Vaticana, 2005. See esp. chap.,"Seven Sacraments of the Church."

35987718R00194

Made in the USA
San Bernardino, CA
09 July 2016